About

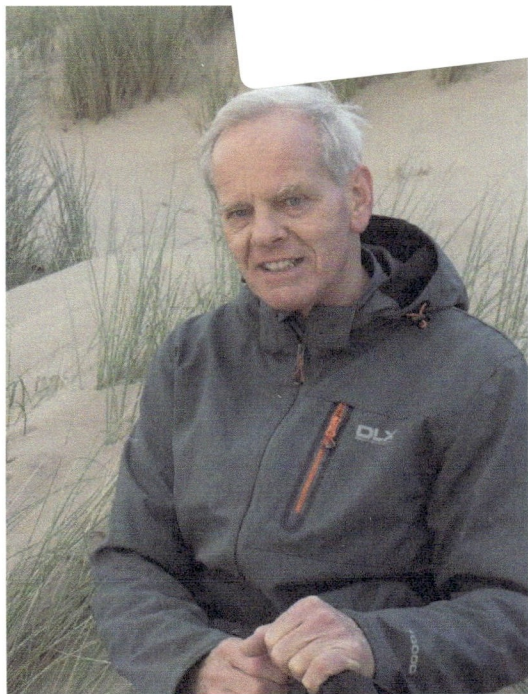

An agriculturalist, John spent much of his working life in Africa involved with development before being ordained into the Church of England and serving, first in an urban parish near Coventry, before moving to rural ministry in South Warwickshire. Now retired, he continues to help in a group of rural parishes although retirement has enabled him to turn his parents' wartime letters into a book.

BEHIND THE WIRE: A PRISONER OF WAR IN NAZI GERMANY

A story told in a collection of love letters written between 1940 and 1945 highlighting the pain and separation of war but enlivened by hope.

JOHN HORTON

BEHIND THE WIRE: A PRISONER OF WAR IN NAZI GERMANY

Vanguard Press

A CIP catalogue record for this title is
available from the British Library.

ISBN 978 1 80016 259 4

*Vanguard Press is an imprint of
Pegasus Elliot MacKenzie Publishers Ltd.*
www.pegasuspublishers.com

First Published in 2022

**Vanguard Press
Sheraton House Castle Park
Cambridge England**

Printed & Bound in Great Britain

Dedication

This book is dedicated to Alan and Peggy Horton

Acknowledgements

I would like to acknowledge the help of my wife, Elizabeth, for thoroughly checking the manuscript on numerous occasions.

My sister, Anne Moore-Bick, for discovering some of the photographs and papers used to illustrate the book.

Roger Pringle has also read the book and made a number of extremely constructive comments which have added greatly to the text.

Finally, my sincere thanks are also due for all the help given to me in preparing this book for publication by the staff at Pegasus.

Christmas 1943

They pass us by, these changeless, empty years
Each the twin of that day which went before,
For age-old Time forgets the charge he bears
And here lies sleeping while the sirens roar.

They say in the world so far away
The sun still shines, the birds sing at dawn
And people laugh, and children careless play;
But maybe that is just a wish unborn.

Can it be true that this New Year of Grace
Will prove a year of Grace in very fact,
That peace will shine o'er Europe's tortured face?
We can but wait and hope — we cannot act.

Captain Randall Sly, the Royal Warwickshire Regiment
23rd December 1943

Contents

A List of Abbreviations

A.A.	Anti-Aircraft.
A.M.P.C.	Auxiliary Military Pioneer Corps.
A.T.S.	Auxiliary Territorial Service, the women's branch of the army.
B.E.F.	British Expeditionary Force.
███████	Censored
B.C.	Battery Commander.
B.H.Q.	Battery Headquarters
B.S.M.	Battery Sergeant Major
B.Q.S.M.	Battery Quartermaster Sergeant Major
C.I.S.	Chartered Institute of Secretaries
C.G.M.	Chief General Manager
C.S.M.	Company Sergeant Major
C/O.	Commanding Officer
E.N.S.A.	Entertainments National Service Association
F.A.N.Y.	First Aid Nursing Yeomanry
G.H.Q.	General Headquarters
H.E.C.P.	Harbour Entrance Control Point
JU52	Junker 52, a German aircraft
M.E.F.	Middle East Forces
M.C.	Military Cross
M.T.	Military Transport
N.C.O.s	Non-Commissioned Officers
O.C.T.U.	Officer Cadet Training Unit
O.O.D.	Officer of the Day
R.H.Q.	Regimental Headquarters
R.A.M.C.	Royal Army Medical Corps
R.A.	Royal Artillery
R.A.S.C.	Royal Army Service Corps

R.M.P.	Royal Military Police is the usual definition but I do not think that is the case here and have failed to find a suitable alternative.
N.A.A.F.I.	Navy Army Air Force Institute
U.S.N.R.	United States Naval Reserve
V.A.D.	Voluntary Aid Detachment
W.A.A.F.	Women's Auxiliary Air Force
Y.M.C.A.	Young Men's Christian Association.

Introduction

"Daddy, what's that mark on your leg?"

"It's where a bit of shrapnel hit me in the war."

"What happened after that, Daddy?"

"It went through my leg and out of the other side."

"Where did it go then, Daddy?"

"It went into the head of the person lying next to me."

"Did he die?"

"Yes."

As a small boy in the early nineteen-fifties, I can well remember that rather gruesome conversation with my father, Alan Horton, just a few lean years after the end of the Second World War. It was a time when rationing was still stalking the land and we lived as tenants in a somewhat drab first floor flat in Cheltenham where Alan worked as a sub-manager for one of the main high street banks.

With the continued questioning of a persistent child, I eventually learnt that the shrapnel came, not from the Germans, by whom he had been captured in Crete and then carted by cattle truck across Europe to Germany, but from the Americans. They had come, with great force and minimal accuracy, to the rescue of those in the prisoner of war camp as part of their liberation of Europe. Unfortunately, on this occasion their extravagant enthusiasm had resulted in the deaths of nine prisoners and the injury of a further fifty men (figures vary according to sources). An unknown number of Germans were also killed or injured in the attack.

One reason for remembering that conversation was that it was pretty much the only solid fact about his years as a prisoner of war that Alan ever disclosed. As far as one can tell, a strong, reinforced shutter had been drawn firmly across his mind, blocking it off from the many unpleasant memories that must have been held captive there. I later learnt that this was a phenomenon common to many veterans of any war.

Very occasionally, there were glimpses behind the shutter, such as when we were watching television one Christmas many years later. One of the well-known and popular wartime escape films was on and Alan said at one point, "I remember that I was standing just there." He never elaborated further.

My mother, Peggy, did once mention that she understood Alan had been on a camp escape committee helping others to freedom, but she knew no more. He did not attempt to escape himself, but numerous escape attempts were made. Captain John Mansell records in his diary on the 4th of June 1943 that, '67 chaps had got out of a tunnel', although no one he knew of had any knowledge of the planned escape. Sadly, he reports the following day that a number of this group had been recaptured[1].

In a letter written to Alan shortly after the Battle of Crete, Peggy wrote, 'But think, in years to come how your son will love to say "Daddy, tell us about the war". I can see you puffing out your chest and saying, "Well son…" That never did happen. Even on the rare occasions I asked, Father certainly never puffed out his chest and he never spoke seriously about the war.

Once or twice, Alan referred to a humiliating incident when an officer stuck a ping-pong ball on his nose and pushed it around the

---

[1] The Mansell Diaries edited by E G C Beckwith T.D. published privately in 1977.

camp mud in order to obtain some reward from his fellows. As a child, it seemed hilarious, but it must have had its grisly, degrading side for a desperate prisoner. Sometimes there would be mention of roll calls that lasted all night because the prisoners would not co-operate with a pompous, dictatorial Nazi camp commandant. That was about the extent of Alan's revelations.

Even when asked to give after-dinner speeches about his years in prison camp, he gave precious little away. His notes read like a comedy script explaining that there was no truth in the rumour he overtook a hare as he fled from the field of battle. They also confirmed that, as a prisoner, it was his task to eat as much of the enemy's food as he could. It made those attending a dinner, who knew nothing of such an existence, laugh but revealed little, if anything, about the reality of life as a prisoner of war. It was off limits, and we never attempted to go there.

When, on one occasion, he was challenged by a well-intentioned vicar, concerned with human rights abuses, to say if he had seen the Germans commit any kind of barbaric acts, Alan refused to confirm or deny such things, stating that he knew the British had done much the same and he felt there was no point in raking over such memories. In war, all sides indulge in atrocities, and he was doubtful whether any one should be entitled to claim the moral high ground.

There were times when Alan would accompany Peggy to see films about the Second World War, but he would quietly admit that he went to please Peggy, not because he enjoyed war films. He had seen too much ugly violence in real life to want to see more of it depicted in glorious technicolour on a vast silver screen.

For a year in 1956/7, Alan was very seriously ill with tuberculosis and both he and the doctors attributed that to his long, hard years in prison camp with poor rations, Spartan conditions, and hard labour. Many years later, he confided to me that he felt prison camp had probably left him rather depressed and it had taken him years to rid himself of it. I recalled dark winter evenings when he would don his coat, seize his walking stick, and set out into the night for a walk, slamming the door behind him with scarcely a word to anyone.

He certainly never sought any kind of counselling or medical assistance. The idea that one might speak to a 'counsellor' never entered his mind and you had to be 'barking' mad to visit a 'shrink'.

When war broke out in 1939, Alan was twenty-eight years old and had been working as a bank clerk since he had left the local grammar school. He came from a modestly well-off family where his father, Frank, had risen from the ranks in the Royal Navy to become a lieutenant commander — quite an achievement in those far off days when commissions might be seen as the preserve of the youngest sons of the gentry. Alan's brother, Cyril, was carving out a career for himself in the Royal Marines. Alan too would dearly have loved to obtain a commission but the early death of his father, from stomach cancer, soon after retiring from the navy, rendered this impossible. The modest family finances could not stretch to two commissions. Alan did, however, join the Territorial Army some years before the outbreak of war and he loved it. It enabled him to gain confidence and independence from a very possessive and lonely mother who had the capacity to be quite manipulative when it suited her.

Peggy, at twenty-one, was the eldest of five children, whose mother had died in 1938. Their father, Frederick Sutcliffe, was a London architect of some note having worked on *The Daily Telegraph* building, the Epsom Grandstand and some large hospitals including Saint Thomas's. He spent considerable sums of money freely but found himself unable to cope with his four daughters and one son, plus his business, once he no longer had the support of his wife, the bedrock of the family and inspiration for much of his work.

My parents met sometime in the cold winter of 1939/40, but the first two letters addressed to Alan from Peggy were written in the early spring of 1940. The letters are really quite formal and end, 'Yours sincerely, Peggy', suggesting their relationship had not developed greatly at this time. However, despite a fairly nomadic lifestyle for Alan, by now enlisted in the army, their relationship developed quickly. Indeed, they were married in November 1940.

In those days, the weather was the least of their worries. On their wedding anniversary, they would often remind themselves of the sound of spent cartridges clattering onto the roof of the church from a Battle of Britain dogfight taking place overhead during their wedding ceremony. Thankfully, few people today have to carry such memories of their wedding day into the rest of their life. Unsurprisingly, there are few photographs of the wedding. Posing outside for photos at that point in history may not have been a particularly good idea! A very brief three-day honeymoon in the home of old family friends followed in Suffolk before Alan returned to his regiment, 'The Gunners', of which he remained immensely proud all his life.

Within a few short weeks of marriage, these same Gunners embarked on the S.S. City of Canterbury and sailed south down through the Atlantic Ocean, round the Cape of Good Hope and northwards up the east coast of Africa and, eventually, via Egypt and the Mediterranean, to Crete. Here they set up their guns to defend the island, remaining until the last when they had no option but to spike their guns and surrender to the Germans by whom they had been soundly defeated.

As prisoners of war, Alan and his comrades were transported to the Greek mainland and placed in cattle trucks to begin the long, gruelling journey across Europe to the prison camp in Germany. During these months, Peggy had all the letters she had written to her husband of only a few months returned stamped simply, 'CERTIFIED MISSING/PRISONER OF WAR/ DECEASED'. It would be well into 1945 before they were to meet again, although they were able to carry on a correspondence during the intervening four years.

Following Peggy's death in 2003 we discovered a very large part of that correspondence together with *A Wartime Log for British Prisoners*, written in a little hardback notebook supplied as a gift from The War Prisoners' Aid of the Y.M.C.A. in Geneva, Switzerland. Scribbled on the inside cover is 'A. E. Horton; Lieut. (Army). No. 3275, Block VII B, Room 2'. The first entry is a poem under the heading 'Christmas 1943', written by another inmate, but the main text does not start until 30th June 1944, by which time he was a prisoner in Oflag VII-B, at Eichstätt, Bavaria, Germany. This was his third and final camp of the war and where he remained longest.

The log also includes some photographs of family members. There is an unusually large number of Alan's niece, born the same year as the war started. The explanation for this is that the Germans liked blond 'Aryan' children and were sympathetic to people whom they thought to be parents of such children. Alan never claimed his niece as his daughter but neither did he rush to contradict any assumptions his captors might make for themselves. It was some four years after the end of the Second World War that Alan was able to claim that he was indeed the 'Daddy' to two little blond children of his own — twins!

The correspondence contains some letters written before Alan travelled overseas, others he wrote whilst on the S.S. City of Canterbury, but most were written during the years he was a prisoner of war. Staff of the Imperial War Museum informed us that it is one of the most complete sets of correspondence of this kind ever to have been found. It certainly reflects a much more formal era than the one we know today. Christian names have now replaced surnames, whilst few people today begin a private letter, 'Dear Madam'.

No one used the term 'cool' in relation to anything but the weather or a drink in those days. 'Grand', however, was used to describe a wide range of items and situations. The place of women in society was very different to that of today and racism was more overt. The letters contain phrases that Millennials would never consider using; they make all of us squirm with embarrassment but that was how things were three quarters of a century or more ago and we should not try to kid ourselves otherwise.

Without even reading the letters, one can see from their envelopes the pain that the war must have engendered, especially in Peggy, a bride of less than a year, many of whose letters were returned stamped simply 'Undeliverable For Reason Stated, RETURN TO SENDER'. Another stamp callously states, 'Addressee Reported Prisoner of War'. There is no information given about the prisoner's whereabouts or his condition. That would have come later in the form of a printed card and signed 'Alan Horton'. We think it finally arrived in September 1941 over three months after the Battle of Crete. No texts, emails, WhatsApp, Twitter, or Facebook in those far off days.

Other letters include ones written to Peggy by relatives of fellow Gunners who were reported either dead or missing, as they too tried to discover the fate of their loved ones. These make especially poignant reading and could bring a lump into any throat. There is also some interesting correspondence Peggy had with the Red Cross as she tried to learn more for herself of Alan's whereabouts and condition.

Additionally, papers have revealed a very simple code devised and used by my parents to indicate where Alan was because he could not write openly that he was in Egypt or Crete, for security reasons. There is also a meticulous record, prepared by Alan, showing the fate of comrades in arms. All letters were censored by both sides.

Peggy's own letters are more numerous because, whilst discouraged from writing too many for fear of clogging up the censor's table, she was free to write many more than Alan. Prisoners were only permitted a few postcards and aerograms each month. Peggy held in contempt many in authority and could also be very forthright and any idea of being 'politically correct' was utterly alien to her. Thus, in one letter she informs Alan that, 'No more (perfume) can be found because the Bosch have helped themselves to it all for their fat Fraus!'

Peggy was an excellent cook and, occasionally, there are insights of how inventive one needed to be to cook good, tasty food using the very limited wartime rations available to any cook in this land. Meals out were also of comparatively meagre fare compared with what we have come to expect in even the most modest of restaurants in twenty first century Britain.

Together with the prisoner's log, we found notes Alan had been making before his death, of the lives of his father and six uncles. All but one of these seven men had died before my twin sister and I were born in 1949 but each one had lived the sort of life of which, today, we can only catch glimpses in novels and films. Their example is one of exemplary service and together these two generations span some of the remarkable events of the last part of the nineteenth and early twentieth centuries. In February 1900, Queen Victoria sent the mayor of Sandwich the princely sum of £5 to pass on to their mother, Alan's grandmother, because so many of her seven sons were serving in her armed forces. Alan Horton was following in a distinguished family tradition, and he knew and honoured that fact.

Today, with twenty-four-hour rolling news cover, Zoom, Skype, social media, mobile phones, and other technology, it is hard to imagine having to wait so long for news of a loved one. It would take weeks, if not months, before a letter received a response assuming it ever reached its intended destination. This book aims to provide a glimpse into one small and very personal corner of the Second World War through some of the many letters Alan and Peggy wrote to each other around eighty years ago as he dwelt in three German prisoner of war camps and in the months leading to his incarceration. This is supported, where appropriate, by Alan's log and with correspondence and other papers left by my parents. These letters highlight a personal side to war especially among the wives and families whose lot it was to remain at home and wait for the duration of some eternally long years.

Only when reading these papers did I appreciate just how much both Alan and Peggy, along with millions of others, must have longed for victory day throughout many tedious years of conflict. Unfortunately, most of the letters we have from the early stage of Alan and Peggy's relationship are those written by Alan making the account a little one-sided, however, they do help to construct a picture of the difficulties of a wartime relationship. Later in the war, considerably more of Peggy's letters survive than those written by Alan.

Finally, where letters allude to events in the camp that are not explained, I have drawn on other documents, held by the Imperial War Museum and others, to provide the necessary background. Otherwise, I leave the letters of my parents to narrate their own all-absorbing story.

John Horton
January 2022

Getting to Know You

Rosemount, R.M.P. Bobbing, Near Sittingbourne, Kent.
4.2.40.

Dear Daddy,

This is a little note to say thank you very, very much for the grand evening I had with you on Saturday — I am afraid on leaving you at Twydall my manners weren't at their best — and my "thank yous" somehow got mislaid in the black out.

Pam has gone to bed with her cold and so there's only Treadgold and myself left.

Your chocolates are fast disappearing — Angela works with them on her desk — I'd better remove them. Once again my very many thanks and I hope you can call on us again very soon. Yours sincerely, Peggy.

PS: my first whisky was excellent!

(At twenty-eight, Alan was quite a bit older than many of the officers and so was given the name 'Daddy' by his fellow officers.)

234/89th A.A. Regiment R.A. The Drill Hall, Crown Quay, Sittingbourne, Kent.
23rd March 1940.

Dear Peggy,

Peter rang me up yesterday and told me the sad news. It is very bad luck getting it now after passing through the thick of the 'flu epidemic unscathed. I hope it is only a slight attack and you will soon be well again. In view of the later developments perhaps it is for the best.

It is a pity about the party but perhaps we can hold it at a later date. We hope to see you back soon. Yours sincerely, "Daddy."

Hatton Cottage, Lubbock Road, Chislehurst, Kent.
27.3.40.

Dear Daddy,

It was so nice of you to remember me with your letter — yes — I was furious on finding that such a childish complaint had caught me. Polly Porter sent me home straight away, so I have leave until April 7th and come out of quarantine this Thursday.

Do you have much time free on Saturday and Sunday — if so perhaps you could manage to come over for a meal? I can't promise to fetch you as Pop's away with the car — but some of us will meet you at Bromley South as the Green bus stops there — anyway ring me and we can arrange something.

This is my first day out of bed and it is surprising how weak one's pins feel. Isn't the spring air grand?

Am afraid this is a rather chatty letter, but it gets boring talking to dogs all day long.

Hope you can manage to come over. Yours sincerely, Peggy.

Officers' Mess, A.A. Command School of Instruction, Biggin Hill, Kent.
3rd April 1940.

Dear Peggy,

This is a somewhat belated letter to say "thank you" for the grand day I had on Sunday. I enjoyed every minute of it and was glad of the opportunity to meet your cheery young brother and sister. Thank you very much.

I hope you are well settled in at Bobbing again and are reconciled to the loss of that week's leave. That was undoubtedly "a bit 'ard."

The Major is here with me now, but I do not see much of him as most of my time is spent in my quarters preparing for passing out examinations on Saturday.

Please give my kind regards to all at Bobbing. I hope to see you all again soon.

Yours sincerely, "Daddy."

Rosemount, R.M.P. Bobbing, Sittingbourne, Kent.
4.4.40.

Dear Daddy,

Thank you for your letter — so glad you liked the hooligans of the family; you've still got two more girls to meet. They are as bad as the rest of us.

This note is really to wish you "Good luck" for your exams — it must feel like school again — cramming up for the fateful day.

There's not a great deal of news — Angela has a new car — a scarlet Talbot 10 — a Red Devil! Another Padre has attached himself to us — R.A.S.C. — can't make out whether he is Northumbrian or Irish by his accent.

Well cheerio and best of luck for Saturday. Yours sincerely, Peggy.

234/89th A.A. Regiment, R.A.
12th April 1940.

Dear Peggy,

Many thanks indeed for your letter and the cloths. It is very sweet of you both to think of us — they will brighten up our mess no end — you must come and have dinner with us next week when we will use them for the first time.

If you are free on Monday evening what about coming to a cinema with me, and we can then arrange a party for the end of the week? Once again, thank you from all of us.

Yours sincerely, Alan.

13th April 1940.

Many thanks for your letter. I am sorry to hear that you too, are confined to barracks and hope soon the ban will be lifted and you will be able to call on us again. I look forward to your visits very much.

Well, here's hoping you will get up to see us again. Ooh, what I wouldn't give for an evening off and a shout. I will certainly pass on any good stories I hear.

Yours sincerely, Alan.

Rainham
19th May 1940.

Many thanks for your note. First, I must apologise for the "pansy" notepaper, but I won this in the boomps-a-daisy competition on Tuesday.

We had a foul night again last night and were out until nearly three o'clock. I am very cheerful today but devilish tired and miss the support of my field boots which I cut off early yesterday evening. My brother paid me a visit on his way up to the Admiralty. He has got a new job and has promised to call in tonight and tell me all about it.

I shall look forward to seeing you again soon and as you say, we can have a chat.

What shall we celebrate that night? If it is Saturday the excuse is good enough as one is allowed to get tight on Saturdays because they are Saturdays. I have a great deal to do and look like having to do without sleep for some time to come so I am afraid alcohol will eventually get the better of me as my one and only source of energy. I am messed about so much here that it is impossible to do myself justice and I am leaning towards doing something wild to get slung out and let some other poor so and so try it. It hurts my professional pride very deeply particularly as all criticism reflects directly on me and I am powerless to improve it. However — perhaps twenty-four hours leave will brighten the horizon. Au revoir, your, Alan

234/89th A.A. Regiment R.A. Sittingbourne.
6th August 1940.

Thank you very much for your letter. Today has been a typical hum-drum day on site and it was a great joy to come in tonight and see it in the rack. Your letters have a happy knack of reaching me just when I need them the most and telling me just what I want to hear and what you can never tell me too often. I, too, am very happy and find my tongue and pen inadequate to express my inmost thoughts. Your quotation from Rupert Brooke is very appropriate — how I wish I could write like that. It has set me thinking of others. I send you one which I have always carried with me since I found it and which if followed, would clear up many of our troubles today. What a pity Hitler hasn't read it!

"Thinking seldom of your enemies"[2] is a difficult one to carry out when one's whole life is towards his destruction. I can almost think well of him now though as he indirectly brought us together.

Well, my love, I must say good night now for the mess is filling up and concentration is impossible. Until tomorrow then — All my love, Alan.

Rainham
8th August 1940.

Beloved, I have been filled with remorse since I left you at the disgraceful state I was in last night and have been hoping you can find it in your heart to forgive me.

Can you, my dear? Your, Alan.

---

[2] Henry van Dyke (1852-1933).

School of Anti-Aircraft Defence, Gunnery Wing, Manorbier, S Wales.
12th August 1940.

Well, as you can see, here I am. I came straight to the mess on arrival and found your letter — a better greeting I cannot think of except finding you yourself awaiting me at the end of a journey. It was a very sweet thought of yours, so typical of you, and one of the many things that endear you to me.

We had lunch on the train in Newport Station and were very amused to hear the "Raiders Passed" sounded on the sirens after we had been in the station some considerable time. The platforms were packed with people, and everything appeared normal. It was the first indication we had that anything was wrong.

There was a large party of us on the train and I met Fish, whom I had met previously at Rainham, with a friend of his. We three had lunch together with a young Welsh civilian Padre. He was a likeable fellow and parted from us with "May God bless you and keep you safe." For once in my life, I prayed fervently that it would be answered and inwardly repeated it for you too.

Your verse from Rupert Brooke is very beautiful. I shall never forget that day we spent in the heather on the hill. He must have known such a day as that and voices the thoughts that rise in my mind, but I am incapable of committing to paper. How I wish, my dear, that I could write such words for you.

If we are to be parted soon, we must make a second trip to that very spot again before I go. I can close my eyes now and picture you kneeling on that rich carpet and feel the wind again on my face; the woods in the distance; the blue sky and the white clouds overhead...

You have done much for me Peggy, more perhaps than you can ever imagine. At times when I have been despondent some word of yours has put fresh life into me and fresh hope; for months past your visits have been the one thing I have looked forward to. You have raised me up from the coarseness of that squalid army life that we know; it was bringing me to and turned my mind again to the things I used to love books, music and ordinary things of everyday. With you Peggy I believe I can do almost anything. I remember reading somewhere, "to have love is to work miracles[3]."

Your ring is a constant reminder to me of you and the promises we have made to each other. I shall guard it well and all that it means until I return. I hope by then to have your father's consent. Goodnight, my darling, All my love, your, Alan.

15th August 1940.

I was delighted to find two letters from you awaiting me when I came in for lunch today and have read and re-read them several times already. Your news is very good too. Particularly I am glad that your father will raise no objections to our engagement. As you say, it makes for a much happier feeling although nothing and no one can stop us now.

I will certainly write to your father as soon as I know what time I shall get back to town but before I do will you please let me know his initials and degrees, I should hate to offend him now by addressing him all wrong.

I have "clicked" for duty manning the defences over the weekend and was also on duty the second night here and did a two-

---

[3] "To have love is to work miracles" — the origin of this is unknown.

hour look-out in blinding rain from 05.00 hrs to 07.00 hrs on the second morning. I've no doubt they will find something amusing about that at Rainham. I didn't and neither did the man with me!

I have not had much chance to look around here yet and have only had a quick walk into Manorbier. The castle looks very attractive; indeed, the whole place is very charming in a quiet way.

Now I look forward only to the time when you are really mine. I shall love you always and will then be able to look after you as well. Let us hope it may be soon.

"Au revoir" my darling and all my love, Your, Alan.

17th August 1940.

Thank you very much for your letter — as for being inundated with them — I can never have too many.

It must have been rather fun meeting your father's friends in the circumstances. I wish I had been there with you for their reactions on meeting would be amusing to watch. I wonder what they will think of me? Above all I wonder what Diana *(Peggy's youngest sister)* will think of me? Obviously, I must make a good impression with her if I can. Has she any weaknesses I can exploit to that end?

So, the fun and games have really started in earnest at last. It is just my luck to miss a shoot having been on the site for nearly twelve months but above all I am glad nothing happened to you. Do you remember the old song about taking care of yourself? Please do so. We seem well away from all the fun here although two dull crumps were once heard in the distance. If anything is to happen, I hope it happens today or tomorrow for I am on a gun from 17.00

hrs today until 17.00 hrs tomorrow. We actually have to spend seventeen hours of this on the gun park at the weekend.

I went into Tenby yesterday with the object of finding my cousin's camp at Wiseman's Bridge. It seemed such a difficult place to get at that I stayed in Tenby for the evening. It's a charming little place — a good place for a lazy holiday.

The sun is shining today and it's quite warm so a party of us are going down to bathe in one of the coves. How I wish you were here, my dear, and we could roam about together. The country is beautiful; the sun shines; it only needs you here to make it perfect.

I started this letter early this morning but before I could finish, I had to go to lectures. Now I have your photograph by my side and very good it is too. Thank you very much. I shall keep it by my bunk so that you are the first person I shall see in the morning and the last one at night. I am longing to get back, Peggy, so that I can hold you in reality again. Can you wrangle some leave on Sunday? You are always in my thoughts, and I send you all my love. Your, Alan.

Monday.

Your letter with the bad news in it reached me today at lunch time *(We have no letters that record what this bad news was that Alan had received from Peggy).* It is bad luck that having been at war so long this must happen now. It is typical of the services and war and must be accepted as part of the show. I am terribly disappointed though, darling, and hope that it will not be for long. You must cheer up my dear, for even now it may not happen.

I hate to be here living in peace in marvellous surroundings while you are having such a hectic time. It is just my luck to be out of it when things start to happen. I do hope "B" Troop is giving good account of itself, and hope when I return to find the Bosch planes piled in heaps around the gun park. Whatever happens take care of yourself Peggy, if for no other reason than for my sake. Everything will sort itself out in the end and you and I can be happy together. I think of you every day and look often at your picture. I feel sure that when two people love as we do, nothing can keep them apart indefinitely. The war must reach a decisive stage soon and then our turn will come. It makes me livid to think these Germans and Italians can affect us directly and I shall have no mercy on them if any fall into my hands.

I long for the time when I can see you again and hold you once more in my arms.

Au revoir my darling and all my love, Your, Alan.

PS: Please don't forget to let me have your father's initials and degrees, Your, Alan.

20th August 1940.

I have come to expect a letter from you every day and was very disappointed not to find one in the rack this morning. It was more than offset, though, by the one I found this evening. My heart goes out to you, now you have Bradley as a patient. Many is the time I would gladly have wrung his neck although for all his escapades I can't help liking the little blighter. Hackett, I don't know. Is he from 234 as well?

It all sounds very exiting down there and I look forward to hearing all about it from Charles. I am very annoyed with him though for he promised he'd send on to me my watch and boots and up until now nothing has happened. I am hobbling about in shoes that cripple me and never have any idea of the time. Perhaps he is too busy to worry about these trifles?

You had better watch out tomorrow for the course is doing a shoot. Heaven only knows where the shells will go, and some blinds are quite likely to land in Kent!

The mess at the moment is packed with officers. It is almost impossible to get a bath in the morning — one is very lucky if room can be found to shave. Several men I know came in last night — Felton from 235, Taylor who is with 205; Streetfield from the 75th and Crawford who used to be in the 75th but went to the B.E.F.

I have written to your father tonight and hope to arrive there about noon on Saturday. I shall catch the night train from here on Friday and want to do some shopping in town on Saturday morning. The news Felton brings is making me look to my kit.

I heard from Mother tonight, and she said she was writing you. I am very glad that you like her and that she, too, has taken such a liking to you. We must try and go down together and see my new home. I have not, of course, broken the other news to her yet.

I look forward to meeting Diana on Saturday and hope I will pass the test in her eyes. I shall get away fairly early for I am anxious to be with you again at the earliest possible moment.

Hukins has not answered my letter about leave yet but I suppose we are asking rather a lot if we are to expect him to make up his mind so soon. Between us I feel sure we can make it all right. What fun we shall have. The thought of a whole week with you seems too good to be true. I count the hours darling, until that time. Still seems impossible that you love me as you do and I too, hope I shall never fail you either.

Take care of yourself until I get back. Good night my darling. All my love, Your, Alan.

Lieutenant Alan Horton

22nd August 1940.

I intended to write to you last night as usual, but I was manning from 17.00 hrs in very bad weather and felt fit only for bed when I came in. There was a terrific gale blowing bringing with it clouds of sand and after an hour and a half on look-out and five hours standing too we all came in exhausted.

Well, the course is nearly at an end. Today we have been firing (great fun) and tomorrow we give our lecturettes. I hope to catch the night train from here and arrive in town at 05.00 hrs. (What to do then I can't think), I shall do some shopping, visit Chislehurst, and be down with you as early as possible — about seven o'clock, I hope. Go to Rainham at the usual time and I will join you as soon as I can.

The Major has written to me at last to say that my leave is OK for the 4th unless something unforeseen happens. Charles has at last sent my watch and boots — the night before I leave. However, he has apparently been very busy, so I suppose there is some excuse. Both letters were very reticent hinting at terrific news to come. It amuses me considerably in the circumstances and I am trying to make up my mind whether to appear surprised when I hear it or whether to admit that I know.

Well, my dear, owing to the lecturettes an air of gloom pervades the course and like everyone else I must do a spot of revision so I will again say "au revoir". Only forty-eight hours and we shall be together again. Good night sweetheart and all my love, Your, Alan.

Build-up to a Wartime Wedding

There is no record of the date on which Alan and Peggy became engaged although, in her letter written to Alan on 1ˢᵗ August 1941, Peggy reminded him that it was nearly a year since they were engaged. Alan writes elsewhere about their engagement in September! In a letter dated 2ⁿᵈ November 1941, written by Peggy, it is clear that wedding preparations did not begin until shortly before the wedding. 'It was November 1ˢᵗ that we finally decided to be married before you went away. On the 5ᵗʰ we broke the news to Mother and went off to a hotel together — what scandal!'

From this point on some very frantic and last-minute preparations were made for their 'big day' but with Alan working long hours, much of the preparatory work was left to Peggy.

234/89ᵗʰ A.A. Regiment R.A. Sittingbourne.
7ᵗʰ September 1940.

My own darling,

Thank you very much for your note this morning. You are always in my thoughts, and it is grand to hear from you.

Life here is a terrific change from leave and when Atwell brought my tea in this morning you have no idea how much I should have welcomed being back at Chislehurst. I shall never forget those morning visits of yours and look forward only to the time when we can be together always.

Thank goodness you are free tomorrow, and we can get together again. I will come in for you in the late afternoon and bring you back. There is a good deal to do here at the moment getting hold of the strings of my section otherwise I would come in tonight. I am sorry I could not get this ready to send by Talbot (*Captain Ian*) but most of the morning has been spent trying to find ink and writing materials. Lloyd is coming through this afternoon so perhaps he will bring it.

"Au revoir" then my darling and give yourself a big hug from me (If that is possible).

I send you all my love. Your, Alan.

16th September 1940.

Beloved, every time I have tried to call you up today the sirens have gone, and I am greeted with "emergency calls only".

The Major's answer today was an emphatic "No," so the Canterbury trip is off. (The old…!) I can only suggest that you come up here and spend what is left of the day helping me arrange my "flat". Please come as soon as you can. All my love, Alan.

22nd September 1940.

If you do not turn up for tea today, as I hope you will, I plan to send this by driver tonight. I know you will have looked for a letter from me when the mobile returned this morning and am very sorry that I failed to keep my half of the bargain. Actually, Lloyd had arranged a route march for us this morning to get everyone out of the way. Before we went, we had a trial evacuation so there was no time to write then. I only knew about ten minutes before we left and just had time to get ready.

Your description of the view from your window sounds very attractive indeed. I was astir quite early and attended Roll Call Parade (!). The marshes looked about as well as I have ever seen them with the sunshine in the mist turning everything to gold. The scents too, are so delightful both in the morning and evening.

I really thought last night something might happen and slept half dressed with my revolver by my side. I half laughed at myself for having it, until I found that Lloyd spent most of the night roving about and even some of the men did not undress.

The route march this morning was great fun. The men were in good spirits and sang all the time and had a good feed of pears from a farmer who said they could go in and take as many as they liked from under the trees. From the mad rush after "Fall Out" one would have thought they were starving and never had fruit anyway. No one would have believed that they live in an orchard. It rained for some miles, but we let down our capes and carried on. It was very pleasant.

I often think, my darling, of the times you and I will have when this war is over. Together we shall be able to do justice to just such mornings as these. I often picture you coming home to tea on an autumn afternoon, with a dog at your heels, and that inevitable armful of flowers or branches. They will be great days. Au revoir darling, all my love, Alan.

28th September 1940.

I am writing this now in time to be brought in by Peter to let you know that you are always in my thoughts. Your letters to me have done much to bridge the short gaps between our meetings and I know you look for them as I do. I fear I must often fail you in this respect for with the many trivialities making up my day I often leave writing until too late. You know, my darling, how my mind turns, and I know you can forgive these things.

Tomorrow should be an easy day here although I have had to ask the C/O over to deal with a "drunk and disorderly" but with luck it should all be over early, and I will be with you in the late afternoon. We must then lay our plans for the future and come to a decision. The course I want to take is very clear in my mind, but my conflicting duties and loyalties make it hard to fix a line of action. You know the thoughts doing battle in my mind and must know that always uppermost is my thought for your welfare in these difficult days through which we are passing. Tomorrow then Peggy. Until then my thoughts will always be with you. I send you my warm love, Your own, Alan.

8th October 1940.

Although, as you know, there is but one person in the world I want to be with tonight having taken forty-eight hours leave instead of twenty-four I cannot justify another night out on any grounds at all. Lloyd is still away and Wilson and Corbett both went into the town, so I am left in solitary state making arrangements for tomorrow's move.

Yesterday and the day before will live in my mind — particularly the time on top of our hill. It is against such backgrounds as that I like to picture you in my mind. Misty sunsets, hills and heather, flowers and trees, of such is your setting.

9th October 1940.

The beginning of this letter will read strangely after what actually did happen last night. It only shows how easily we may be wrong and how soon we may be together again in spite of the way things look now.

The motorcycle did its stuff well and I got back without incident although the wretched thing kept stopping whenever I throttled down. It must have seen you and wanted to go back in answer to my unspoken thoughts.

I am sending you a code with this as we arranged so that if we go you will have some idea at least of where we are. I know it is unnecessary to add — keep it safe and tell nobody at all even that we have such an arrangement. It is for you and you only that I do it and for anyone else at all to know might mean disaster.

Well, my love, I must come to an end. May God bless you and keep you safe until I return. Until then I send you all of my love, Your own, Alan.

As they arrived in Egypt, Alan mentioned in his letter 'Woolworths', thus ensuring Peggy had an idea of what part of the world he was in. Crete, sadly, did not feature in this code! It is interesting to note how many of these, once well-known brands have ceased to exist.

The Code:

    Woolworths — Egypt
    Marks and Spencer — Haifa
    Burtons — Gibraltar
    Hepworths — Malta
    Harrods — Portugal
    Gamages — Kenya
    Swan and Edgar — Singapore
    Selfridges — Cape Town
    Scotts — British Somaliland
    Boots — West Africa
    D. W. Evans — Greece
    Timothy Whites — Albania
    Dolcis — Cyprus
    Bourne Hollingworth — Hong Kong

"B" Troop. 234 A.A. Battery R.A. Station Road, Ince, Nr. Chester. 11th October 1940.

As you can see, we really are here after a hectic day and night of work and travelling. It is now 00.15 hrs and after this I propose thinking seriously about some bed. But first I will start from the time we waved you good-bye and tell you what happened to us.

We stopped the column on the road near Gravesend and while they had a drink at a wayside pub, we reconnoitred a route and had a very nice meal (at the Major's expense) in the White Hart, Gravesend. We entrained about eight o'clock during an air raid and I was very impressed by the sight of the Battery marching section by section on to the Platform in single file in the darkness. There is something "Je ne sais pas quoi" about the orders echoing in the darkness, the rattle of riffles and the tramp of feet… the dim shapes of the men. I think a man who has never been a soldier has missed a good deal.

The journey passed without incident but at one station, early in the morning an old porter informed us, "that there bridge which you just come over, were bombed last night mister. Lucky, they didn't hit 'un or it's in the river you'd be zur." It caused us much amusement, but I was very glad they "didn't hit un."

We arrived at Birkenhead about ten o'clock and hung about for some time before we could find out where we were to go. Eventually the Major told me to take my section off in a bus to a gun site to get breakfast, adding that all arrangements were cancelled, and we were to return that night. I thought that was typical of the army but was glad to hear it. However, off we went in a double-decker bus and eventually had breakfast on this site some miles out of Birkenhead. We had scarcely finished when the Major rushed up again and said the arrangements were now on again and our section was on the wrong site. We em-bussed again and went for miles and miles until we arrived here. Kirk-Smith's section came in later and we took over about seven thirty this evening. The other Battery moved off about ten o'clock to go to Practice Camp. The place is miles from anywhere and is quite pleasant and we have already been in action. As I write the sirens are going again. It looks like fun and games.

Well, my darling, I can't write much more now but my thoughts are always with you, and I live only for the time when I can take you in my arms again and kiss you. I seem to be miles from where your grandmother is living but I hope to get along sometime before we leave. Thank you for your last letter before we left.

May God bless you and keep you safe until my return. Until then,

Peggy Horton

12th October 1940.

It is now quite late, and all is quiet for the moment, so my thoughts naturally turn to you. I wonder where you are and what you are thinking?

As I believe I told you we are some twenty miles from Birkenhead and Hukins has refused to let us have any leave so it seems unlikely that I shall be able to see your grandmother unless I can find some means of escape. This means one of your letters may never be opened but the other I kept until last night. It was very sweet of you and so typical of you. I am very proud indeed to have your love and only hope I shall be able to justify your faith in me. I feel your presence always with me and with your help, hope to do much. As you say we can never be parted, for each lives in the heart of the other and we are truly inseparable.

One or two things have happened since I wrote last which will interest you. Sonia arrived this afternoon and Kirk-Smith has rooms for her near at hand. She is very well and asks after you. How I wish you were here too.

Peter, Corbett, Allchin, and I went to a William and Mary talk at a place N. E. of Liverpool and were amazed to meet Farnworth there grinning as usual. He is in fine form and congratulates us on the engagement. Allchin had bad news yesterday for his sister-in-law was killed by a bomb in Canterbury. There were several casualties besides and I am feeling rather concerned about Mother.

The local vicar called on me today and has asked two of us over to dinner on Sunday evening. Wilson and I hope to go. He is quite a pleasant old boy, and it should be rather amusing.

One point about this place is we get plenty of fun and games. It is grand to hear the guns speak again and see the flashes close to. We strung up a Dornier the other day but got no conclusive result worse luck.[4] I hope however to bring you back a piece of Bosch plane just to prove what we can do.

---

[4] The gunners trained their guns on a German Dornier plane to shoot it down but there was no proof of success.

Well, my darling, here's hoping to see you soon and until then, all my love and thoughts are with you and for you. Your own Alan.

16th October 1940.

I have had three letters today from you and very welcome they were too. You certainly seem to be having plenty of excitement with your Pilot Officers, Germans, and bombs, don't you? I can just picture Charles walking into the R.M.P. behind a prisoner complete with revolver. How is it that one managed to have dinner at the R.H.Q. without being shot by the Colonel and his scalp removed to adorn the door to his bunk? That is, I believe, the correct thing to do with scalps, isn't it?

How I wish I could join you in your sherry and fish and chips at the Bull. As a matter of interest how many sherries had you had by the time you had finished? My guess is about eight. Can you think why?

It is interesting to read your remarks about R.H.Q. expecting to be there still at Christmas time. It will be grand if we are all still there and can spend Christmas together.

It will be grand if you are able to take your father down to see my mother. I know she will be delighted to see you both. I have heard from her in a letter dated 10th but she had had no news of my brother then. The chances of my being able to call on your Grandmamma seem about nil at the moment, but I certainly will if I get half a chance.

Needless to say, we have the inevitable camp dog here — a rather pathetic looking animal with a limp in one leg. It is strange how these animals attach themselves to our camps. The men are usually very kind to them, and I believe in them, is an inherent desire to care for something which shows itself in this way.

You ask about this site. Well, I have since I started this letter, had three opportunities to see it in the pouring rain after dark for we have had three alarms and have fired once. I love to see the great flashes and feel the shake and roar as they go off. They are grand guns, and we have grand instruments. We all feel quite at home with them now.

The site is well out in the country near an old church and nearly fifteen miles from B.H.Q. which is a great advantage. Actually, there is nowhere near at hand to visit, for Chester the nearest town is six miles away. It is quite pleasantly situated in a field surrounded by tall trees. Life is much the same as on the site at Rainham, but I do much less having learnt by experience. We do however crack off quite a lot.

My darling, I long to be with you again, to hold you in my arms and gaze into your eyes again. One does not really live like this but only exist between meetings. With luck, however, we should be together again within a few days. I long for that moment. It makes me angry when I think of all the people who you can talk to when I cannot. Your letters are a great help and do something to bridge that gap but only you can fill the void in my heart.

Take care of yourself, Peggy, and until we meet again, I pray with you — May God bless you and care for you until I return. All my love, Your own, Alan.

Witham Green.
30th October 1940.

I am sorry I could not get in yesterday, but it was 8.30 p.m. before I could really breathe freely and then I found the telephone was disconnected so I could not ring you from here. It was far too late then to get in to see you, so Wilson and I walked down to the "Local" about 9.30. We have quite a comfortable place here, but it has one snag — no lights, you must come and approve the place soon.

Well, Darling, I hope to drop in and see you tonight if I may and look forward to seeing you again and holding you in my arms. It is only for times like that that I live at all. Here I am just a machine and do things automatically, but it is with you that I live.

Please don't ever think because I may appear to neglect you that you are any further away from me. Your picture is by me on my desk and is by my bed when I sleep. Your handkerchief is always in the pocket of my tunic and comes out in quiet corners many times a day. Always you are in my thoughts.

Until tonight then, darling, I send you all my love. Your own, Alan.

Poste Restante, Clacton-on-Sea.
12th November 1940.

Well, here we are at Clacton. We got in last night about 7.30 and found a big and almost deserted station. There was, of course an air raid and no light, there were of course, no lorries, the school where we are billeted was, of course, nearly two miles from the station: finally, of course, it was raining in torrents. Apart from these things everything went splendidly. When we got to the school there were very few lights, a splendid hot meal but nothing to eat it with. The place was very dirty but there were straw palliasses and blankets. The kits were very late arriving, and we slept between the most evil smelling blankets, I have ever seen.

Leverton was Troop Orderly Officer, and I must say he behaved grandly. The more I see of him the more I like him. He is hardworking, cheerful, and full of resource — a splendid combination. The Major arrived in the middle of the night looking for his kit. He woke nearly every man in both troops and became very unpopular. I was not agreeably impressed by his conduct. I suspect someone of intentionally jettisoning his kit.

You will think from all this that we had a very miserable time. Actually, the men and the officers (!) took it all in good part and the whole situation was really quite amusing.

Well, darling, I have not thanked you for your letter yet. You always time such things so well and just when there is nothing I would like better than a charming letter from you — it arrives. Yesterday it came just when I was feeling somewhat harassed and cheered me up no end. If possible, I think I love you now even more than ever. God grant that all will go well, and we are married before I go and shall end our days, as you say, in the traditional Darby and Joan style. I shall never really be happy again unless I am with you. You have become an essential part of myself.

I have not had news from the Padre yet. Do you know anything yet?

Well, my darling, there is nothing for me to tell you yet so I will say "au revoir". Like you, I shall write every day. Chin up. All my love to you. From, Alan.

234/89th H.A.A. Regiment, R.A., Butlin's Camp, Clacton-on-Sea. 13th November 1940.

Let me tell you something of the place in which we live. It is an elementary school, and the men sleep in the classrooms and eat in the assembly hall. We have one classroom in which to sleep, and we eat and make our office in the headmaster's room. It leaves much to be desired but at least we are our own masters. The other troop is in a school near at hand and their officers live in a small, empty house.

Last night I marched the entire Battery down to Butlin's Camp where we saw a very good E.N.S.A. concert in the theatre there. There seemed to be miles and miles of them. We had a drink in the mess before the show and although it is very comfortable the decorations are very garish. It reminded me of an Odeon Cinema.

The town seems practically untouched by bombs, but it is like a city of the dead. The streets are almost entirely empty, and I understand that practically the entire population has been evacuated. Kirk-Smith and I have been to the local cinema tonight to see Hedy Lamarr and Spencer Tracy in "I take this woman"[5]. The place was practically full of troops.

I had a letter from you today posted on the 11th. I know just how you feel my dear, for I am just the same. Your hymns are grand, and I thoroughly approve. If possible, I will arrange that solo for you. As you say, it would be grand if we could only arrange all this together *(There is no record of the hymns chosen for the wedding or if there was a solo, however, from what Peggy said, 'Love divine, all loves excelling' may have been included).*

---

[5] *I take this woman*, film starring Hedy Lamarr and Spencer Tracy, directed by W.S. Van Dyke.

Life is very empty here without you Peggy and I just long to see you again and hold you close to me. Your picture is always near me, and I can still faintly detect "Numero Cinq" on the handkerchief you gave me to keep. Why, oh why, must we be separated? It makes me impatient to be up and away, to do our campaigning, destroy our enemy and come back to build up a home for you and I. I am impatient for promotion and responsibility, for a chance to do something that you may be proud of me, and I feel worthy of your love. Above all I want to give you a home worthy of you and to erase for ever from my mind the lurking fear that I may fail you and you may suffer for your faith in me. You are my only inspiration and, as you know, I shall give you of my very best.

"Remember me in the hour of leisure, spare me a thought in the hour of pleasure, and should you forget me in the hour of care, remember me in your prayer[6]." But then I already have your faith and your thoughts and your prayers.

Well, my darling, take care of yourself and let me know directly you get any news from Padre Haig. I send you all my love, your own Alan.

Priority Post Office Telegram
Priority — Sutcliffe — Rosemount — Bobbing — Make arrangements for about 20th. Stop. Letter following. Love Alan.

Around this time, a priority telegram was sent to Peggy with some very basic planning for the wedding. Clearly wedding arrangements have developed a little over the last eighty years!

---

[6] Source unknown.

Further arrangements were made in letters the week before the big day.

14th November 1940.

Many thanks for your letters (two) which reached me this morning and for the one you forwarded to me. You would have been very amused had you seen the contents. I had a letter from my brother, and he is making arrangements for the renovation of our flat.

I am glad you have seen the other Padre. He is probably speedier than Haig. I have not contacted the local vicar yet, but I hope to, tomorrow.

This mess is very, very small and as I write all four of us are in it and it is almost full to overflowing. Leverton is sitting on the table by my side and asks to be remembered to you. He has made friends with a telephone girl over the phone and keeps us in fits of laughter when he converses with her as he does several times a day.

Kirk-Smith is talking to Sonia over the 'phone and trying to persuade her to come down here tomorrow. Allchin is sitting by the fire smoking. The atmosphere is thick with smoke.

We all had to go down to Butlin's this afternoon to have a fitting for our tropical kit. On the way back we had tea at the Royal. It seems to be almost full of officers' wives. We met Mrs Stebbings, Mrs Hukins, Mrs Lloyd, and Mrs Sutton there. We all decided it was no place for us in view of the regulations in force here and we have found some very reasonable rooms quite near here and away from the eyes of senior officers. If you are able to stay here it is the obvious place.

I do hope you enjoy your trip to London and Jerry does not worry you while you are there. I only wish I were able to come too.

Well, my darling, in spite of all I have said to you I am getting very excited at the thought of our wedding. The only link missing in the chain of arrangements seems to be the most important one of "where". As soon as that is known definitely, we can go straight ahead. Please let me know directly you have anything definite from one or other of those Padres and we can then fix a date. What a grand thought it is. I am simply longing to stand by your side and say, "I will". Take care of yourself darling, and until that time I send you all my love. Your own, Alan.

16th November 1940.

I have had your letter from London and your telegram tonight and I hope, before this reaches you, to have spoken to you on the 'phone. In case that fails, however, I will try to get all the facts laid out on paper. As we must be married in Sittingbourne I am afraid that you, my darling, will have to make all the necessary arrangements. The best time will be about the middle or end of next week, about the 21st. I shall have to come down the day before. It will mean arranging for the church, the Padre, the licence, and the details in connection with the ceremony, i.e., hymns, choir, etc. etc. not to mention the reception, transport, invitations, etc. etc. please wire me immediately you know the date and the time. I hate having to let you do all this, much of which is undoubtedly my job but see absolutely no alternative. In the meantime, I will issue "warning orders" to my mother, Cyril and Jennie. *(Alan's brother and sister-in-law)*

Incidentally have you arranged with Lintgenich for the ring? If not, I will arrange it from a local jeweller here when I know your size. If you did see him, did you arrange for him to send it here?

As for numbers I will only ask my mother, Cyril and Jennie, the Colonel, and officers. I should imagine about six officers only will be able to come. If we extend invitations to any more of the family or to any more friends, the numbers would be completely out of hand.

You are what I would like as a wedding present. Really darling, I am at a loss to know what to say but make it some small personal thing I can carry with me in my travels. Say a propelling pencil that will be in constant use and remind me of you in all possible situations. Not that I shall ever forget you but all these things like my shaving tackle, your photograph, Rupert Brooke's poems — they bring you very near to me whenever I handle them. Give me something like that.

Now then, what can I give you? It is at times like this when I give myself away for when I try to think what it shall be I just have no idea where to begin. It is no use my pretending I am much of a man of the world. Please tell me something you really want and save me the agony of fruitless thinking. I shall never be able to make up my mind unaided.

Well, my darling, I am so excited I scarcely know what I am doing. I have tried to write logically and with thought. If I have forgotten anything you must write me, telegraph me, or if possible 'phone me at Clacton 993. How I long to see you again and to hear you called "Mrs Horton".

I send you all my love. Your own, Alan.

PS: I have quite forgotten the honeymoon. In the absence of anything else how does Goudhurst strike you? It seems to be within easy striking distance of Sittingbourne, and I believe is very attractive. Give the matter thought and let me know but remember to keep travelling down to a minimum unless we can raise a car. Alan.

17th November 1940.

I have just had your telegram telling me all the arrangements are made for Thursday. That's grand. I saw the Colonel yesterday and asked his permission to get married. Needless to say, he granted it with "four- or five-days leave". He tells me he has a very high opinion indeed of you!

Doubtless by now you will have had my letter. I will come down as early as possible on Wednesday and check up on the arrangements. I am so excited I scarcely know what I am doing. Practically all the officers of the Regiment have their wives down here now and they are all staying at one hotel, the Queen's. The place is particularly full of them. Sonia arrived last night, and she too, is there.

We had a Regimental Church Parade today, a grand show and held in very good weather. We all marched passed the Colonel. It is amazing how many men there are in the Regiment now. Even the Battery seems a terrific length.

Well, my darling, it is impossible to explain how happy it makes me to think we are to be married so soon. I just live for the time when I see you again.

18th November 1940.

The mail has just come in and the much-awaited letter from you has not come in. You must be very busy, and I only wish I could be with you so that we could plan things together. Communications being what they are, it makes things very difficult for I have no idea how far you have got with things and what I can do to help. The ring at any rate has arrived but I am in the extraordinary position of being married in three days-time and do not know the time or the church. I wanted to put the notice in "The Telegraph" but could not owing to lack of knowledge of the situation. Incidentally has anything been arranged for a photographer to appear.

My application for leave has gone in and the Colonel will only grant me four days which is a curse. It means I shall have to return on Saturday. We shall have to make the very best of that time darling.

Life is somewhat hectic, and everyone is getting rather under the weather. It is not that we have a great deal to do but life is full of very annoying details which keep us constantly at the grindstone. Being out of operations is a bad thing for all concerned.

Well, my darling, I suppose it is quite unnecessary to say how exited I am and how much I long to see you again. Things are very empty without you, and I think of you constantly. It comes home to me particularly when I see the other officers with their wives. How I long to see you among them and how proud I shall be of "Mrs Horton".

I had forgotten all about a photographer when I wrote on Saturday night (or was it Friday?) but tonight I had the photographs from home and that reminded me. I am very pleased indeed of the one of you. There are two of me for you to pick from and a very grim and terrible old warrior I look. Strangely enough I look exactly like a Spaniard and have a beautiful black eye in each. I'll bring them down when I come.

As I write Jerry is flying round and round in the darkness outside at about 1,000 feet if it were light, we could see him easily and probably be able to use a machine gun on him. I have just been outside to make sure we are blacked out in case he decided to use a machine or other novelty. Touching wood — he has been very quiet with us lately.

Thank heavens, darling, only two more days and I shall see you again. I keep looking at the ring I carry in my pocket and longing to slip it on your finger.

As ever, beloved, and all my love until we meet again. Your own, Alan.

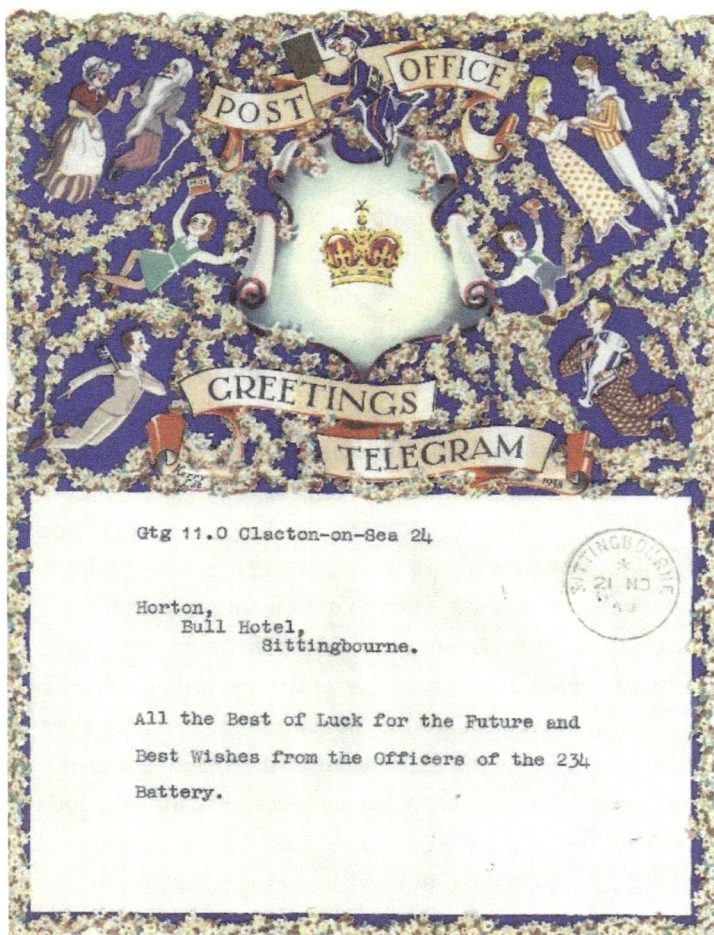

Gtg 11.0 Clacton-on-Sea 24

Horton,
    Bull Hotel,
        Sittingbourne.

All the Best of Luck for the Future and Best Wishes from the Officers of the 234 Battery.

Married Life — The Early Days

234/89th A.A. Regiment R.A. Butlin's Camp, Clacton-on-Sea.
29th November 1940.

My very own darling Peggy,

Now that you are gone from me, I feel that some essential part of my being is missing. You leave a gap in my heart that nothing and nobody can fill. At least that is what I thought I felt. Actually, now I know you are never far from me. You are always waiting in my mind ready to step into my consciousness and cheer and hearten me when I am down; to share my happiness when I am glad; to quieten my thoughts when I make a decision and generally to brighten and colour my life and be my constant companion.

It is strange, looking back, to think of the way you have grown into my life, from an ordinary (?) acquaintance, to one who is more than the whole word to me. Though now we are torn apart it is rather as though there is a definite and concrete bond between us, an elastic bond, which grows stronger as we go further away and will drag us through everything until I reach your side again. God grant it may be soon and we may start upon that journey together. Those bonds of trust and loyalty are stronger than I have known, and I shall never rest until I am at your side and can whisper again — "Heart of my heart, our heaven is now won".[7] How great it will be when

---

[7] From "The Hill" by Rupert Brooke (1887-1915).

we meet again and give each other that hug and kiss of welcome —
when we trace our steps once more over the places of our memories
— Cobham, Rivers Hall, when we think of today and laugh and
laugh at our unhappiness, thinking only of our joy. Until that day,
my love, may God bless you and keep you safe for me. Your very
own and ever-loving husband, Alan.

1st December 1940.

I am writing this in the office after tea. Kirk-Smith and Leverton are
out, and Allchin and I are keeping each other company. Since I
wrote yesterday Martin and I have visited the Odeon to see "Blue
Bird"[8] — a very pretty little film. We also had the usual Church
Parade this morning and a walk this afternoon. The weather is of
the best possible English winter variety, frost, and sunshine, but it
is marred slightly by a mist tonight. We have restarted local leave,
and, for the moment, all is quiet.

I forgot to mention yesterday some changes which have taken
place in the Battery. Several N.C.O.s from other Batteries have left
us owing to ill health and as a result Bingham has gone to 205 as
B.S.M. Old Brown is now our B.S.M. and Playford becomes
B.Q.S.M. we have also lost Sergeant Rye to 235. Sergeant Major
Bingham is very annoyed at having to go — he has been with this
Battery for 22 years. My own feelings in the matter are mixed.

Well, Peggy, how do you like life at home now that you are a
married woman? Your flowers are by my side as I write, and the

---

[8] *Blue Bird* — a black and white film directed by Walter Lang and
staring a young Shirley Temple, Russell Hicks and Spring Byington.

heat of the room has made them wither. I can't bring myself to destroy them yet.

Our first group of vehicles has left on its journey, and I am pleased to say I have got some excellent drivers for my heavy stuff. They pulled out of here after dark and I watched them go with inward excitement. I wonder what adventures we shall have together? They are grand things, just run in and excellent condition. Their power is tremendous.

As I told you on the 'phone this afternoon we treated ourselves to a real meal last night — steak and chips and a bottle of Niersteiner Superior followed by pineapple chunks (out of a tin!), biscuits and cheese and coffee. It was very nice indeed and the way Leverton tucked into it and licked his lips was too funny for words. Our Stephen certainly likes the flesh pots and makes no secret of it.

It is grand hearing your voice, darling, when you ring up. I have got to look forward to those rings of yours very much. But doesn't it give one a feeling of so near and yet so far? I feel I want to dive into the receiver and struggle through the wire to your side. I fear that even I am not so thin as that though.

Well, Peggy, that is all the news to date and so I'll say "Goodnight" and wait impatiently for your call tomorrow. Don't forget the advice in the old song to ensure you take care of yourself, and remember that you are mine. All my love is with you darling, Your own, Alan.

2nd December 1940.

Once again night has fallen. The usual pile of stuff has gone into B.H.Q. and I sit down to write my letter to you.

The day has been quite uneventful really. I turned in very early last night and the day started in the usual way with nine o'clock parade in a world of white frost. I had the place cleaned up for an inspection this morning and then changed and did some PT with No. 3 Section (the old body is beginning to rebel already!). The men spent the afternoon marking their kit bags and I took the opportunity to kip down for part of the afternoon. — Hence the lazy voice you heard over the telephone.

A lazy feeling is aggravated by the foul atmosphere in which we live. It seems impossible to get fresh air in the place whatever we do.

I am sorry to hear you have got a cold. The best thing for it is lots of fresh air. For my complaint I think a large dose of salts is the best.

Life is getting quite gay here — tonight we are going down to Butlin's to see an E.N.S.A. Concert and on Wednesday there is a Battery Dinner at the Royal. I have not been there since you left, but someone brought in your parcel from Harrods, and I have sent it on to you tonight. Apparently, there is a large number of A.M.P.C. Officers there now and (strange to relate) still one or two wives. Mrs Harrison, Mrs Boyce, and Mrs Lloyd are still there. I think we are all ready to move off, but it may be some considerable time before we go. I see tempers getting very frayed between now and then. I say we are all ready but several of us, including myself, have not yet got our drill uniform. It is promised for Wednesday.

I have got some drink in the place and tomorrow we are going to entertain the sergeants. It is to be a bachelor party so remember me in your prayers. Actually, it is only going to be a modest affair during the break tomorrow morning for they all like to go out in the evening.

My rug from Cyril arrived today and very nice it is. I am glad it came after you left, or I feel sure you would have wanted it.

Well, darling, time is getting on and I am going to walk to Butlin's to get some air so I must say "au revoir". Take care of yourself and avoid all "Blitzs" until we meet again. Until then. All my love, your very own, Alan.

3rd December 1940.

At last, I have had a letter from you; it was on my desk when I came in tonight. It was grand to hear from you, darling, and I still get a great thrill out of your endings when you sign yourself off as my wife. I never thought it possible to be so proud and happy at being married.

I am writing this later tonight, for soon after I spoke to you this afternoon, I had to go to a Battery Conference which lasted until 7.30 and from there Kirk-Smith and I went to a cinema. These conferences are rather fun for they develop into a battle of wits among the section commanders. Each is all out to get promotion for his men and tries to get the best N.C.O.s of the Battery. I've done rather well although (shame) I've lost Sergeant Cooper to B.H.Q. I have wrangled two "gunners" however, who are really good mechanics and drivers. I've got a very strong team of drivers and mechanics with one or two spares up my sleeve. I got the last one out of Wilson's Base Details by bribing him with a whisky.

The show last night was very good, and the pianist was a woman who had been twice to Rainham while we were there. She recognised the Major at once (?). After the show we all had a drink in the mess and wandered home about one o'clock. Leverton made tea and tongue sandwiches and served them to us in bed. It was very like a dormitory party at school.

In spite of Hukins' threat, I walked in the town this morning for some shopping. It was a fine frosty and sunny day — one of those mornings when you feel glad to be alive and walk on with a spring in your step. I went marching off down the road with my cap on the side of my head feeling no-end of a dude. I collected the photographs and enclose the negatives but unfortunately, they are very poor.

I have heard from Mother and Everett today and also have received my stuff from Canterbury. The Everetts are waiting to hear what we want and so also are the McConnells (You remember the little dark laddie). Think it over and drop Everett a line. Mother too says that my people at Deal are asking the same question so you might deal with them in the same way through Mother. I shall be glad if you will do this as it is more in your line I think, than mine. Do you mind, darling?

I am enclosing an official notice received today which may be of use for urgent communication when I am away. Allchin tells me the Post Office will give you special rates for cables if you ask for them.

4th December 1940.

Well, here is evening again and I sit down to write your daily newsletter. I have had two letters from you today and was very pleased with the photographs of Rivers Hall. I shall never forget the time we had there. Those memories will live with us forever. Thank you too for the letter from your aunt which is very sweet. I am sending it back in case you want to keep it. My mail today has been quite large; a parcel from Mother; a letter from a dear old aunt of mine who wants to meet you very much and your two letters.

There was a soccer match against the A.M.P.s this afternoon which the Battery won 8-0. We sent the men down to watch and I seized the opportunity to visit the Royal for a bath. I met the Boyds and the Lloyds on my travels and changed in the Lloyd's room. It is the first time I have visited the place since you left, and I found it haunted. I escaped from the Lloyd's room into the fresh air as soon as possible for the ghosts were troublesome to me.

I did some PT with the section this morning in my endeavours to get back into condition again. Actually, skinny as I am, I find I can compete quite favourably with the men in both strength and speed. I have cut down considerably on cigarettes and am much better for it.

There is still no news of our move but, (one must only whisper this) we may not move until after Christmas. Just what inferences can be drawn from that I do not know but even now we may meet again before we sail. How I should love to spend a Christmas with you. Would you let me kiss you under the mistletoe this year? Just think of Christmas in our own home darling — holly, mistletoe, dim lights, and a log fire...I would take you to a Carol Service at Canterbury Cathedral on Christmas Eve.

As I write the "Poker School" is settling opposite me. Leverton is humming a medley of popular songs, each one of which reminds me of different times and places I have been with you. However, enough of this — you must take care of yourself and get out of "Blitz Country" as soon as possible. I long to hear you are settled safely until my return.

All my love and kisses are yours, Your very own loving husband, Alan.

6th December 1940.

Another letter from you today — the one in the blue and violet ink. I just love to see the mail come in and your letters addressed in that well known hand tossed over on to my desk. I know you feel just the same and I am sorry, for that reason, I let yesterday pass me by without writing to you. Actually, time overtook me and before I could get down to it, I had to get dressed and be off to the Battery Dinner. We were down at the Royal until about one o'clock. All the officers were there except Corbett who was so man-handled by the dentists in the afternoon that he is still in bed. The guests were the Colonel, the Adjutant, Gus Gore and Bill Murray. It was quite amusing, but I cannot honestly say it went with a swing. The bright spot of the evening was a story told by Leverton to a large group of us — including the Colonel. It was quite clean and one of the funniest things I have heard for years.

I visited the dentist this afternoon, but he treated me more gently than Corbett. I am to be x-rayed at Colchester tomorrow as there may be some trouble with a dead tooth I have, and they want it confirmed before they begin their performance. I want to get it completed before I go.

I have had another wedding present today. An old Aunt of mine has sent me another Ronson Lighter similar, but not the same, as the one you gave me. I am going to keep it as a spare and you shall have it on my return. It is rather nice and has the Gunner's crest on it.

It is getting late now and there is a biting wind blowing. It fairly roars through every crack and cranny of this place. I am going to say "Good Night" now and wander along to my bunk and go to sleep thinking about you. God, darling, how I wish I were with you.

All my love is with you beloved, Your very own, Alan.

7th December 1940.

Two letters again today. How I long to get them. One of them had enclosed the cutting of our wedding notice and I am forced to the conclusion you do not mean me to forget I am married! Actually, I had seen it before and meant to tell you about it when I 'phoned you. Did I, or didn't I?

Well darling, "Hubby" has been seeing life. Last night we went down to Butlin's and saw a very good evening's boxing. The Battery was very well represented and put on some good fights. Yerby — Leverton's batman is very good.

This morning I went to Colchester with Captain MacCormack and had an x-ray of my tooth. It was a fine, sunny morning and the journey was very pleasant. I thought of you all the way along the road and of the last time we traversed the same road — Remember? We had a coffee in a rather pleasant café there and returned for lunch.

This afternoon I have played rugger for the battery, and we won 12-0. Corbett and Peter Stebbings played very well but I was almost out on my feet after ten minutes. The second half was not so bad, but I cannot honestly say I am in training. Tonight, I can hardly move and hate to think what I shall be like tomorrow. Martin played quite a good game at three quarter, but he too is very stiff tonight. He and Leverton have gone off to the Cinema and Allchin and I are toasting in front of the fire. Leverton does absolutely nothing and is getting fatter and fatter. I hate to think what he will be like at thirty.

With regard to you coming down to Colchester, darling, or to Rivers Hall, I should just love it. Transport is the curse for the last bus leaves there at 7 o'clock, and if I took a chance and slept out, I could not get back in time for parade in the morning. At this stage I do not feel inclined to take the chance in case we get a sudden move.

If you were to come for a weekend though, I could spend a few hours with you on Saturday and Sunday. What about making it next weekend? If anything crops up in the meanwhile I can let you know by telephone. The difficulty about staying at Rivers Hall is that it will be difficult for you to get back there after I have left in the evening, and I should not have time to come over there myself. I think the best thing to do is to fix you a room at a hotel from Saturday morning until Monday. Let me have your opinion. It will be grand to see you again.

I hate to think of you living in the heart of the "Blitz Country" and make every effort to get somewhere to go at the very earliest moment. I should feel happier about you when you are well away from the London Barrage.

Give my best wishes to all your people and take care of yourself. Good night my darling. All my love is for you, your own, Alan.

8th December 1940.

Since I phoned you this morning a fair-sized flap has started. The originator, a certain major of your acquaintance, started it by appearing just after lunch hopping about from one leg to the other as though he had a wasp in his pants. The cause I need not mention, for you can guess that, but it appears to be so remote that it is hardly worthy of consideration. However just in case communication with me should cease suddenly my address will be:

No. 71325, Lieut. A E Horton R.A. 29849C, G.H.Q 2nd Echelon, C/O Army Post Office 725.

Please address correspondence exactly like this. Nothing else should be used. I do not think you will have to use it for some little time though.

I do hope your weekend here will materialise all right. I miss you more and more every day. If all remains quiet, I will book a room at Waters for you from Saturday to Monday and we can be together on Saturday afternoon and evening and Sunday afternoon and evening. Saying "Goodbye" again will not be so good but I would give everything to be with you if only for a few hours. Once we start on our way I can drown my thoughts in work for a time although the ache is always there. At present I miss you intolerably and nothing takes you from my mind for an instant. What a grand day it will be my darling when we meet again on my return. I shall count the hours and minutes until then. Our love is a wonderful thing, a means of overcoming all our difficulties. I remember reading once "To have love is to work miracles"[9] but I did not understand its significance then.

Today, apart from the "flap", has been the normal Clacton-on-Sea Sunday. We marched to Church and back again this morning and spent the afternoon getting one or two things up to scratch. Wilson and Leverton have played cards all day and I took a short walk alone before tea. It was a grand, sunny winter's day, the sort of day you and I love to be outdoors, and I just longed to have you at my side.

I was slightly stiff this morning after the match yesterday but not much considering the length of time since I played. I would like to get a game twice a week and get back into the old stride again. Allchin, Leverton and myself, have vowed to start serious morning training tomorrow but I cannot honestly see it coming off. Leverton

---

[9] To have love is to work miracles: Source unknown.

has become incredibly lazy and scarcely moves from the room except to go out in the evenings. Then more often than not he gets a car from somewhere.

Well, my darling, Allchin and I have promised ourselves a drink tonight, the first for three days, so I am going to say "au revoir" now and will look forward to your call tomorrow.

All my love and kisses are for you, and I remain as always, your very own loving husband, Alan.

10th December 1940.

My own beloved Wife,

I know that what I have to say will hurt you as it has me, but the flap has materialised, and your weekend visit is off. I have looked forward to it as you have, and now regret bitterly we did not arrange it sooner. For obvious reasons I cannot commit any details to paper and as, officially, I know absolutely nothing, it will be better if you do not mention yet that it is off. I live now only for the time we meet again and hope and pray it will not be long.

I have had four letters from you today. It is sweet of you to write so often for your letters mean a great deal to me and I can never have too many. You must never worry about your stammer for to me it is part of your charm. It is one of those many things that go to make up "my Peggy".

It is strange that your thoughts and mine should turn to Christmas together in similar circumstances at practically the same time. Unfortunately, our wishes will not materialise this year, but I mean them to next year if I have to kill the Fuhrer and the Il Ducé with my own hands. At the moment I feel I could do it and enjoy it.

This afternoon I visited the Dental Centre and had a consultation on the x ray results. The verdict is that about one month's treatment is necessary when once the job is started and in view of all the circumstances, they advise me to wait until I can be sure of continuous treatment under one dental surgeon. I am taking the plate with me and will have it done at the first opportunity.

The "keep fit" campaign is doing well. Leverton, Allchin and myself, have become early risers and our room is like a gymnasium in the mornings. We wonder — how long?

Martin and I visited the cinema again tonight and saw Gordon Harker in "Saloon Bar".[10] It was very amusing and cheered us up considerably. I think our thoughts and reactions to present events are much the same and we each use the cinema as a means of escape.

13th December 1940.

My very own darling Peggy,
The other officers here are all commenting on the terrific mail I get each day. Today I have had five letters and a parcel from you. One was Jennie's letter. It was grand to hear from you and I never tire of reading your letters. How I shall look forward to mail drop in the near future.

I thought Jennie's letter was very nice and I quite agree with her remarks on starting a home entirely on our own. Our method has definite disadvantages, but I feel that war conditions make us accept many things which one would not accept normally.

---

[10] *Saloon Bar*, 1940, film staring Gordon Harker and directed by Walter Ford.

As I told you we had the whole Battery on Parade this afternoon — the first time it has ever paraded as a whole. The size of the column was enormous, and I got quite a thrill out of marching with such a large party. Poor Hukins looked very insignificant in front of it all for he has none of the bearing of a commander as you know. He looked more like a guide than a Battery Commander.

The service was quite impressive, and the Padre gave the men a good short, and I thought, very good talk. It was all very solemn, and the usual undercurrents of levity associated with Church Parades were absent.

The men are all in good spirits and glad to see things moving at last. We are confined to Barracks now until we move, and tonight we have "laid on" a party. We have bought no end of beer from the profits of our canteen and are going to have a sing-song. Last night was the night after pay-out and the men's last night out before we sail. You should have heard the noise about 10.30 p.m. Nearly every man in the place was half shot and they all came in singing like blazes. I turned a blind eye to it all of course. The batmen were in a shocking state. Yerby pitched over on his face while removing his boots, Saddler had considerable difficulty in negotiating the corridor. Leverington was his cheery red self (he has been very miserable lately) but had difficulty finding his mouth with a cigarette. Salt was more or less sober, mainly less. They all looked shocking this morning when they brought in the tea. Incidentally, Kennett is due back from sick leave tonight so with luck he will come with me.

The news from the Middle East is very good, isn't it? It is grand to think we are attacking at last and successfully too. Did you read Lord Lothian's last speech? It is great to have such optimistic news — just think of a victory by 1942. Great stuff!

Your letters telling me how you feel about our parting, darling, describe my feelings exactly. I often lay awake at night thinking of you and longing to have you at my side. I always fall asleep with you in my thoughts and think of you again when I wake up. I feel somehow this parting is really worse for you than for me as I shall have the work and the experience to help me through this time of waiting but for you it is just the waiting and wondering. Do not, whatever happens, worry about me darling for I am determined to be with you by next Christmas and our love has given me added strength and I know I shall get safely out of any holes I may get into.

I had almost forgotten, you mentioned in one of your letters today that you had a pain under the "Pinny". I hope it is not very bad and will soon be well again. Do take care of yourself my dear. Well, au revoir Peggy until tomorrow. Here's all my love to you now and forever, Your very own, Alan.

14th December 1940

My very own darling Wife,

What a terrible state of affairs. I have let another day pass without writing you. I am very sorry about it but after the rugger match yesterday I had just time to wash and change, then tea, then a Section Commanders' Conference, then off to Butlin's for guest night. I had meant to write to you after tea, but the Conference came on us as a surprise.

Guest night was rather fun. The A.M.P.C. gave their mess to the Artillery for one night and there were one hundred to dinner. The darts and the snooker cups were on the table and were presented to the Colonel as the regiment won both of them. He gave one of them back to the A.M.P.C. Colonel to be played for continuously.

The letters are very nice, and I am returning them for you to keep. I cannot think of anyone else to whom we should send cake. It would be a grand idea to send some to the Sergeant's mess and to the servants, but I fear it is too late now. It will never reach us in time.

There now I have got round to that topic. Have been trying to leave it out but there is no escaping it. I hate not being able to tell you anything, but I know you understand. Darling, it fairly tears my heart for now more than any other time I want to be near you, to protect and care for you as well as I am able. I cannot, at the moment, find much consolation in the fact we are indirectly protecting you by engaging them on another front.

May God bless you and take care of you for me until my return and make our campaign short and successful. My love is with you always, Peggy.

16th December 1940.

I am writing this in the train in a very poor light. There is just a chance I can post it to you, and it will reach you just a few days after we have sailed, and I know you will look forward to a letter no matter how badly it is written.

Well, darling, there is practically nothing I can tell you except that the journey so far has been very comfortable, and all is well. Your photograph is in my pack, and you are in my mind; each will remain so until we meet again. Pink tickets[11] are not required for

---

[11] This is a phrase used by my parents but I never knew what it meant.

your husband for thoughts of you will suffice as his entertainment throughout the campaign.

Remember, my beloved, courage, and faith. These are ours and will see us through. Chin up. I send you all my love and kisses to keep you safe for me until that great day.

Officers of the Battery, Alan middle row second from the right.

All at Sea

18th December 1940.

My very own darling Peggy,

The last short letter I wrote you was written on the train under somewhat difficult conditions. I really thought then that it would be the last chance I should have of communicating with you until I cabled my safe arrival. This chance has cropped up, but it is definitely the last.

I am writing at sea where, up to the present, we have had quite a reasonable journey. I was Ship's Orderly Officer yesterday and in consequence had very little sleep but apart from that I am very fit although rather sad at the thought of leaving you. "Rather" is actually a mild term, I should, however, be very sorry to have missed the experience.

My thoughts are a queer mixture of gladness and sorrow. There is something about the life — the sea air, the mess decks, the creaking of the rigging at night which stirs the blood in a man as nothing else can. I think the real answer is I shall be very, very happy to be back with you again and to have put these experiences behind me. As something to talk and laugh over but be secretly glad that they are behind me.

I am sharing a small cabin with Peter Stebbings and have bagged the upper birth for obvious reasons. He swears he is a good sailor, but I am taking no chances. You can doubtless imagine what sharing a cabin with Peter is like — his kit is everywhere but he can find nothing.

These letters are, of course, subject to censorship so there is nothing much I can tell you but when I come home you must ask me to tell you the name of the ship. Therein lays a coincidence.

Well, my darling, all the things I have told you and written to you in the past hold good and will do for ever. Your pictures are by my bunk where I can see them before I turn off my light and immediately [when] I awake. You are always in my thoughts and will remain there. Take great care of yourself until I come back to look after you myself.

21st December 1940.

It is about 8.30 in the evening. I have just been forward to see the troops are OK for the night, paused for a while on the deck and watch the sea and now I'm in my cabin to write to you.

The ship is rolling terribly tonight and the wind howls in the rigging just like the noises-off in a wireless play. In spite of this the men are better now for they have got, or rather are getting, their sea legs. For the first two days the mess decks were indescribable. I will leave it to your imagination rather than try to describe it. Strangely enough I have not been ill at all although the mess has been but thinly populated for the last two days. Majors Harrison and Hukins went down very quickly. Kirk-Smith, Corbett, Clarke, and Felton are but a few of the subalterns who have appeared but for brief and irregular intervals. Peter is very well and in high spirits.

Tonight, at dinner, the plates, knives, forks, and spoons were careering madly up and down the table and one had to hang on to one's food for dear life or it was lost forever before it reached one's mouth. It is rather amusing if one is fit but it must be dreadful if one is not. The food, incidentally, is very good and for the only time on record we are living like lords at the expense of H.M. Government. Drinks and tobacco are, of course, very cheap. Gin is 2d[12] a glass and cigarettes 1/8 d for 50 so it should be a very cheap trip. Our only expenses are our servants and the Lascar[13] stewards.

The Colonel was asking after you yesterday morning. He talked to me for some time in the lounge and told me many of his personal worries. He is a great admirer of yours I think and is very interested in your welfare.

The rolling of the ship is growing steadily worse. Twice since I started, I have slipped off my chair and brought up under the bunks under the far side of the cabin, so I am going to say "Goodnight" my love and sleep tight. My thoughts and prayers are with you, and I will write more tomorrow."

23rd December 1940.

I was rather too optimistic when I started this letter, Peggy, for although I was in to all meals and did my round of duty I felt far from well and spent most of the day on my bunk. Writing was impossible for the sight of a piece of paper moving up and down before my eyes, was more than I could endure. Today the weather is somewhat better although the ship is far from steady, I can have the porthole open in my cabin and get some fresh air. It is the first time for two days, for had we opened it, we should have been

---

[12] 2d was in old currency. There were 12d in a shilling. In Decimal Currency 5p was one shilling.

[13] Lascars — Ship's crew from the Indian sub-continent, the Arab world or S.E. Asia. Some British Officers called all servants Lascars.

flooded. Actually, according to orders, they should be closed continuously in case we get hit. She sinks more slowly if everything is shut down. Needless to say, blackout is very strict at night, and we always carry lifebelts when on deck.

The three B.S.M.s have all been ill and a queer trio they made until they got their sea legs. Our "Q", Playford, has been very bad and appeared on deck yesterday for the first time looking like something the dog had brought in.

24th December 1940. Christmas Eve.

Well darling, today dawned bright and clear with a fresh wind across the quarter. I stood for a long time this morning on the forward part of the promenade deck looking out over the bows. It was a magnificent sight. The waves were slapping against the port quarter and great clouds of spray were obscuring the forward deck. The sun glinted through the spray and on the waves. The beauty and grandeur of it surpasses my powers of description. An escort vessel passed to starboard of us about noon. She made a picture to paint as she rose and fell to the waves. At times she seemed engulfed only to rise again with water pouring in cascades from her decks. A thing of living beauty!

This afternoon the weather has grown worse. The spray is coming right up to the promenade deck where the ship's band (may God forgive them) are murdering Christmas Carols as they slide backwards and forwards on the reclining deck.

Incidentally, I forgot to mention that Peter cracked a rib in the lounge the other night. The ship's rolling was so bad that all the officers and all the furniture started to roll with it. Peter brought up against a table leg and got a nasty crack. He is quite fit although wrapped tightly in plaster.

I have just read yesterday's news bulletin. More raids on London and the S.E. I hope you are unscathed.

25th December 1940.

Well darling, our Christmas Day started with a bang — many bangs to be exact. At 07.40 hours the convoy was engaged by a surface raider. The weather was rough and misty, and our first indication of danger was a salvo striking the water to starboard. Nothing came very close, but some shots fell between us and the next vessel to starboard. The escort vessels laid a smoke screen around us and then made off into the mist and gunfire was heard for some time. The result we have not heard. It has been rumoured that the raider was the Admiral Scheer and that she engaged us at 28,000 yards. I can get no confirmation of this, and I do not think it is true. We saw no vessel at all, and the weather was such that to engage accurately at that range would have been impossible.

No damage was done, and our Christmas festivities went off as arranged. The sea was very rough, but we served the troops with soup, turkey, pork, potatoes, greens, plum pudding and beer and each man had fifty Players. I think they all enjoyed themselves.

We had a very good meal in the evening and some bubbly to go with it. Needless to say, our second toast was "those at home". You were very close to me at that time as, indeed, you were all day.

After dinner, about nine o'clock, Allchin and I groped our way forward to our mess deck getting drenched in the process. We went below and played pontoon with some of the boys for a time. Getting about on deck at night is quite an adventure.

27th December 1940.

Yesterday was uneventful and the weather was much warmer, but a strong wind made the decks rather unpleasant. Towards night, the sky cleared, and the wind dropped considerably, and I spent nearly an hour on deck before I turned in breathing the fresh air and watching the phosphorescence in the bow waves. Our cabins are dreadfully stuffy and smelly as we have to keep them battened down and fresh air last thing at night and first thing in the morning is essential. I started early morning exercises on the deck some days ago. The first morning all went well; then the second the decks were slippery with spray and the ship was rolling badly. I did one bend, slipped up and brought up on my back in the scuppers which were full of dirty water. I haven't tried since, but I hope to continue tomorrow.

I have not told you much of the routine on the ship. Reveille is at 06.30 and breakfasts begin about 07.30. I am Messing Officer for our mess deck and present to see most of the meals. Next the mess decks have to be cleaned up and all the hammocks, haversacks and kit bags stowed neatly away in the racks overhead. At 10.30 the Officer Commanding Troops and sometimes the Ship's Captain inspects the ship. The latter, incidentally, is a grand fellow, Percival by name. A typical sailor in whom one can place complete trust. For the first few days we rarely saw him for he lived on the bridge and had practically no sleep. He is relaxing somewhat now but only comes below for brief spells.

The crew and stewards are mainly Lascars. Their dress is composed of the most motley assortment of garments. Some go in for colours and some look as though they obeyed the advertisement "Let Montague Burton dress you" many years ago. I've seen some jackets with that unmistakable stamp on them although they are very shabby now.

There seems to be a good chance that I can mail this to you so I will bring this to a close and start another.

I enclose a copy of the Ship's newspaper, The Christmas Number. The name is a queer coincidence, isn't it? Well, my love, I remain as always,

Your ever-loving husband,
Alan.

28th December 1940.

Although I brought my last letter to an abrupt end as I thought we were touching at a port this has not turned out to be the case. The rumour brought in a letter from practically every man on board for censorship and I spent several hours last night dealing with some of No. 4 section's mail.

Although censoring letters gives me a great deal of useful information about the men it is a job I would much rather not have to do. It seems to be prying into that part of a man's life which is his and his alone and even in the case of some of the most illiterate letters it seems like sacrilege. One interesting point though is the different ways in which the same things are regarded. The Christmas Dinner ranged from "very good" to "B...dy lousy". About 80% decided it was good.

Today has been the best day we have had aboard. The morning dawned bright and warm, and we had some PT on deck. It was grand taking exercise in the fresh sea air and after a saltwater shower I felt like ten men.

I long to have a letter from you telling me all the news — how you are, where you are and what you are doing. Even the most trivial everyday things at home are meat and drink to us here my darling. Write often please and with much news.

The Ship's Captain held a service on No. 3 Deck this morning at 11.00 hrs. The ship's band (of whom I've written before) murdered the hymns with a piano, several saxophones, and a trumpet but in spite of this the old hymns and prayers brought back my thoughts of home. The ship's bell was tolled for five minutes before the service and sounded for all the world like the bell of the old village church where I once lived.

Life on board is very pleasant just now. After the morning inspection there is very little to do except read and lounge about in the sun. I have read several novels and am now turning my attention to my textbooks. I propose to concentrate on administration and organisation and leave others to worry about the other side of the work. There is a great deal of gambling going on in the ship all day and a good deal of money changes hands every night. I am avoiding these parties like the plague, but I am getting Kirk-Smith to teach me bridge on the quiet. There is a great temptation here to eat, drink, smoke, and sleep far too much and take no exercise at all. I am doing myself pretty well on all four but make a point of getting some exercise each day. Actually, I am very fit indeed.

Well, my Love, according to the news bulletin London and the S.E. caught it again the night before last and there is still talk of that much threatened invasion. I hate being so long without news of you and being so far away should anything happen.

30th December 1940.

The weather is truly magnificent, a light warm breeze and blazing sunshine. It is very invigorating, and we are all fit and well. Overhead is a great stamping of feet where a PT Squad is in action. I am getting very enthusiastic about PT and Vivian *(a fellow officer),* and I do some, every morning before breakfast. We have some medicine balls and spend some time each day throwing these about. I am going to get a crack PT squad from our boys and train them under Bombardier Scoates. Unless we interest ourselves in something of this kind time hangs heavily on our hands.

There is one thing I have not mentioned which is not good about this ship, the tea is simply lousy (Please forgive the expression). Water and milk are the main sources of offence, and these added to the Lascar tea making produce the most sickly and unpalatable concoction. I have given up drinking it completely and just have fruit in the morning early, coffee for breakfast, nothing at teatime and drink lemonade most of the evening although occasionally we launch out and have a cigar and liqueurs to finish off our dinner and drink either gin or beer during the evening.

31st December 1940.

New Year's Eve and it's even hotter than yesterday. It's nearly eleven thirty here my Love, and for you it is already New Year's Day [sic]. I wonder where and how you have spent it; what sort of weather are you having; how you are?

You have been at the forefront of my mind all day, my darling. I have not been able to forget all that 1940 has brought to us. In many ways it has been a very happy year, certainly one we shall never forget. Do you remember the cold warmth of its beginning? Those happy meetings in the snow when we were both rather shy. Then the spring with the sunshine and the blossom. I remember particularly our walk to Hartlip and how much I wanted to kiss you when I sat on the gate by your side but somehow felt it would be a bad thing and break the spell. How stupid of me! Finally, the happy September of our engagement, our wedding, Rivers Hall, Clacton and on to this. Yes, my Love, it has been a great year, but this will be greater.

The year will be aging when this reaches you but with all my heart, I wish you a very happy New Year. You must too, give all your people my best wishes for 1941. I hope all are well and avoiding Jerry's explosive toys.

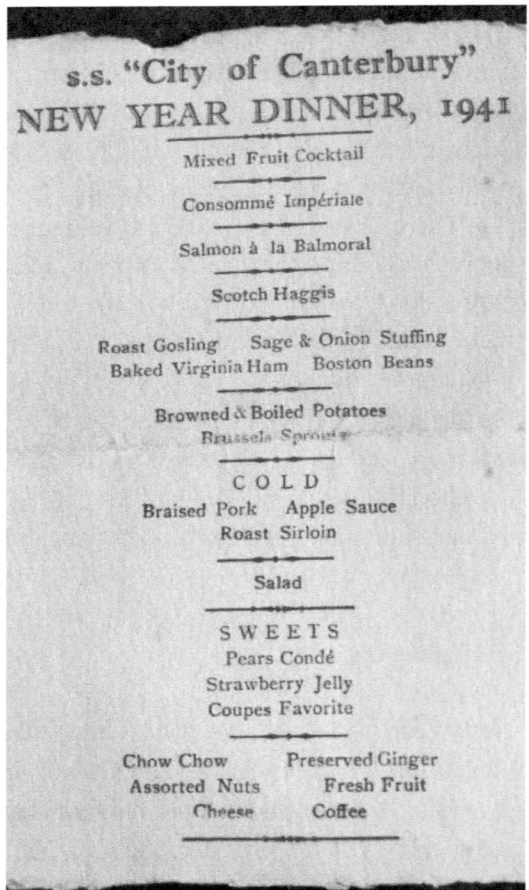

s.s. "City of Canterbury"
NEW YEAR DINNER, 1941

Mixed Fruit Cocktail

Consommé Impériale

Salmon à la Balmoral

Scotch Haggis

Roast Gosling   Sage & Onion Stuffing
Baked Virginia Ham   Boston Beans

Browned & Boiled Potatoes
Brussels Sprouts

COLD
Braised Pork   Apple Sauce
Roast Sirloin

Salad

SWEETS
Pears Condé
Strawberry Jelly
Coupes Favorite

Chow Chow   Preserved Ginger
Assorted Nuts   Fresh Fruit
Cheese   Coffee

1st January 1941.

It seems that soon we may be able to drop some mail so today I am going to bring this, my second letter, to a close.

The first day of the year has dawned warm but misty. The Ship's Captain gave us all a talk on the mess deck this morning on tropical diseases, the sun, food, and various other things. It was very interesting, and he spoke very well. We are advised to bath twice a day although the weather is not unpleasantly hot. Salt water, both hot and cold, is very plentiful but needless to say the fresh water is scarce and we use it but sparingly.

We have heard over the wireless of the strafing that London had on Sunday night, and it has put everyone's blood up and I feel sure it will have the opposite effect to what Jerry hoped. It's damnable to think of such a place as the Guildhall being burnt out. Allchin worked there and was very upset about it. I hope that if you are not already away from Chislehurst you very soon will be for it will be a great load off my mind to know you have moved further west. How I long to hear from you and know for certain you are well and safe.

Well, My beloved, the gang has gone for lunch, and I must bring this to an end and get it in the rest of the mail in the Orderly Room. You would be amazed if you saw the number of letters collected in there since we sailed. God bless you, darling, and keep you safe. May this separation end soon.

Au revoir beloved.

Your ever-loving husband,

Alan.

9, St. Michael's Road, Maidstone, Kent
3.1.41.

My very own beloved darling Husband,
Alan, It's the missus feeling very fit and cheery but just longing for her dear "old man". I keep thinking of so many intimate little things to tell you but daren't as I really would hate the old censor to see them, but you find just those sayings in your heart. You dear, dear darling, I feel absolutely and completely yours and so proud to be your wife — oh roll on our great day and all those many, many years to come. I long to hold your face between my hands and look up into your eyes and whisper, "Look out a woman is going to kiss you." Later. Darling, this was absolutely brought to an end, and I've unexpectedly had to come on night duty — how I wish you could ring me up — I miss those phone calls such a lot but then I miss everything connected with you Dear heart. Ah! When I think of those phone calls at night — I wanted to whisper nice things to you, but we were somehow still a bit slow. I believe '42 is a lucky year for us. What about a birthday kiss for me? I'll wake you up that morning by a wifely privilege. "Some while before the dawn I rose, and stept softly along the dim way to your room, And found you sleeping in the quiet gloom, and holiness about you as you slept. I knelt there; till your waking fingers crept about my head and held it. I had rest unhoped this side of Heaven, beneath your breast. I knelt a long time, still; nor even wept."[14] — Another memory of ours, he must have known and committed to verse so beautifully. In my dreams and thoughts, I often imagine creeping, finding your bunk in the half light and watching you sleep, like I did on those beautiful days together when perhaps I awoke before you and just

_____

[14] A Memory (From a sonnet-sequence by) Rupert Brooke, (1887-1915).

watched your sweet face so peaceful at my side. This rambling on of my thoughts can continue for hours. In 15 minutes, I am having a 22 o'clock cup of tea with the night nurses and then to bed. We are to sleep in our clothes, however, so will end this darling by wishing I could post myself to you. Good-night my sweet, sweet dreams. May God bless you and keep you safe and well. All my love and kisses and hugs from your own ever-loving wife, Pegasus.

No. 71325 Lieut. AE Horton R.A. 29894C, G.H.Q. 2nd Echelon, C/O Army Post Office 725.

5th January 1941.

My very own darling Wife,
I must sit down to night and write to you for today has been one of the happiest and most interesting of our trip. I want in some measure to share it with you as I want indeed, to share all things with you.

First, I must try to describe the night as it is at present. We are at anchor quite close to land. The night is hot and still with a bright tropical moon shining. The sea is an oily calm. Wonder of wonders, there is no blackout here for the first time since the voyage started, we can fling wide our ports, open up the windows in the saloon and smoke on deck. I have just come below from the promenade deck where all the officers are sitting talking, drinking, and smoking in the light from the saloon windows. From my port I can see another ship which is a blaze of light and clearly beneath it is its reflection on the water. From ashore too, can be seen lights from windows and from cars. In spite of the fan and my light clothing I am wet with perspiration for it is very hot. The relaxation of these restrictions has had its reaction on the men. They are having a sing song on the deck forward where the ship's band is entrenched beneath the awning. The strains of Loch Lomond, the Quarter-master's Stores, She'll [be] coming round the Mountain, Deep Purple, etc. etc. etc. are coming to my ears. They are all as happy as can be.

The good news of our success in Libya and the fall of Bardia have added zest to the jollifications. We hear of blizzards in the Straights of Dover. How strange it all seems as we swelter in the heat and what a contrast to last year, but I would willingly barter this port and all there is in it for a party such as we had at Bobbing last year.

The work I have to do in the ship is practically nothing, but I make a point of reading technical stuff for an hour or two every day. We have to give technical lectures for about half an hour in the evening and I am trying to learn enough to "Shoot a Line" when my turn comes. I hope I can pull it off for it might do some good. I might add that the competition for promotion and the methods employed by some, need seeing to be believed.

The mail containing Series 1 of these letters left this morning and I hope you will have it in about three weeks-time. I know how much it will mean to you to know we are still safe. I can visualise how you must feel knowing how relieved and glad I shall be when I hear from you.

We are still at anchor and believe me it is hot with a capital "H". Last night I had a party with Major Boyd, Gus Gore, Cobb, and Seaton. We drank a good deal of beer and I slid down the awning from the promenade deck to the forward well deck into a pool of water wearing my new Khaki Dress. It seemed a good idea at the time but not so good this morning! From now on I am Tee Total all the time we are in the heat.

9th January 1941.

Well darling, we're at sea again. The restrictions waived in port are now in operation again and believe me, in this heat it is not much fun. The ship is again blacked out at sundown and the saloon quickly gets like an oven. In addition, smoking on deck is taboo after sundown.

We had a concert in the saloon last night despite the heat. Vivian arranged it and the artists came from the whole ship. Some are very good indeed. One man does "In Town Tonight" making all the noises from start to finish with his mouth and I am quite sure anyone would take it for the real thing coming over the radio. We have good pianists, good accordion players and some good singers.

There is one thing I certainly must not forget to tell you. Sergeant Cooper was Sergeant of the Guard last night and in the darkness opened a wrong door and stepped straight into the engine room. It was a considerable step to take being some 20 or 30 feet in depth. He is in hospital today, but you will be pleased to hear he is not seriously hurt. (Is it a libel to say I arranged this in order to do away with a fool?)

12th January 1941.

They played the wrong tune for "Onward Christian Soldiers" which no one had ever heard before and played an extra verse at the end while we all waited impatiently for the "Amen". That was the first hymn, they did better for the others and the saxophonist surpassed himself by "Swinging" God Save the King. I could understand his feeling.

You know, darling, until one has seen it one cannot imagine how much sea there is in the world. In nearly four weeks we have only seen, at the most, twenty or thirty miles of coast. It reminds me of the old adage about joining the navy in the hope of seeing the world, but only seeing the sea.

Did I tell you I have a namesake on board, one 2nd Lieutenant G B Horton? It's rather strange isn't it? He comes from Reading and is no relation whatever.

16th January 1941.

This letter is getting so long I think that if I write every day, by the time I am able to post it, it will make a small parcel. It is because of this that I have missed a few days. You must not think that because I have missed a few days I have not been thinking of you. You are in my thoughts constantly and I miss you more than I can possibly say. At times it becomes almost unbearable and sends me pacing up and down the decks, smoking cigarettes and thinking of the grand times we have had together.

The weather is now much cooler; in fact, at night, it is definitely cold on deck. I have had a slight chill and a terrific pain in the side of my face from going on deck at night from the heat of the saloon. The shower baths have a definite sting to them now and are very refreshing after a game. Incidentally, I've beaten Charles at last in three successive sets of deck tennis which is something of an achievement. He now owes me 2/6 d.

Lectures and Morse code lessons are still in full swing, but I have not given my lecture yet as the captain spoke on the stars on the night I was to have given mine. My turn comes round next Wednesday.

18th January 1941.

Very soon now, darling, this should be on its way to you for we have just had orders to get all letters ready for Wednesday. I hope it will reach you safely and find you still your cheery self and in good health.

Have been thinking of old England as it must be now. I have never before realised how much I love it for all its faults — particularly the climatic ones. You know Peggy, I do not believe that you and I could live long away from it and still be happy. I see the country in my mind's eye in all its varying moods and just long to be back again. I think of autumn mostly with its cool winds; the stubble giving away slowly to ploughed land; the trees and the hedges touched with those delightful russet hues; the smell of damp undergrowth and the newly turned earth. I think of English homes and English firesides — you know, my Dear, those grand comfortable places with crumpets on the hob for tea.

We have now been at sea for over four weeks and have only seen land once since we passed Ireland. It will be a great treat to get ashore, as we hope to at our next port of call and get a change of scenery and see some fresh faces. I am keen to know how the men will react to it — can you imagine what a trooper is like after four weeks at sea without seeing a woman or having a decent glass of beer?

Needless to say, their welfare gives us some thought as we lecture them on the dangers of these foreign ports and give them fatherly advice. Can you imagine me doing the heavy father act and talking of the dangers of wine, women, and song? Strangely enough they listen very attentively and ask, at times, some very shrewd questions. Can it be that they regard me as an authority on these things?

Last night I had the honour of being a guest of the captain's at dinner. We take it in turns when he comes down to dine with us. He is a typical seafaring man with a ruddy face, heavy features, and very humorous eyes. He told us many tales of his career which were both interesting and amusing.

Well, Peggy, if I write much more, I shall not be able to fit it all in to an envelope so I will bring this to a close and write another before Wednesday. You are always in my thoughts and dreams and have all my love now and always.

May God bless you and take care of you until my return.

Your very own,

Alan,

19th January 1941.

Things have taken a very different turn since I finished off my letter to you yesterday. Whether for better or worse I am at a loss to say. This afternoon the sea is covered with white horses, a very stiff breeze is blowing, and the ship is rolling and pitching to such an extent that it is difficult to write at all.

Being Sunday, we had the usual Church Service this morning given by the Master. I always enjoy these for he chooses hymns which we all know well, and the men sing them with zest. I love to stand swaying from side to side, surrounded by the troops and hear and sing those fine old English hymns. There is something fine too, in listening to our tough old skipper offering up prayers for, "the ship in which we serve, protect us from the fury of the sea and the assaults of our enemies… until… we can enjoy the fruits of our labour." There is always a very fervent "Amen" to the prayer for those at home. The men too, like these services and I have not noticed a single man attempt to dodge them. They are short, cheery, blunt, and to the point — no sob stuff and no eye wash. We all appreciate it.

Major Boyd is sitting opposite me as I write. He holds the record in the letter writing stakes having written over 100 pages to his wife. There is considerable conjecture on board as to what he could find to write all that about. I talk to him a good deal at times and have grown to quite like him. In many ways he resembles Vivian with whom I have also struck up quite a friendship. I find though that I have very little in common with most of the new young officers. Felton and I often say how we should like to see them in a Battery with Colonel Sadler as B.C. Their professional outlook is very different from ours.

20th January 1941.

I mentioned yesterday a change in the weather, but it was nothing compared with what is happening today. This ship is rolling and pitching in a most disconcerting manner and several faces are green already. It is grand on deck in this weather. The sea is a very deep blue and covered with white horses.

22nd January 1941.

The ship is still rolling considerably but the weather is very pleasant. I gave my lecture last night after all and think and hope it had the desired effect. In a way I know it has for I have already been called in to arbitrate in several arguments on the subject.

It is amusing as I write to look up and watch the albatrosses. There are several of them following the ship now. They are great things similar to seagulls but much larger. Some appear to have a wingspan of about 6-8 feet. Occasionally we see "Mother Carey's Chickens".[15] They are like moor hens and often go floating by looking very unconcerned.

Well, my Sweet, time to say au revoir again. All my love and kisses are yours always and I live only for the time when I re-join you.

23rd January 1941.

We are not making as good time as was expected so there is still time to write you another letter before we reach our next port. Since I finished off my last letter my slight indisposition has improved immensely. Today has been magnificent, a calm, blue, sparkling sea, hot sun, and clear sky. I am now writing this before getting down to a real evening's work. I shall go on until about eleven o'clock and then go on deck for my nightly breath of air and undisturbed thinking about you. I always look forward to that time each day.

Latterly I have felt somewhat worried about you. Will Bevin's plans affect you? If so, in what way? Let me know at once if they do and I'll take up the cudgels. Further I am wondering how you can possibly manage on the meagre pittance I am able to send you at the moment. You have given up so much for me, My Love. I often wonder what I can possibly do for you in return.

---

[15] Mother Carey's Chickens are not dissimilar to a Storm Petrel.

I hinted but did not say in my last letter that we have crossed the line. I thought the censor would take exception to it but as that is not the case so here goes. Neptune, Mrs Neptune, the "Doctor", the "Barber" and the "Court" came on board about three o'clock one afternoon and the fun began. The Third Officer, "Tiny" (he weighs eighteen stone) was the Barber. Various people, including myself, were tried, found guilty, doctored with vinegar and pills made of soap and pepper, shaved with a whitewash brush and wooden razor about a yard long and finally ducked in the pool until we were nearly done in. The troops loved it and it really was a damn fine afternoon. In the end the pool was so full — so many people having either fallen in or been thrown in — that one could hardly get across it. I hope to get a certificate signed by the master, as a souvenir.

It is great news about Tobruk falling, isn't it? Darling, the poor old country should be ready to deliver a knock-out punch to finish this b---dy war once and for all. No. 4 section is developing marked murderous tendencies as we get nearer to our destination. The spirit is good and will pull them through anything. I am taking an excellent view of young Bradley, who you will remember, was always in trouble at home. He just thrives on the thought of adventure, and I could do with many of his calibre.

The general spirit is, we don't mind where we go, we don't mind what we do but let's get at these ████████████████ finish the job off properly, then, home sweet home.

24th January 1941.

There is a great air of expectancy in the ship tonight for it is rumoured that tomorrow we may put in at a port AND GO ASHORE. I wonder, darling, if you can appreciate how much that means to us after five weeks at sea. Just the pleasure of walking on land again is worth a good deal. I might add we have all been dared to send any cables or letters while we are ashore so it looks as if I shall not be able to keep my promise to you after all, the reason for the order is fairly obvious if one stops to consider.

Take care of yourself, my beloved and have no fear for me. The future is far too attractive for me to miss and soon I shall be back at your side again. Until then I send you all my love and kisses, keep our love locked safely in my heart and work and think and dream of our future. Your very own, Alan.

In view of what the previous letter says, it was interesting to see this among the correspondence:

POST OFFICE TELEGRAM
Durban
Horton. Hatton Cottage, Lubbock Road, Chislehurst.
OK Love Alan Horton.

Also written at this time is a brief undated note — Saddler was Father's batman:

Darling,
Whenever you get a cable from me saying I am OK will you be good enough to write to Saddler's wife: Mrs G H Saddler, 96A, Cannock Road, Chadsmoor, Nr. Cannock, Staffs.

Hatton Cottage, Lubbock Rd, Chislehurst, Kent.
5.2.41.

My very own beloved Husband,
Though I only wrote this afternoon to you I must write to you again my darling. I look forward so much to writing these epistles — I am still walking on air after receiving your three grand letters this weekend. You have a happy knack of writing them so nicely. Don't miss me too much darling — I know how it hurts — it's a deep gnawing pain — but my God, it's worth bearing, isn't it? And think of the happiness, almost unknown to us, to come afterwards. I am not losing heart, far from it, but there are times and remarks that bring realities far too near. War is the most hateful thing man can be faced with. I pray our children never see one.

As this will be airmailed it will reach you earlier than others so I will tell you my latest plans. If our doctor says my innards will stand the life I plan joining Angela and Joe Harrison at their transport work — I am doing this to avoid conscription — so far 18–21 years old are to be called, so I can wait a while then join nearer the spring and warmer weather. Kay Sutton and Sonia may join us too. You do understand this move of mine darling, don't you? But it all depends on what the doctor says — you see all that floor scrubbing at Bobbing didn't exactly suit my tummy, but driving should be all right.

A positive Armada of our planes trekked home today at dusk — now the Bosch is paying us a casual call, the first in the evening for a long while.

It's still very cold here and we've had another fall of snow. I treated myself to some lovely, warm sheepskin over boots and for once my feet aren't perpetually asleep with cold. They'd better be my next birthday present from you darling. Lillywhites had a few odd pairs at 47/6 d. They are rare these days as the Air Force is taking more and more of the material required for their manufacture.

I bid you sweet dreams — you are forever in my thoughts and heart — your spirit is a great comfort to me these days darling heart. God bless and may he hear my prayers and keep you safe my dear husband.

All my love and kisses are always yours,

Your ever-loving wife,

Peggy.

No. 71325 Lieut. AE Horton R.A. 29894C, G.H.Q. 2nd Echelon, C/O Army Post Office 725.

5th February 1941.

Last night, Major Harrison spoke to all the officers and N.C.O.s of our Battery in the dining room after dinner. He called upon me to speak on something and as I spoke slowly got wet around the shoulders and chest. It was incredibly hot. After dinner he talked to Charles, Wilson, and I until nearly midnight when Porter, Doc

Talbot, Bill Murray and Boult (all somewhat pickled) started singing bawdy songs. We all joined in, and a grand party ensued. Just when the party was reaching its zenith the master sent a peremptory order down from the bridge: "Master's compliments Sir, Stop that bl—dy row now, AT ONCE". Some walked and some I regret to say, staggered down to bed. For what it's worth, I walked!

14th February 1941.

We are now in what I always regarded as one of the hottest places in the world. Although winter here we were all expecting to swelter in terrific heat and have had a pleasant surprise. The breeze is fresh and cool all day. The sun shines and the sea is deep blue, but although quite warm it is not hot in the same way as some of the places we have been are hot. The nights are particularly pleasant. I spent some time on the boat deck after dinner last night and the scene was most entrancing. The moon is full and very bright. The whole ship and the sea are lit by its silvery light and I can watch it almost indefinitely. You would just love it.

There are lots of things I should have told you about our last port of call which I have not done. On rereading what I have written I feel the description is very inadequate so I will try and add some more to it. Seen from the sea it looked very attractive indeed for many of the buildings were tall, twenty stories in some cases, and the whole waterfront had a clean and colourful look about it. This was mainly because nearly all the buildings were white with red roofs. The tropical vegetation among and behind the buildings added greatly to its attraction. It is so far away from the war that no blackout is necessary, and it was a real treat to be able to walk about well-lighted streets again. You can have no idea how fascinating well lighted neon signs become when you have not seen them for a long time.

Shops were good and, in the main, not much more expensive than in England although pay for white people is at least twice what it is in England. I think there is much to be said for us living there when the war is over. Many of the big stores we know have branches there and one of these is Woolworths. Rationing is unknown and everything seems very plentiful. Fruit is cheap and there are many varieties of excellent quality.

Desert Conditions

234/89 A.A. Regiment R.A. Middle East Forces.
22nd February 1941.

Before I started this letter, I had already written a long letter to you in diary form and was awaiting an opportunity to post it. Unfortunately, I found it contained a certain amount of information which is taboo here, so I had to scrap it. I have had a very interesting time and have lots to tell you, but censorship leaves us with very little scope. I sent a cable to you the day before yesterday which I hope will reach you safely. It was very dry but that was because of the price. I was anxious too that my new address should reach you as soon as possible. I have had no news of you for ten weeks, but I know that is not your fault for we are all the same. News of home is the chief desire of us all.

My quarters at the moment are quite comfortable. I live in a roomy tent with Allchin and at the moment we are "doing ourselves proud". This is a land of sand, sun, flies, lizards, and wind insects. During the day it is very, very hot but at sundown it drops with a bump and the early mornings are very cold. So far, I am feeling very fit indeed and I'm steadily becoming like a local in my appearance.

As I write there is a slight breeze blowing through the tent and the air is like a blast from a furnace. Although it is very hot it is a dry heat and so not as unpleasant as it might otherwise be. Flies are a confounded nuisance and play around one's face all day long (They spoil my afternoon sleep). Such natives as I have seen leave a lot to be desired. It is not until one has seen a country such as this that one appreciates the cleanliness of our homeland. Even the very worst places in England cannot compare with some of these for filth.

We have bought ourselves an earthenware vessel in which to keep our water. The evaporation from the outside, draws out heat, and water keeps remarkably cool in it.

28th February 1941.

Although it is about noon it is very dark, and the tent is lashed down but flapping like blazes. Outside a sandstorm in raging. It is rather unpleasant but rather thrilling. About twenty minutes before it reached us the sky turned black and had all the appearance of an ordinary storm. Small sand devils began to appear, whirlwinds which carry the sand along like waterspouts standing some hundreds of feet into the air. As the storm approached one could see it was a great mass of whirling sand and the whole surface of the desert rose up to meet it as a vast wave. By then we had everything lashed up and ducked inside as it reached us. For a time even the tent about ten paces from us completely disappeared. It is dying away now, and some rain is falling but it still hangs over the desert like a fog. Needless to say, sand is now in everything. The desert is certainly the devil's own country.

Today is cloudy and dull with some rain. It is most extraordinary weather for the desert, quite different from anything we expected to get when we arrived here at first. We are still wearing warm clothes for the day is very like a March day, in England. I believe the weather starts to warm up soon which will make it very hot again. Last night it was very cold, and Allchin and

I piled on all the clothes we could find, and we were still none too warm. The wind has been quite high, and several tents left their moorings during the last three days to the consternation of their owners. One canteen tent blew down and everything was saved except the "tick book" so they now have no idea who owes money. Someone was very quick on the uptake.

Hatton Cottage, Lubbock Rd, Chislehurst, Kent.
4.3.41.

At the moment I am lunching particularly well on a tray by the fire — cold duck, Russian salad, and prunes to finish up with. Tomorrow we shall be finished with duck and back on rationed meat, so lunch will be toast and coffee.

You'd laugh, darling, at things in the food line that thrill in these days. The grocer has found us 2 lbs of Golden Syrup and 1 lb marmalade — the first for weeks. This rationing is teaching us English people to appreciate plain food.

Letters written from this date are marked 'Return to Sender' and 'Certified Prisoner of War'. It is probable that they never reached Alan before he, and many thousands of other allied troops, were captured in the Battle of Crete. Many were eventually returned to Peggy by a fellow officer who managed to avoid being taken as a prisoner of war.

Hatton Cottage, Lubbock Rd, Chislehurst, Kent.
10.3.41

"Dearest love, I am listening to the radio with some lovely tunes on by either Coward or Novello, Never mind who — but it is lovely to hear them.

Mother wrote me pages this morning — she's very well and was meeting Cyril at the Bull on Saturday then he was taking her to Chatham. Kay Sutton & Angela wrote also — old Titch wishes to be remembered to the "Old Man"! Indeed, cheeky little so and so. Kay says Charles mentioned in his cable that no one had received any mail on arriving at — darling what a terrible shame. I had hoped you'd find a month's letters and a parcel at least awaiting you, at least 60 or 70 letters. However, I hope you have them now. If this Battle of the Atlantic develops, we may have to lose a few letters now and again, so I'll still keep writing much and often dearest love.

Old London looks still as gay as when you last saw it — the spring sun was shining on Regent Street as I came out. We passed the bombed restaurant in Leicester Square. Jeanette had four friends dancing in there when the bomb fell on Saturday last — one has a splinter in the shoulder, he's at the War Office; his girl-friend has a piece in her lung; someone else in the skull, but they are, at least, lucky to be alive.

I get terribly proud when little troops I give lifts to in the car ask where I got the gunner badge that I wear. I proudly reply, "My husband" and equally proud when they ask where you are serving. My reply is the "Middle East". The majority envy you people. Gosh, you know you are lucky serving the world like that — how I envy you.

234/89 A.A. Regiment R.A. Middle East Forces.
14th March 1941.

Yesterday I had two letters and a copy of the "London Opinion" from you — the first letters for nearly three months — and I must hasten to answer them. You have no idea what a letter means to any of us here. The letters were dated the 9th and 20th January and sent by air mail, or rather were marked and stamped for air mail. How they came, the Lord only knows.

Officers in the desert, Alan back row third from the right.

18th March 1941.

I had a rather interesting trip into a village some distance from here the other day to see some of my men in hospital there. I went by road and passed through some picturesque places. I saw a great many Falanakas or native barges with their characteristic short masts and very long booms taking the luff of the sail up about ten times as high as the masthead. Near water, the country is very green and attractive. There are orange groves and little banana trees as well as various sorts of palms and cactus. Always there are tracks beside the water and haughty looking camels stalk majestically among the lowly donkeys. Women fetching water are a source of constant delight to me. They carry it in large earthen vessels balanced on their heads and in their long robes look very graceful. The villages are terrible. One can smell them many miles away and they are tumbled down; masses of indescribably filthy mud huts and houses all jumbled together.

We often see Libyan prisoners here and there is a story going around that guards for them try not to prevent them escaping, but to prevent the natives joining them. One Officer Commanding a prison camp is reputed to have twenty-three more men than he should have. The extras have attached themselves to working parties at various times to get the two Piasters a week and their keep. The poor wretched prison wallah doesn't know one from the other now — I can't vouch for the truth of this.

21st March 1941.

You are so much in my thoughts today. I must start another letter for you. I am sitting in my tent feeling very hot and sticky and surrounded by a cloud of flies awaiting lunch (I am awaiting lunch, not the flies). The weather is very changeable and unpleasant. Last night it blew a gale and was very cold. This morning I have been working in a dust storm and now it has become still and very hot. Dust storms are the very devil and give one pains in the throat and chest. A respirator is useful at times to keep it out.

I had a very pleasant surprise the other day. Charles Sutton's batman came in and asked to see me. He had been out on leave and met a man who asked if he had ever heard of 234 Battery. When he told him he was in it the man gave him a note for me. It was from Charles Lock. He is in a camp some considerable distance away, but I have written to him and hope to have him up here to split a bottle with me. In his note he told me he only asked Newman because he was a gunner, and he was the first man he had asked about us. The arm of coincidence is a very long one in this case. What do you say?

The moon is growing towards full now and the desert at night is magnificent in its light. It makes me think of those nights at Rainham when the moon was full and shone on us through the window.

22nd March 1941.

Well darling, another day has passed since I wrote yesterday, another day nearer our reunion. It has in a way been an eventful one but for that we shall have to consult my diary when we are together again, or the censor may take exception. I went into R.H.Q. to hear a criticism of some papers in common with other officers for the Colonel to mark. You will be pleased to hear that he put "VGs" on mine — the only one. I hope it is a step nearer to that third pip.

I have seen in the papers that Jerry has had another big crack at London. I do hope his eggs kept well away from Chislehurst. I hate reading such things knowing you are still so near to London.

Yesterday I had a pair of leather wool lined gloves and a letter from my dear old Mother. It was addressed to me at Clacton, and they were "to keep me warm on the voyage". It is rather amusing to get them out here in the desert but as Saddler said, "We may be glad of them if we reach Berlin in the winter!"

From the newspapers it seems we are doing very well in the war at the moment and undoubtedly Germany's difficulties are on the increase. At the moment the Battle of the Atlantic is the thing. When we have won that I shall feel it is in the bag. General Sir John Dill[16] addressed the troops out here on the wireless last night he sounded very heartening and cheered us all up by promising a speeding up of a more regular service for our mail. He spoke of the morale of the people at home. How grand it is and how everyone expects a worse hammering than they have already had and how they await it with courage and confidence. My God, darling, it's good to be English, isn't it? (I should of course have said "British" after my education by the old Scottish Chief Engineer). It almost amuses me when I think of the number of countries that have thought we are without courage to fight, of the number of people who have thought us easy victims when once we have decided to fight. How few realise the tenacity of the British to finish a job once begun until it is too late.

While writing I am smoking a cigar which Sergeant Minter gave me this afternoon and which arrived from England last night. I thought it was a very pleasant gesture of his at the time but I'm not so sure now. I rather think he wants to do me in. It tastes and smells like army socks and cabbage leaves. Perhaps he means well though.

I sometimes wonder what you must think of this writing paper and of my writing on both sides of the paper. Actually, it is very expensive here and being exceptionally thin I can write to you to

[16] Field Marshall Sir John Dill, GCB, CMG, DSO, 1881-1944, Chief of Imperial General Staff, then Chief Joint British Staff Mission & Senior British Representative on Combined Chiefs of Staff, Washington, DC.

my heart's delight and get it away by air mail for the usual 10 Piasters. Wilson has gone to town today and I meant to give him a cable for you. I know you will look for one fairly frequently now.

31st March 1941.

Since I wrote to you last, I have had a fire in my section's lines. One tent was burnt out completely and seven men lost all their kit. They were all out except Gunner Dyer (Do you remember him?), who has been transferred to me, very much against my will from B.H.Q. We shall never know exactly what happened, but I have no doubt he did something stupid.

5th April 1941.

I have been to an open-air service and attended Communion in a tent. The Colonel was there and said afterwards that he wondered if you and Mrs Stebbings had gone to the village church. Did you, darling? It is as hot as — well — hell — today and the flies get worse and worse.

On Thursday we attended an E.N.S.A. Concert in a big wooden enclosure with no roof. We waited an hour and a half before they could get the lights on and then saw the type of show they put on at a small summer seaside resort. It was really quite amusing, and one woman sang very well. We appreciated it very much as it was the first show we have seen for a very long time.

10th April 1941.

Today the heat has been truly intense, tempers have been somewhat frayed in consequence and as invariably happens on such days, all sorts of things have happened and gone wrong. Yesterday I took the day off and went into a local town for a few hours. We were able to hire a sailing dinghy — Wilson, Captain Mac and I spent a very pleasant afternoon. Our seamanship was not of a very high standard, but we managed somehow. It is a very cheap form of sport for the whole afternoon cost only 2/- for the three of us.

Magpie Cottage, Marsh Green, Nr. Edenbridge, Kent.
25.4.41.

Alan, dear, dear darling, you can imagine how excited I am — after your letter of 5th April, yesterday, two more today from— They were marked series 2. Pages and pages — they were truly wonderful letters — I cherish all your letters and hang on to them wherever I go.

Your account of ship's life was very interesting and amusing. I must say life was gay parties. Incidentally did the drowning ruin your khaki dress very much? You do need a wife with you darling. You made me laugh giving lectures to troops in a fatherly manner. How did you get on Daddy, OK? You do have a fatherly way with you I admit — you should be well qualified to lecture on wine, women and song!

Mother and I nodded over the fire this afternoon and now I must away and pack.

Darling this is a very difficult time to write. Mother and Dorie are chatting away over you and the regiment being called up.

Mother's terribly thrilled with you and all your doings. She's been telling us about your escapades as a youth — the boat "Violet"[17] and cream buns! How I wish I'd known you all those years ago.

Hatton Cottage, Lubbock Rd, Chislehurst, Kent.
27.4.41.

Here I am at Chislehurst again — but not for long I promise you my own love. I plan to stir things up. I have just rung up Bobbing as Phyllis is spending her leave here and Pam answered. They are dying to have me back and want me to go to see them. R.M.P. work is more in my line than military hospital. Then Cyril suggests a job in Cairo — but I have time to think it all over and act for the best.

Ssh- ssh — Churchill's speaking. He's a grand old Bulldog and equal to all Hitler's tricks. I rather gather your third pip may be up any day now — think of me when you celebrate it. Cyril suggests you get into a staff college. Can you, darling?

Michael's talking away 50 to the dozen. His room is full of games caps but cricket, the traditional Sutcliffe game, is hated by him — its rugger, boxing and swimming and now soldiering — he's a machine gunner on the Abbey tower in the Sherborne Home Guard and dying to pot at the Bosch.

Old Winston has made a good speech tonight. How I long for this awful war to end but dear heart, courage and faith and we'll be together sooner than we think. My prayers and love are always yours alone.

---

[17] Alan & Charles Lock owned a boat called "The Fidget" but never mentioned "The Violet" — a slip of the pen?

3.5.41.

Three little words have been going through and through my head all today. Can you guess what they are? "I love you". That little sentence isn't just in my head today but always and always.

But I must tell you of the last 24 hours — Phyllis Hill spent 36 hours here from Bobbing. I met her at Victoria under the clock at 10 am. We went shopping to Peter Jones in Sloane Square. We explored furnishing departments and got ideas for our homes. She's engaged to a signaller (now in Singapore). In my mind I chose chairs, a bed, china, glass and silver plus materials — Interruption No. 1 Phone rings. Pam's boyfriend wanting to meet her at Grosvenor House tomorrow as he's off on a 14-day course at Manorbier — these extravagant youngsters — when I suggested a day out in the Kent orchards Pam looked horrified and said a night club was preferable to them! — Well to continue about yesterday — from Peter Jones we went to Leicester Square and had lunch at a nice "Quality Inn". A light lunch — had cod, mashed potatoes and carrots. We then went next door to the Odeon and saw a very excellent film. Rex Harrison (who incidentally resembles you!), Wendy Hillier (who was in Pygmalion), Emlyn Williams and Sybil Thorndike — a truly good cast in G B Shaw's story, Major Barbara, an exceptionally clever satire on the Salvation Army. You'd like it very much. We also saw Donald Duck too and the news which gave photos of the taking of Keren and Mattapan. We went to the Odeon at 1 p.m. and got exceptionally good seats for 3/-. We then had tea at a homemade tea place called the "Green Lizard" just off Oxford Circus.

We had an alert last night but nothing much happened. 16 planes were brought down though — good, isn't it?

Have you heard the dance tune based on Chopin's 6th Waltz — "Weep no more"? It's rather a lovely thing when not swung too much.

Tomorrow I'm going to see the Commandant and C/O: V.A.D. detachment to fill in my re-joining papers. I pray my sweet darling you aren't worrying over me. I will let you know at the earliest moment where and when I go. Nowadays everyone is doing some sort of work — my age group will have to register in a week or so — I will register if I am still at home, even a V.A.D. on active service is exempt — but that does not mean I'll be called to munitions etc. as I shall be awaiting my "posting" orders.

God bless you and may he take very great care of you for me. My love is always with you wherever you go.

234/89 A.A. Regiment R.A. Middle East Forces.
4th May 1941.

This is the first attempt I have made to communicate with you by this means *(Alan was using an aerogram)*. I have just recently sent a cable and a letter so one of them is bound to reach you. It seems ages since I heard from you but in the circumstances, it is to be expected. I hope soon to get a whole bundle of letters. Anyhow, I am still safe and well and hope soon to hear that you are too. I am just living for the day when I set foot in England again — that happy day we have waited so long for. In the meanwhile, however, life is reasonably pleasant; the weather is good, and we have lots of sunshine. We would all change it willingly for the vagaries of the English climate though.

6th May 1941.

For a time, we lived on bully beef and biscuits only and the first pangs of hunger but now things are really quite good. The scenery is truly magnificent and there is some good bathing near at hand which, up till now, I have not enjoyed.

Hatton Cottage, Lubbock Rd, Chislehurst, Kent.
7.5.41.

Well, I set off for London in my costume and feeling full of spring; met Pop and Mr Hoare — you remember him, short, white-haired man, red faced whom we met at Odie's last September. He's Rupert Brooke's first cousin and Lloyd's Chairman's best friend. He said again if you wanted to return to the bank, he'd be bitterly disappointed if he wasn't allowed to help you through the influence of his friend, so darling, it's worth remembering up our sleeves. While in the bar, drinking gin and French, I had three, nearly three too many. We had a very good lunch, considering stricter rationing. Quite a good hors d'oeuvres — pea soup, jugged hare and jam roll; after that enormous amount of food, I just couldn't eat another thing today. You know this rationing seems to have shrunk our stomachs, to the capacity of one peace-time meal a day spread out over the day. It only goes to prove we used to eat too much.

I heard some very interesting facts on the Blitz, but I better not tell you in case the censor objects, but on one night 98 bombs fell on Bromley — one every 3–4 minutes! Thank goodness I was at Magpie, though it was pretty hellish there from 8.45 – 4 a.m. A solid roar and one bomb 200 yards from us, killing 27 sheep. I slept all night and was about the only villager on bed those nights, I was not nervous of them, but I do admit they are Hell with a large "H". However, we'll finish the brutes off soon. I want to fire a machine gun in slow motion at Hitler. Your very own, ever-loving wife, Pegasus

10.5.41.

A very sweet little letter just found its way to me — written 28th Feb after an outing to a town.

I am very sorry you weren't the first in the Regiment. I intended you to be. I airmailed some in December to be awaiting you and had planned a cable to be there too, but I expect, as Cyril told me, cables of no importance are often deferred or left aside for more important military ones that have to go over the lines. But I know by now you must have received news — I have written every day, cabled fortnightly, sometimes more often. Cables should only take 3 days, many take over a week. I airmail one letter a week and often more.

12.5.41

My head's in a whirl I have so much to tell you. My thoughts are a queer mixture of happiness and sadness, you will see why in a minute. However, firstly thank you darling for the cable gram on Saturday. "Well, all my love Alan Horton". I look forward to your fortnightly cables so much.

Well, now for the weekend. No worries about the recent blitz on Saturday please. I was out of town at Bobbing. My guardian angel looks after me very well — touch wood — the last three blitzes I have been out of town.

13.5.41.

Today is a wonderfully warm day — almost the promise of a heatwave at last. This morning I stood by the open window and felt the cool, fresh air on my naked body. It seemed horrible to have to put clothes on. I'm sure my ancestors went naked till quite recently as I hate the feel of clothes at times. I love bathing in my birthday suit. I feel the sharp cut of cold salt water on my body is so lovely a feeling. I used to bathe like this before breakfast on a friend's beach near Southwold. I walked down in my nightie and dressing gown, slipped them off and in I went. It was a heavenly spot; the bracken came right down to the water's edge.

Mother's been far too kind — she's spoilt me again this morning. I had ½ lb Cadbury's Milk Tray, ¼ lb mixed chocolates and 2 slabs. You know darling, she ought not to spend her money on me like this. Next time I am in town I will get Harrods to send some red roses from us both darling. Her sweets came from Crump's in Deal — remember it? I don't as I've never been there. However darling, you must take me to meet all your aunts on your return. They keep asking Mother if they can see me. I should love to meet them all; you will take me, won't you, sweetheart?

Pam's busy packing her things to go off to the W.A.A.F.s tomorrow — Ron has written her from Manorbier wanting to know how he can get her out but there's none of that now you're registered till you are demobbed — unless of course you are in the family way.

I suppose you've heard about our visitor to England from the Devil's nest. Hesse — the papers are full of him. It's like a film story.

Pat arrived home in a whirl today. Her first words to me were "marriage has made you prettier". You see she has not seen me since August '39. Apparently on the holidays at the farm Mike, Pat and Diana had discussions on you and I. They think we are out of the Victorian era — rather proper. Diana described you as "OK, a large beak, not bad, like Peggy for primness!" Also, they think we are wealthy and can give them good Xmas presents.

This afternoon I wrote and mailed 28 PCs to the troops' families — I must buy some more tomorrow and send the rest off — you'll be sure to let me know darling if there's ever anything I can do for them beside this. I fear some of them are in the Blitzed areas. If I hear from them anything important, I'll air mail it to you to tell the men.

As I write I'm listening to a host of old tunes from the Great War — you will remember the original shows they were in darling? Before my time!

I have been sitting on the floor in Pat's room amongst mountains of untidiness as she's having a blitz. She wanted me to give her some motherly advice — Poor Pat's heard bits and pieces and got all muddled. I think schools ought to tell the girls in their early teens all they ought to know like boys are told. That said it was a shock to her — I bet it was! However, she was relieved when I told her I hardly knew anything till I was a V.A.D. (I must have been asleep during the lectures on peace time, was her remark!). I've given her a little book to read and then to come back and ask me any question. It makes me feel like an old grandmother.

Mother wrote yesterday, she's at Sandwich in her brother's new house for a while. She gets so worried when London's blitzed and couldn't reach me on the phone — indefinite delay and telegrams take 3 days. Pop can't even get to the Government departments about Government contracts he's doing. Bl--dy- awful little Nazi man.

Mrs Callow, Lance Bombardier Callow's mother wrote me a short note, in return for my P.C. asking me to tell Callow they are all well and fit — will you do that darling? I should imagine they are all very poor and are in a very unhealthy area these days of the blitz, so I've written her a letter containing news and how well you all are, etc. and begged her not to thank me for my cards — 2 ½ d is a lot of money. All my love and kisses and hugs are forever yours alone.

16.5.41.

Before I settle down to writing can you enlighten us to the meaning of the following phrase; I heard a compere on the radio say, "Slosh him on in the kisser" or is it "Lesser" or "Kesser"? It's been puzzling Pat and I and we don't want to make a faux pas in asking the wrong person and I am sure it slipped out of the compere's mouth by accident. It sounds rather vulgar to me. Is "Kisser" similar to arse — the latter being a word I learnt recently. My vocabulary is growing. *(Alan's response to this question is not in the correspondence).*

There's a lousy smell over the house. Pat and I found some horse flesh to feed Chummy on today. The Ministry of Food says we'll have horse meat in sausages and pies — well after seeing and smelling this, I'm a vegetarian. When it comes to meat mixtures well! Bl—dy awful!

I am getting several very nice notes from troops' parents — they are so appreciative and wish me to convey their sincere thanks to you my sweet. You know darling, if you came back here and went round damaged areas you'd notice a change in the population — people no-longer have that cheerfulness but a grim determined expression. I remember Kipling saying somewhere that an Englishman was dangerous when he had that grim and determined hate, and it was then that he gets down to business. From the news it looks like it, but we can expect grimmer times before the end. I always try to cable you after a bad blitz in the London area, but many cables get deferred and take a long time.

19.5.41.

Alan darling, two letters, very sweet ones, from you today mailed after Durban. One for Pop and Michael arrived today too. Though they are late news, nevertheless, I loved reading and re-reading them. Your letters comfort me and at times, bring tears to my eyes. You say the things I love to hear so sweetly, it's so painful being apart.

I spent nearly two hours writing news to some of the poorer families of your troops — they have written me such nice letters. On my next card I will mention that it's not necessary to reply, and to some I have said if they ever have any urgent news I will always air or cable it, for me the least I can do. For the majority, I gather have only had the letters from the ship so far. Thank God we can at least afford air mail and cables, you know, you can always find people in far worse plight, especially these days. I've told them how proud you are of your troop and that the food is good.

Gunner Wright's wife wrote this morning and nearly accused me of corresponding with her husband and sent a stamped addressed envelope to know why and how I'd heard so quickly, and not her! I must reply to her and save my honour — she said her husband is in Egypt and always writes to her only!

The Battle for Crete

In June 1944 Alan received A Wartime Log for British Prisoners. *In it he wrote reflecting on the period from leaving home to the Battle of Crete:*

We embarked at Glasgow in the SS City of Canterbury (8,000 tons) and, after touching at Freetown and Durban, disembarked at Port Lewfik two months later (Dec 18th – Feb 18th). The journey was pleasant and without undue incident apart from a short engagement with an enemy cruiser on Christmas Day. We remained in Egypt until April when we embarked once more at Alexandria (the Battery only) and sailed for Crete. Weather was good and excitement plentiful. All was well until the German attack started in earnest and A Troop was almost completely wiped out in the first few hours.

There is a much later version of Alan's log typed only a few years before he died. In this he includes an extra, but very significant, paragraph.

I was on deck with Peter Stebbings, the Colonel's nephew, in the SS Ulster Prince at first light as we sailed into Suda Bay. Peter and I were great friends and rivals. He was considerably younger than I and had been a medical student at the outbreak of war. He had boxed as a heavyweight for Guy's, and was a wild, laughing, always-cheerful extrovert. To my astonishment, he turned to me and said without emotion, "We're going to die here, Alan. Well, possibly, you will get away, but I shall not. I shall certainly die here."

Why, I wonder, should it have been? Peter and the others instead of us? From then on fear and danger were constantly with us. It's worth remarking that never had I felt so vividly alive and so keenly conscious of all the natural beauty around me. Finally, orders came to blow our guns and move south. We were licked.

Fatigue, thirst and danger were constant companions. At 5 am on that fateful morning, when we heard the island had surrendered, I felt so weak and tired that I (and those with me) honestly believed that we could move no further. When the Germans finally took us and we were ordered to march back over the road we had traversed, we had our first lessons in what one's body can do if necessary. We had many more.

Hatton Cottage, Lubbock Rd, Chislehurst, Kent.
21.5.41.

Good morning my love. Darling, are you still, OK? Because I fainted early this morning when I woke up — I'll tell you why — I had a lousy pain in my stomach. Shooting pains and then I just passed out. Fortunately, I was in bed, so no one knew — but the same thing happened when Mummy died. God, I pray all's well, my darling heart. I'm sure it is.

The news from Crete is grim, but so I should imagine shooting down a 52 is rather an excitement when it is full of Bosch Troops — is shooting a Stuka like shooting a grouse flying quickly down-wind? Do you have to follow the flight and then fire? I should imagine your new type of warfare is more interesting than in England but many times more dangerous. God, darling how I wish I knew where you were and what life is like with you — I'd give the world to be at your side no matter how dangerous the situation, but my spirits are always helping you with all my strength. How I pray this awful war will end and we can be together, no matter how big a struggle the future holds, so long as we are together.

22.5.41

Good morning, Sir. Will a vegetable pud suit you for dinner tonight followed by tapioca and rhubarb? M & B[18] to drink. My beloved one, you will have gathered I spent most of the morning trying to make a suet pudding. There's no suet to be had so when Sunday's joint comes, we cut it off and save it. It's coarse but answers the purpose, so I've been chopping it up fine and making a tablespoon go further by adding lard then breadcrumbs to lighten it, and flour. It is a work of art, so is the inside — a spoonful of last Sunday's beef chopped and then masses of chopped veg ranging from spinach to carrots and bone stock to give one the goodness of meat. It's rather fun making dishes from oddments, teaches one to be economical too.

Chin up darling, that wonderful reunion is going to be far more wonderful than we can imagine — "All this and Heaven too"[19] — My prayers are with yours, that this campaign must be short and successful.

---

[18] M. & B. — Mitchell and Butler, brewers.
[19] Novel by Rachel Field (1938), Film from Warner Brothers adapted by Casey Robinson starring Bette Davis & Charles Boyer (1940).

All my love and kisses are with you Alan, you wonderful darling — your very own loving wife,

Pegasus.

2.6.41.

Pop's out and we are eating a precious boiled egg each by the fire — I've dropped mine and lost half the yoke on the floor, what a tragedy! The old man's improved the last day or two and given me 40 players and a Black Magic box like you used to give me. Where does he get these luxuries from? He has a friend however who owns a chain of suburban sweet shops.

Later. Oh darling, I simply do not know how to write and what to say. Kay Sutton's just phoned me about Peter — poor dear Pam. I cannot write her tonight, nor the Stebbings family — but please darling my heart goes out to you all in the 234th. Will you tell the others, also the Colonel? I'd like to write to him in a day or so, but to you my love I can feel just how you feel — someone so vital as old Peter is no more — but he's at peace before us and will be happy waiting for Pam to join him one day. Keep the old chin up my love, it's a hard life — I'm fighting at your side, and we'll weather the storm together. I'm going down to Kay's for the day tomorrow. She had a cable from Charles on Thursday saying all OK. You're with him now, aren't you darling? I still can't believe Kay's phoned me — apparently her mother forbade her to tell me in case I didn't know you were in action. I knew for, as I told you I felt you sapping my strength to help you pull through the hell — am glad you need my strength darling. I'm afraid I can't write any more for a while, so I'll bid you good night my sweet — forget the war and dream about me and us. Faith, hope and courage are in our hearts — we are young and strong and full of our love. Chins up, sleep tight my angel — God bless you and keep you for me and our future. My prayers are joined with yours my darling husband. Good night, my arms hold you tightly and I kiss you to sleep.

3.6.41.

Hello beloved — I've spent the day cheering up Kay Sutton. Did your and Charles' ears burn? We sent you a joint cable. God, darling I pray all is well — we hear frightful tales coming out of Crete. But here's something to cheer your weary self with — Kay joins with everyone else, they are amazed at my tranquillity and tremendous faith. I love hearing people say that, for its only you darling to thank for that faith. Together we'll pull through and then my sweet I'll support you as you've never been supported before. I love and worship you so much darling.

The bus conductor put me down at the wrong turning and I had half an hour's walk down a narrow country lane banked by ferns and sweet-smelling lilac. I walked through a water splash — the day was dull, and the air was heavy with lovely perfumes. The conversation was all you and Charles. We are very glad you are together again — level heads go a long way and I imagine Charles is nearly as level-headed as you are in a hot moment — am I right? Tell Charlie, Kay was very well and chirpy. Peter had knocked us badly but a long walk; hatless in the Scotch mist was lovely as you will know. How we talked about you two darlings.

All my love and kisses are yours and yours alone for ever,
your ever-loving,
Peggy.

The following letter was sent to Peggy by Colonel Stebbings whose nephew, Peter, died early in the Battle of Crete.

89th H.Q. A.A. Regiment, M.E.F.
14.6.41

Dear Peggy,
You will have heard that the battery took a horrible knock — Peter Stebbings, Douglas Jones, and Everdine all killed together with many men of that troop. Corbett is back here with a bullet through his cheek.

Greville Man, Charles Sutton and Wilson together with a large party of men arrived back in this country safely. They saw Alan, Hukins, MacDonald alive with another party about six miles from the beach and hoped they would be embarking. But now everyone is back who can probably get back, so I am horribly afraid they must all be prisoners of war. Oh Peggy, I am so, so sorry to have to write, as I know the appalling uncertainty. It will be many weeks before you get the names from the Red Cross of those who are safe but prisoners. I just hope and pray that we shall get news that at any rate they are safe.

We know that a few were lost on the way back, but I have not heard of any at all of our people being included, so we must presume that many were unable to get away and had to surrender.

Peggy, so please accept my deepest sympathy in the doubt and uncertainty. But you know I am doing everything to find out and of course will let you know immediately we get news.

Poor Pam, I wrote to her but what can one say? — Our grand, happy laughing Peter — dying, lived with his men but what finer death, a gunner dying amongst his guns, fighting to the last.

Oh Peggy, I've a heavy heart these days. My prayers are with you all, the women whose lot, so horrid, to wait and hope. Have faith Peggy as I have.

All our dear love.

Yours ever,

Stanley Stebbings.

89th A.A. Regiment R.A. M.E.F.

1.8.41.

Peggy my dear,

It was grand to receive your P.C. dated 1.7.41. and to know that you are bearing up cheerfully. I am wondering if you have received the letter I wrote to you, and if Kay has passed on all the permissible news. I hope so. By all means Peggy, I will be delighted to do anything for you both and I sincerely hope that soon you will receive Daddy's address and letters will be possible. Yes, it is a blow that he was so unlucky. I can't imagine what happened as he was about 6 hours ahead of me, as were the others. The last I saw of him was about 30 miles from the end of the track riding a motorcycle. We had a chat and he said he was going forward to find Mac who was in the front with food and water. However, we did not see them again. The last of our boys to get back did see him with the others about 5 miles from the beach. These boys, all walking wounded were allowed to go forward.

I hope the optimistic views of an early end materialise, as you say — the future. Yes — I would love to be a Godfather! It is good to know that you see Kay and are able to phone each other. Some of Bobbing's beautiful flowers would be more than appreciated out here. What a place this is!

This conscription of women is a blow, isn't it? I am rather worried about Kay and what she will do — I hope not the services. I am sure Dad would prefer to know that you are a V.A.D. than taking your chance with the multitudes. We talked about it in Crete and cursed — you will remember his pathetic moan — "Why did I volunteer?" I have heard of Angela's promotion, and I am very pleased — she will make a grand little officer. Please give her my best wishes.

The battle: Well, bouts of fairly decent Blitz, ack-acks from dawn to dusk, bombed, dive bombed, machine gunned. We reduced 9 to small bits and hundreds of others must have turned back — the scars of 234 determination. We were alone to fight the Luftwaffe — no R.A.F. We hit back as hard as we could — the end blowing up our guns and instruments, was not at all pleasant. They tried their hardest to put us out of action but failed — lucky for us. Other news and heaps I can assure you, until the good old piping days are ours again and old Hitler is reduced to a frazzle.

Best wishes to all, keep smiling Peggy and let's hope for an early reunion,

Yours,
Charles.

Captivity — Lubek

Alan's Wartime Logbook contains the following paragraph:

So, we embarked upon another journey — Spartea to Canea, Canea by JU52 to Athens — Athens by train and foot to Salonica — Salonica by train to Lubek, hunger, thirst, fleas, lice, bugs and filth. Rather unpleasant but necessary if one is to understand the meaning of "undernourishment", "depressed areas", "slums" and "the demoralising effects of unemployment" — just words before but real things now. 37 in cattle truck, half with dysentery and let out twice a day for 5 minutes! This journey lasted exactly 7 days and nights. At least I was experiencing life. I too had dysentery and later Jaundice. I had always craved for experiences. I was having them in plenty! Lubek was a clean but hungry camp. The thought of food dominated the mind, sleeping and waking. Slow starvation haunted the mind and stayed with us till long after the arrival at Warburg where Red Cross parcels were issued regularly.

Once in prison camp, Alan, in common with all P.O.W.s, was permitted only a very limited number of cards and aerograms a month, meaning that all his news needed to be crammed into a very small space. Whilst he continued to use punctuation, paragraphs were, of necessity, abandoned.

On 25ᵗʰ and 26ᵗʰ June 1941, there were two printed cards sent with exactly the same wording and signed by Alan. It is unclear when Peggy received them, but the middle of September 1941 seems most likely from the content of one of her letters written at that time.

I am a prisoner of war and in good health. In the next letter I will give you my address. It is useless to write before receiving the news.

With best wishes,

Name and Surname: Alan Edward Horton

Military rank: Lieutenant R.A.

Designation for military information: M.E.F.

2 5 JUIN 1941

I am a prisoner of war and in good health. In the next letter I will give you my address. It is useless to write before receiving the new address.

With best wishes

Name and surname: *ALAN EDWARD HORTON*

Military rank: *LIEUTENANT R.A.*

Designation of military formation *M.E.F.*

British Red Cross Society, Prisoners of War Department, St. James's Palace, London, SW1.
16th July 1941.

Dear Mrs Horton,
Lieutenant A. E. Horton A/O/2003
We have been informed by the International Red Cross Committee that Lieutenant Horton is a prisoner of war, and that he is well. It would appear that he is at a transit camp, and his permanent address is not known.

Unless therefore you have heard this from some other source, you may as his next-of-kin, write to him addressing your letters for the time being as follows:

Prisoners of War Post Kriegsgefangenenpost
71325 Lieutenant A. E. Horton,
British Prisoner of War,
c/o Agence Centrale des Prisoners de Guerre.
Comite International de la Croix-Rouge,
Palais du Conseil-General,
Geneva, Switzerland.

Letters should only deal with personal matters, should not exceed both sides of a sheet of notepaper in length, and must have the name and address of the sender written on the back of the envelope. If, however, the writer is serving in His Majesty's Forces, the name and address of the Unit must not be given, but a private address substituted.

Letters to prisoners of war may either be sent post free by the ordinary prisoner of war post, or by air, in which case a 5d stamp and blue air-mail label, obtainable at any Post Office, are required. There is no limit to the number of letters which may be written to a prisoner of war, but it is well to bear in mind that as they all have to pass through two censorships, the greater the number sent, the greater may be the delay in delivery.

If you have already received the camp address, or if it is sent to you from some other source before you hear from us again, will you be so kind as to let us know?

Yours sincerely,

J. M. Eddy,

Deputy Director.

Hatton Cottage, Lubbock Rd. Chislehurst, Kent.
24.7.41.

My very own darling beloved husband, Alan, I do wonder how you are? I just long for even a P.C. from you — it will come in time no doubt, but while I don't know I pray to the good God daily to help you — hearten you and keep up your grand faith and courage. Does it help my sweet? Darling I am so proud of my old man. It's such a pity you never received any of my letters after February. I also sent you several more parcels and a very hot copy of "Esquire". This weekend I am going to Midhurst on Sunday to Monday to stay with Cyril and Jennie, Mother and Mary Rose who all go there on Friday. I miss you so terribly on these parties.

Your Pegasus is getting very busy now. I bottled gooseberries and jammed raspberries this week — all this fruit from the garden in our efforts to "Dig for Victory". It will be a grand day when we can open our own store cupboard and see rows of jams and fruits — next year, maybe?

11.8.41.

Can you imagine the terrific waves of relief that keep sweeping over me daily, when I think how lucky I am to have you safe and alive. It comes home particularly when I read in "The Times" of your men once reported missing and now killed. I am making a list of as many of them as I recognise to show you — do you think when it is completed, I'd be allowed to mail it to you? Old Goldfinch has gone — dear me it gives me a heavy heart. Incidentally, you were in "The Times" the other day as a P.O.W. You have even been mentioned by Lord Haw Haw I hear, so too Geoffrey Towse. Carol Towse came to tea on Sunday — she was up for a few days. If her husband is as nice as her, he should be a good companion.

14.8.41.

I am in the middle of cooking a good 3 course dinner. OK to please you I've been complimented on my cooking! Diana's a grand help and companion. I have written many letters to the families of your men who lost their lives; on your behalf and mine for the men I knew. It gives one a heavy heart. Your sweater is nearly finished in a week! Now some socks for you my sweet. It makes me happy even to do this little amount for you beloved one. More next week, you see I can only write once a week by this address.

    All my love and kisses forever,
    your own ever-loving wife,
    Peggy.

British Red Cross Society, Prisoners of War Department, St. James's Palace, London, SW1.
15th August, 1941.

Dear Mrs Horton,

Thank you for your letter of the 11th August. We are sorry to know that you have not yet had any news from your husband. No information has reached us as to his permanent camp address but as soon as we hear this, we will immediately inform you.

As you say it is not possible for you to send him a parcel until you know his address. We enclose a leaflet No. 88 which will show you what you can send in a uniform parcel. Only one such parcel may be sent to each officer, and it must not weigh more than 10 lb.

The Government is supplying uniforms, underclothing and foot-wear and every effort is being made to make sure that an outfit reaches every prisoner before the winter. You will realise that with the enormous number concerned and transport difficulties in Germany today, the problems of distribution are very great. It would probably be wise therefore, to send any uniform you can to your husband as soon as you have his camp address and prisoner of war number. Uniform may be included in the next of kin parcel and great coats or trench coats are often made with detachable lining, this lining can then be sent separately if necessary. It is also a good plan to make a great coat a little shorter, as this makes it considerably lighter without taking much of its warmth.

Yours sincerely,
J.M. Eddy.
Deputy Director.

Hatton Cottage, Lubbock Rd, Chislehurst, Kent.
19.8.41.

The Red Cross are being extraordinarily helpful re you and your clothes, and I am off shopping next Friday so I can have everything ready to send the moment your address comes through in hopes it reaches you before the cold weather. I just hate to think of you under any hardships.

British Red Cross Society, Prisoners of War Department, St. James's Palace, London, SW1.
21st August, 1941

Dear Mrs Horton,
Thank you for your letter of the 18th August.

We quite understand you wish to have the parcel ready for despatch as soon as you hear of your husband's camp address. The advance floating stock of 40 coupons can be had by application to our Packing Centre at 14, Finsbury Circus, E.C.2. These will only be issued once and will be refunded to you in the same way as your own coupons as explained in the first paragraph of the enclosed leaflet, PW1. They can thus be used as often as you have them refunded by the packing centre, and should they not be sufficient you may use your own, or any that you can borrow from your friends which will also be refunded.

We enclose our most recent leaflets which will give you information as to sending parcels to your husband as soon as you know his camp address and prisoner of war number.

The great coat and suit, by which we presume you mean uniform, can be purchased from a tailor who has previously made for your husband. Most military tailors will supply uniform without coupons as in the case of serving Officers.

Yours sincerely,

J.M. Eddy.

Deputy Director.

84, Huddersfield Rd; Odsal, B/d, Yorks.

August 23rd, 1941.

Dear Mrs Horton,

I was very grateful indeed for your kind letter, it seemed to give more hope and courage than I had seemed to have before, and I gave the Red Cross all details and I have received a letter in return telling me they will do their utmost to try and find my son. Also, I have received a letter from the A.A. Minorities Department telling me a name of Jack Lightollers of B/d. has been heard on a foreign radio as P.O.W. but it gives no country, and they say it may refer to my boy, but I have to treat it as unofficial, but it certainly gives me fresh hope again.

In the meantime, I do sincerely hope you have had direct news from your husband and that he is safe and well.

Thanking you again, I am,

Yours sincerely,

Eveline Lightollers.

Only some parts of this first, short, handwritten postcard (below), from Alan are legible.

Prisoner No. 3275. Oflag X C.
August 1941.

Mr darling Peggy, I just know your thoughts of these last months. My main desire has been to know where and how you are. I am quite fit but have lost all my kit so next letter will be all wants. Before writing get "Communications with Prisoners of War Abroad" from the Post Office. As above put "Gefangennummer" before my name. Please let everyone know my address and particulars of communication as I have you…

23rd August 1941

My very own darling, I must say "sorry" for dealing with wants but we are all anxious to get warm clothing before winter comes. Pamphlet 2280E from the Post Office will tell you all about communications. We have had nothing from the Red Cross yet but hope to, soon. Can you please send me in first personal parcel: 1 set warm underwear, 1 bush shirt (15 1/2), 2 ties, 3 handkerchiefs, bootlaces, 2 pairs long woollen socks, gloves, scarf, long sleeved pullover, balaclava, housewife with thread and wool, safety tin opener, soap and shaving soap, Eversharp refills, sponge bag and as many slabs of chocolate as possible, whilst tobacconists will permit 300 cigarettes a month. Books from approved publishers: Croppers Higher Bookkeeping and Accounts; Company Act 1929; An English-German Dictionary and a good German Grammar. Some Cod Liver Oil and Malt in the Medical Parcel to the Senior Medical Officer might help in the winter. How I wish darling, we were back where we were this time last year. I can only wish you many happy returns and hope that next year we can celebrate your birthday and the anniversary of our engagement together. I am allowed two letters and four postcards a month so soon I will write again telling you of our life here and something of past events. I long for your first letter telling me you are well — I cannot help feeling some anxiety.

My love is all yours, now and always.

Your own,

Alan.

Hatton Cottage, Lubbock Rd, Chislehurst, Kent.
27.8.41.

Darling one, I'm slowly recovering from a 'down' of considerable magnitude. The cause is partly my fault for dreaming of last year — you see the flowers, the trees and weather are growing more and more autumnal — then above all I dwell on our wonderful leave this time a year ago and from then onwards our memories seem to flow beautiful and precious. Incidentally, Mrs Saddler rang up today saying she has just heard he is a P.O.W. What a relief for her — such a nice little thing.

29.8.41.

Today my own, I have so much news of my doings to tell you, I am wondering if this allowance of one page will be able to suffice. However, beloved here goes — Diana and I went to town yesterday for the day. I've bought you a rug (pure wool), a kit bag, 2 vests, 2 pants of pure wool — they asked if you wanted long legs — I couldn't say however and bought short as they seem soft, warm garments. It was lucky being able to buy pure wool, slacks (khaki), 2 Vyella shirts, tie, 6 handkerchiefs.

Mrs Saddler senior has rung up to say Saddler's joined you — I am so glad, and they are most grateful for you to have applied for him. You know they all came to tea here a few weeks ago, John too. We sat out in the garden. I rather let the side down as I'd just washed my hair and it was all pinned up when they unexpectedly turned up, but who cares, we were soon all chatting about you both. Remember me to Saddler and say his wife and I correspond regularly and ring each other up when any news comes through. Many other wives and mothers write often to me, and all say a thing I love to hear — how glad they are their sons had such a grand officer as my husband over them and they know all will turn out OK in time. They think an awful lot of you my sweetheart and I am very proud of you and all of them. I am writing to these poor families and cheering them up for many have only heard their beloveds are missing.

30.8.41.

Beloved heart, whether these reach you, or not — I pray they do. But I want to reassure you and put your mind at rest if you are worrying over your £. s. d. — The Army Bankers have explained to me that £5.8/- is deducted monthly from your pay for you, £3 is also deducted, now that still leaves heaps for Mother to have £3 and I hope to save the rest. Now Everett is back from holiday he is chasing after allowances, etc. I have drawn £5 this month as Pop's not given me mine, otherwise I hope not to draw any. However soon, I hope to be in a job and so live on my pay and save the rest. We may not be able to save what I'd hoped. I'd made up my mind to hand you a balance of £300 on your return. It should however be over £200, that's assuming you are away another 8 months from August; now, however, I pray you aren't sweetheart. Cyril's giving Mother £8 a month now. He can afford to give more if she finds it hard as when in town, he gets £80-£90 a month! Colossal, isn't it? Well darling, I think it's all explained but you must never, never worry. If things do get tight, I shall enjoy a rocky path.

Your very own ever-loving wife,

Peggy. xxx

Prisoner No. 3275. Oflag XC.
2nd September 1941.

My own Darling Peggy, how I wish I could come with this and see how you are, or better still, put the clock back a year and relive those wonderful times we had together. I shall never forget the 5th and 6th September of last year and the days round about. Since then, my adventures have been many and varied. Much must wait until I can tell you personally, but I will tell you something of our life here and what has happened to us. Peter Stebbings, Cocollis and Douglas Jones were killed, and Corbett wounded right at the beginning of our action. Please say how sorry I am to any of their people you may meet. I was taken with the Major, Captain, Towse and Clark on June 1st. Since then, I have been in various transit camps so that apart from one card which I hope you had some time ago, I have been unable to write until recently. Conditions are now reasonably pleasant. I share a room with nine others. Our compound is large and has quite a pleasant garden in it. We have a canteen where various articles of hardware can be bought and condiments, pickles, salted fish, etc. To amuse ourselves there is soccer, basket-ball, lectures and classes — we have specialists in a variety of subjects including law, accountancy and German. Time passes fairly quickly. We are paid £1.16/- every ten days which will come off my pay. Well, my beloved, I hope to hear from you soon and will write as often as I can. My thoughts are always with you, and I live only for our future.

May God bless you and keep you safe,

Your own,

Alan.

Hatton Cottage, Lubbock Road, Chislehurst, Kent.
4.9.41.

My own beloved darling, I have just had a very enjoyable 48 hrs. Sonia's been here so you can imagine how we gassed away — did your ears burn darling? We spent all day in town yesterday and saw a Chekov play, "The Cherry Orchard". It was very good. The whole day cost us just under 10/- each. We "pitted" for seats but had tea in a very select restaurant full of red tapes. Darling, I've been rather extravagant. I've bought a most lovely, large pigskin handbag for myself as a birthday present from you. It was 79/6d! Do you mind for once?

8.9.41.

My beloved heart, just returned from staying down with Mother and Everetts to find the best birthday present in the world I could have had this year — a postcard from you my own Alan. Printed in German — thank heaven I know enough of that language to read it quickly and eagerly as I snatched it up from the letter tray. It's nearly four months since I last heard from you so you can imagine my feelings. But my loved one have you had any of mine? I've written many letters and these all by Air Mail for the last 10 weeks at least — all via Geneva Red Cross. I pray you have as you must long for a letter now more than ever.

9.9.41.

Beloved heart, another two cards from you today June 25th — 26th saying you were a P.O.W. One Everett sent me telling me to go and have a booze up to celebrate — you'd laugh at his ending — instead of saying "Yours sincerely", its "be good"! Why? I really am most awfully good I promise you. Mother's received your card too.

Prisoner No. 3275. Oflag X C
11th September1941.

My own darling, with luck I should get a letter from you within a few weeks. Needless to say, I am impatient to know all about things. There's not a great deal I can say on these post cards except that I am still well and always thinking of you. My letters have covered all the news to date. I forget whether or not I asked before, but I do please want some more photographs of you. Please remember me to everyone.

Your own,
Alan.

Stamped by the censor onto a number of Peggy's letters written at this time are the words, 'Write legibly to avoid delay'. *Her writing was never easy to read!*

Hatton Cottage, Lubbock Rd, Chislehurst, Kent.
13.9.41.

Pat Hukins, Carol and Mrs MacCormack have had letters and cards from their husbands mentioning things they want so I am planning your parcel with similar wants my sweet. The sweater and gloves were made by Mother — I'll send my sweater in the next parcel, the scarf which I hope to finish was mostly made by Diana, socks by Miss Foster and me. I am sending Mother's sweater as she would be very upset if I didn't darling. By the way I'm sending Charles Lock your address; Martin, etc. want it too.

14.9.41.

My beloved Alan, Sunday and a real wintry one. Diana and I had buttered toast for tea by a fire in the little sitting room full of roses — I can smell their perfume as I write this. Can you my sweet? We spent most of the afternoon on the floor weighing out your next of kin parcel — 10 lbs, seems a very small weight when there is so much you must want however. I am sending essentials like a camel-hair blanket & kit bag, shaving tackle, sweater — some shoe trees are for Geoffrey Towse darling. I couldn't find a face flannel for you anywhere so I'm sending a fairly new one of mine — it's clean and hygienic. In three months, I will send another. I do want you to have everything you want. Between these two I am sending a

Uniform parcel with warm shirts, tunics, trousers, gloves and maybe a peaked cap — let me know what fitting shoe you take. I've just been listening to a community hymn concert: Onward Christian Soldiers, He who would a pilgrim be, Fight the good fight and many other lovely tunes that breathe our English spirit.

Prisoner No. 3275. Oflag X C
16th September1941.

My own darling Wife, although I have been eagerly awaiting this letter to write to you, now that I have it I find it difficult to know what to say. Mere words on paper seem too inadequate to bridge the distance between us and satisfy the longing in our hearts. All my thoughts are about you and home. I see you always as you were on our walks together with that happy smile on your face and the wind blowing through your hair with the background of the view from our hill. Scenes of England come particularly vividly to my mind just now, I long for the sight of English meadows and the plough plodding slowly back and forth and seagulls wheeling behind it, for the woods tinted by autumn, for the grey stone churches and thatched cottages. Then too, are the country pubs with their dim interiors and bright fires. There are many fine ones I mean to take you to when I get home. What fun we shall have on our first holiday together. Life here, as I have said, is not too bad. Our classes continue with studying and note taking, time passes quite quickly. The Geneva Y.M.C.A. have been here and asked us what books we want for study. I have asked for a set to work for a BSc (Economics). Oh, my darling how I long to be back with you again to start our life together. I pray that time will not be far distant. In the meantime, I eagerly await the first letter from you. We expect to hear early next month and have a sweepstake on the date.

Your very own,

Alan.

Hatton Cottage, Lubbock Road, Chislehurst, Kent.
17.9.41.

My very own darling, a card dated 20th August has just arrived from you. I am so thrilled to receive a card with your handwriting on after all these months. Yes, we do know each other's thoughts darling, and that's why I've been endeavouring to mail you news of me. The Red Cross gave me an address at Geneva which would forward letters to you, so I started writing via this in June and I can't think why nothing has yet reached you — unless by now you've received a pile. I have been very careful too re saying anything, but personal news and all mine are in the same strain. I have mailed one parcel of warm undies, mending, etc. a camel hair blanket, kit bag, pipe, shaving and washing oddments. I am now completing a parcel of your old tunic and slacks, woollies, shirts, gloves, etc. for you will need warmth I imagine. It's a very similar climate to where I was at school and the same grand scenery. How I want to be with you — I'd be your interpreter! You may meet many of your lads; they are all near you now, as families are hearing from them all in good spirits and health. Have you been able to claim Saddler as batman yet darling one? In three months-time when I can send another parcel, I'll send warm pyjamas, more soaps, etc. and shoes. I have made arrangements re books, cigarettes and baccy. Many people are also mailing you books etc. — your address I put in the papers a week ago darling.

All are very well, including your very own, ever-loving wife, Peggy.

God bless you and keep you safe.

Lieut. C. B. Sutton R.A. 89th A.A. Regiment M.E.F.
Sept 17th, 1941.

Peggy, my dear,

I was so very pleased to receive your letter, dated 30/7/41 today. How glad I am to know that Alan is safe and sound and that you are able to communicate with him. Please let me have his address as soon as you can, and I will surely write to him as often as possible. Poor old Dad, I wish he had been in my party. Never mind — the future now holds lots of parties when we all get back. I have heard also from Kay that Leslie is also a P.O.W. Mrs Hukins, I am sure shares your delight. She has been staying with Kay. I am anxious for news of Mac, Clarke and Towse.

I did not get the joint cable I'm afraid, quite a lot of our mail went astray but it is improving a little now. I have kept all your letters to Dad and the few parcels. I will do as you say Peggy as I am sure the chances of forwarding to Dad are very remote. I hope you will be able to get your "pip", and please Peggy, if Kay is forced to enlist and you can help her in any way, I would be truly grateful. I am hoping and hoping however that she will be able to remain at home and keep the home fires burning. Like Alan, I hate the idea. Yes, he received the news that you had joined the V.A.D.s Again he was gnashing at his bit for several days though I fully appreciated his reactions, but I suppose it is necessary but here we do not fully appreciate what is happening at home.

I managed to keep out of 205, and at present with the Colonel here. Very interesting work but quite a change from gunsights. The Colonel has been most kind to me and I sincerely hope that I will be able to soldier on with him. He has been in hospital with malaria but is now fit again and recuperating at Cairo. This is a dreadful country to be in, everything is rotten and filthy, but it is helping us to win the war and that is everything. I kill billions of flies a day, but still they come, the little devils.

We are all very fit and quite cheerful and enjoy quite a peaceful existence, our nights are often disturbed but not without success, our bag is getting quite heavy. I hope to hear from poor Pam. I often think of her and wonder how she is getting on. I am sure she will be very brave and face up to her big loss. Other news is scarce, but I will write again.

My best wishes to all, keep smiling now, we are always thinking of you at home and well, you can imagine there will be a big rush for the first boat.

Sincerely,

Charles.

Hatton Cottage, Lubbock Road, Chislehurst, Kent.
18.9.41.

My very own darling Alan, your card of yesterday has made me a new woman — I carry it everywhere and it comes out in quiet corners very often. Alan, my sweet you mustn't worry over me, there is no need at all. I have been here since leaving Magpie looking after the children as, after leaving the cottage, I was told I wasn't wanted in my job for some months, so I stayed to help with the children who were home for the holidays. As I am still not wanted as yet, I've obtained my resignation and am joining Angela's corps — not under her however with a view of reaching the rank you were when I first met you, after three months. Apparently, I'm the type they want to look after the new raw girls, morally, etc.!

Prisoner No. 3275. Oflag X C
24th September 1941.

My darling, it is a grand day today, one of those Indian summer days we love so much, just such a day as we would love to have when next we visit our hill together. How I long to be with you again but the main thing at the moment is to know that you are well, and I hope to hear that next month. Please give my love to everyone we know — I do hope all are well — and explain how impossible it is for me to write to them all.

Your very own,
Alan.

Rivers Hall, Boxted, Colchester, Essex.
25.9.41.

My very own darling Alan, it's been a lovely day and I'm browning with my lazy life in the sun. I fell asleep under ye olde apple tree for ages this afternoon. Carol Towse wrote me today saying she'd had Geoffrey's 2nd letter — I am unlucky so far, I've not had a letter, only a card, however it may be at home and will be forwarded in due course. How I long for it — letter No. 1 may not reach us as Carol fears they have disappeared. She told me all Geoffrey's news etc. so I can imagine more than ever now what your life is my darling. Now a girl has come who is unofficially engaged to a man who is with your old friend Charles who is very well I hear. Darling, have you received any of my letters? I've air-mailed piles for 3 — 3 1/2 months now via the Red Cross.

Mrs E Callow, 89, Edward Street, Deptford St. SR8.
September 26th, 1941.

Dear Madam,
I hope you won't think I'm intruding but I thought you would like to know I have received a card this morning from my son Lance Bombardier Callow saying he is a Prisoner of War in Germany. You don't know what a relief it was to me. That is the first news since 11th May. Hoping you heard from your husband.

I remain yours sincerely,
Mrs E Callow.

Rivers Hall, Boxted, Nr. Colchester, Essex.
27.9.41.

My very own beloved darling husband, Alan, my own, can you imagine how thrilled I am? A letter was forwarded from home to me yesterday — it was dated 23rd August and full of "wants". Incidentally I've got two parcels off to you in the third quarter of the year — a uniform parcel and next of kin — so now in a week or two, I can get another next of kin off in the fourth quarter of the year. I've sent everything you've asked for except sponge bag, Eversharp refills, tin opener, balaclava, so these plus more in the next parcel. You should be receiving 470 cigarettes a month and one and a half pounds of baccy — I've sent a pipe, one to follow in every parcel in case of breakages! Your books will be ordered at once.

You are doubtless wondering why I am not yet in a job. When I left Magpie, I wired you my intentions four months ago. Actually, I was told I'd be wanted any day, so on shutting up Magpie and being home a week I was told there was no work for me for months, so I applied for my resignation — this took till last month to come through! But as long as I was still a member, no other association or organisation would take me. Now I've had a commission in Angela's service offered me but after going into it all, I should get only £2 a week, then income tax, messing, etc. in the end you have to draw from private income, so I am remaining in the ranks driving, but private cars, etc. — you know, hauling red tabs over the country, etc.! In this I get my keep, clothes and 11/- a week but am not quite under the stiff restrictions Angela is.

I get many letters from your men's families — all except for a few are safe and well as prisoners and are enjoying themselves at farming, etc. — all the families seem very fond of you and mention how glad their sons and husbands are to have served with you. It makes me very proud to receive these, darling.

Prisoner No. 3275. Oflag X C
1st October 1941.

My own darling wife, several officers have already received letters from home, many of those written c/o the Red Cross in Geneva so I am hoping to hear from you very soon. It is six months now since I had any news of you at all so you can imagine my anxiety. The

Red Cross seems to be a very efficient organisation but so far we have had none of the promised parcels from them. We hope to have them soon. At present I have not even a change of underclothes but apart from washing days life is reasonably comfortable and the weather warm and sunny. In the afternoons we can sit out in the open and listen to the wireless music and German talks in English. This is a big camp, all officers and we have a large number of R.A.F. Officers among us. Occasionally one recently captured comes in and we gather round quickly to hear the latest news from home. It seems strange when one speaks to one who was, perhaps, in London only a few days before. After being away so long and travelling so far England seems months of travel away to me. It has been a great experience but the last part I could well do without. I would love to take you to Crete darling[20] when my memories of the battle have grown less vivid. It is the most beautiful place I have seen, at present though I only want to get back again to England and start our life together. You never leave my thoughts and I plot and plan how best I can organise my life to make you happy. Just go on loving me darling and all will come well.

All my love to you as always,

Your own,

Alan.

5.10.41.

Beloved, there has been something over which I've wept bitterly at times during the past months, and I see in your letters and P.C.s no

---

[20] Alan and Peggy did visit Crete together once or twice for holidays in the 1970s and they loved it.

mention was made of it. Did you darling receive a wire in May from me saying I was returning to Hatton Cottage and working again? Darling, I've kicked myself ever since for sending that wire if it reached you, for if it did, it was at a very busy time for you, and I am very much afraid it would worry you. It hurts me awfully when I think of the worry I may have caused you. From what Charles Sutton remarked on in a letter it looked as if you did receive the wire. I was due to work again soon, then a week or so afterwards they said I wasn't wanted for 6 months so I've resigned and I'm joining something else — driving light vehicles to be exact.

Your very own ever-loving wife,

Peggy.

Hatton Cottage, Lubbock Rd, Chislehurst, Kent.
6.10.41.

I came up to "Grey Stock" with Uncle last night and over a cold supper we opened a bottle of bubbly and toasted your birthday and success. Uncle's writing to you and sending books, etc. I was fairly tired having driven Uncle up at about 60 mph nearly all the way in heavy rain as we wanted to be in before dark. Today he lent me the car and chauffeur and I went shopping for you. I've spent a lot of cash but it's necessary. I've bought you a suede fleece lined waistcoat for warmth and long socks. I couldn't find khaki but under trousers they won't show.

7.10.41.

My mail is so colossal these days — masses from your men's families. I think it would be nice to send them several hundred cigarettes for Xmas from you. I'll send them to one man to divide up and write to him and explain my plan. Their wives and mothers write and thank me for keeping up their faith and hope whilst waiting for news — how very sweet of them. The Red Cross have just told me where your camp is — hence salt fish in the canteen. You aren't exactly where I'd have liked you to have been — you've certainly seen a bit of the world my love, what lots you will have to tell me.

15.10.41.

My very own darling husband, Phew! Can you smell high pheasant — it's stuck to me — I've been casseroling a bird of uncertain age and smell. Mrs Saddler rang me up yesterday. I've asked her and John to tea next week. Saddler's where you left him and a batman, but till he is moved I can't send him any cigarettes from you as I had planned. I am sending 370 odd, to be shared between your men. I am sending it to one of the N.C.O.s to divide up. Tomorrow I am going for my interview ███████████████. I am stipulating and hope to achieve the type of vehicle I want to drive, not like Angela's, that's definite. They sound to be quite decent on the phone, after all one doesn't mind lumping it with decent girls, but with a rough, coarse type it's a bit hard.

The British Red Cross Society, Prisoner of War Department, 14, Carlton Terrace, London, SW1.
15th October 1941.

Dear Mrs. Horton,

71325 WS/Lieut Alan E. Horton. P.O.W. 3275, No.1 Company, Oflag X C.

Thank you for your letter of October 7th which must have crossed ours to you of the 8th.

I am so very sorry to hear that your husband has lost so much weight, and I know how much this must worry you. In order that there shall be no delay I am arranging to have a 10 lb. parcel, containing a good supply of Cod Liver Oil and Malt and some Halibut Liver Oil Capsules and other nourishing Invalid Foods and vitamin preparations, despatched to him c/o the Senior British Medical Officer of his Camp direct from this section without delay.

I think that as he has lost so much weight, we should be quite justified in authorising you to send him a similar parcel every two weeks for the time being and if you would like to send us one for forwarding according to the instructions given in our letter of October 8th, we will despatch it at the end of a fortnight.

After the despatch of these first two parcels perhaps you will let me know if you would like us to send the other parcel direct from here, or if you would prefer to send the things to us for forwarding.

I suggest that we might send Lieut. Horton these fortnightly parcels for the next two months, and after that you will doubtless have further news and will be able to tell me if you think it necessary to continue sending so frequently.

With all good wishes,
Yours sincerely,
Muriel Bromley Davenport.
Hon. Secretary Invalid Comforts Section.

Hatton Cottage, Lubbock Rd, Chislehurst, Kent.
17.10.41.

Angela's just turned up for the night very well and cheery and has some news which I will pass on to you. It will recall a dinner conversation one night in November with Martin, Sonia and Steve. Gus is up a pip, Stuart's going up into a better job, boy David is taking Stuart's place and James F has his third ███████████████████████████████ *(Five lines censored!)*

19th October 1941.

A great joy of joys brought a P.C. from you September 24th and a letter October 1st. You were enjoying a lovely Indian summer. I was too, over those days whilst at Rivers Hall. Oh, my darling how I pray that by now you have a terrific bundle from me.

Captivity — Warburg

Alan's logbook describes Warburg as follows: "Warburg meant mud, dust, filth of every description and, above all, cold. The European winter took the place of hunger as a ghost to haunt us. It marked, however, a new phase in life for me. Better food made sport attractive. Books were available in large numbers. We had music, concerts, and other amusements, official and unofficial. Here I took myself in hand and resolved to make a favourite quotation, "I am the master of my fate, I am the captain of my soul"[21] really mean something.

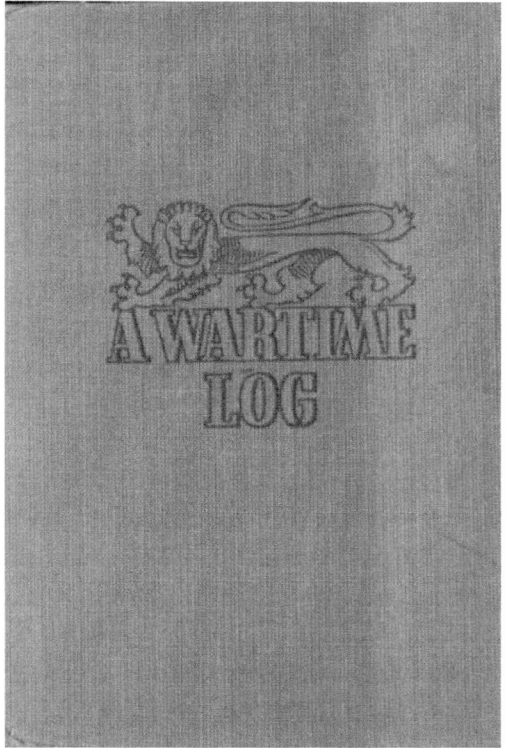

---

[21] "I am the master of my fate, the captain of my soul" — from Invictus by William Ernest Henley, 1849-1903.

Prisoner No. 3275. Oflag VI B.
17th October 1941.

My darling Peggy, my new address is:
    Oflag 6B, No.4 Battalion, Germany,
    I am well.
    Love Alan.

26th October 1941.

My very own darling Wife, Mail is rolling in now and I had another letter from you and one more from Cyril yesterday. We are well settled in our new home now. I am in quite a comfortable room with Captain Mac. There are fourteen of us in it, and we sleep in two-tier bunks. The room is bright and airy, and it is quite a cheery crowd we are with. I turn out about 7.30 am, wash and shave and have breakfast and go on roll call parade at 9.30. After that we are left to our own devices until another roll call at 6.15 p.m. We visit our friends in other huts and fight and battle again over cups of tea, cocoa or Ovaltine. The concert parties have got going and produce some very good shows and we have a very fine library. There is plenty of exercise room here, so life is quite pleasant. We have started getting Red Cross food parcels which are very good indeed so you see Peggy, there is absolutely no need for you to worry about me, and you can assure Mother I shall not come home a physical and mental wreck. My back is still very straight and there is still a twinkle in the old optics. Please tell Cyril that John Willing is here, and many others taken in France. I shall write to him soon. Oh darling, how I long to be back again with you and collect those hugs and kisses of which you write. Needless to say, I have some for you.

Please remember me to everyone.
Love,
Alan

C/O: The White Hart, Salisbury Wilts.
26.10.41.

My own beloved Alan, how we wish both you and Martin were here. Sonia and I are awaiting the arrival of our gin before going in to lunch. We went to watch Michael play a rugger match yesterday, before we took him out to lunch. After tea, at which young Bob Minter joined us, Sonia and I came on here in time for a late dinner. This morning we were lazy and stayed in bed till nearly 10 a.m. so we only just had time for breakfast before going to the Cathedral for Matins. This afternoon we are going to a Poushinoff recital — he's playing Chopin; then I return home after tea. Sonia and I have prattled away the whole time about you and Martin — Sonia's adding a P.S. to this. I'll finish it off on the train going home as its time we went to lunch.

P.S. It's been such fun meeting Peggy this weekend but we've both been wishing so much you and Martin were here and we talk about the marvellous celebrations we'll have when you both come home. Peggy is looking very well (not out of a box!). She has a check costume on with a brown jumper and seems very cheerful especially as she is now getting letters from you.

With love from Sonia.

Hatton Cottage, Lubbock Road, Chislehurst, Kent.
30.10.41.

I am high up in the clouds today, for yesterday teatime, a card dated 24th September and a letter dated October 1st arrived from you. Mother was here when they arrived, as she had come over for the day from her cousin's. She is very well and thrilled when I read out your newsy bits. But oh, how I wished mails — I've been writing as often as I was allowed to via the Red Cross, Geneva till your camp address arrived on my birthday. Then I have written often since. Sent a "Next of Kin Parcel" and an "Officer's Uniform Parcel". Another "Next of Kin Parcel" is going off tomorrow — also you will receive two invalid parcels a month for two months then one every three months, i.e., if you put on the weight you lost, so please let me know when you are receiving them from your senior R.A.M.C. Officer. Red Cross are sending them for me at 10/- a head and Cyril insists on paying for £3.00 worth. Mother has given me a £1.00 towards your parcel this quarter, part of a Xmas gift. It's very kind of them.

5.11.41.

Dear heart, a most amusing post this morning, an aerograph from old man Harrison saying how glad he was to have heard you were safe — decent of the old man. He also wishes you were with him to employ your fly swatter! Corbett's a Captain with him and has won an M.C.! A letter came from Harrison's wife to me, Jo MacLarron who has written to you and hopes you know who she is. She is really amazing the way she writes to us so often. Cobb and Eric Horton have had typhoid, Morley, John and Stuart, malaria but all are well now; a letter from Cyril enclosing a cheque for your invalid parcel — very kind of him. Pat's just bought a new frock and told Pop it was 39/6d[22] — the bill came to £3.9.6d — Pat thought it was the same thing! Everett has been unable to find your birth certificate in your sealed envelope of your past darling — were you really born? However, we've applied for a copy to claim our 6/- a day marriage allowance. Tomorrow I am going ███████████████ for my medical and have to take an overcoat or dressing gown. I resent having to undress in a cold room and I resent having to have a medical at all by a strange doctor. Never mind, I will find some amusement out of it just as I did at the Labour Exchange on registering. Your very own,

Peggy.

7.11.41.

I went for my medical, first however after Pop had dropped me I went to fortify myself with a gin and French in The Star and who do you think I walked into? Mrs Everett and a young Captain friend of theirs. This called for a 2nd gin and on an empty stomach I turned up for my medical in high spirits and so I found amusement in that quarter. When I arrived at 1.05 p.m. there was a queue a mile long. None of that for me. I marched right up to the curtained off rooms till I found someone and said I had an appointment at 1 p.m. and had come a long way and hoped I didn't have to wait. My dear after that it was Mrs Horton this and that. It took nearly an hour signing forms etc. Then I was told to undress except for coat and shoes!

---

[22] Before decimalisation of the currency 39/6d would have been £1.19.6d considerably less than £3.9.6d.

Taken before a funny old boy who decided to be rude and called me "recruit Horton". I replied "Mrs Horton". He told me to sign my name. I gaily put my full Christian name as always and he crossly said no need for all that, just initials. So, I piped up I never put my initials etc. Well anyway he tested my eyes and teeth. The latter he said were perfect ███████████████████. Then I went to a nurse who asked me to perform a physical impossibility! Don't laugh too much; actually, I thought it very funny, crude as it may sound. So, on that I have to return next Thursday.

Prisoner No. 3275. Oflag VI B.
7th November 1941.

My very own darling Wife, How I wish we could be together on 21st. I thank God daily for that great day last year and for your great love. We shall at least be very close in spirit. All you have done, both for me and the men, makes me very proud of my wife. I am glad about the Saddlers. I have not seen him since Crete so please ask his wife to send him my best wishes. I can quite understand events leading up to your going to an O.C.T.U. and though neither of us will be really happy until we are together, I hope at any rate you will find it tolerable. I feel I could help you with the raw girls! Please thank Pop, Lady Minter, Mrs Muir, Cyril, Jennie and Mother for letters and everyone for their gifts with a special word to Diana. I will write Pop and Diana soon. The parcels sound grand and the wants are now ONLY occasionally toothbrushes, tooth powder and shaving soap. Chocolate and food in parcels or via American Red Cross always welcome but not essential. Most prisoners have made as many American contacts for the despatch of the latter as possible. Here's hoping that lovely song about walking beside you will soon have real meaning for us and you will be making our jam and arranging our flowers and looking after our home. Oh, my sweet, how much I love you and long for you. The day cannot be far distant now. Your very own Alan.

89th A.A. Regt. R.A. M.E.F.
9.11.41.

My Dear Peggy,

It was good to hear from you again with news of dear old Dad and others. I bet the old boy is fed to the teeth and I am so glad he is able to pursue his studies. You, little woman, have done well with the savings. How on earth do you manage it? Kay and I are very broke and likely to be, as far as I can see. I have written to him, but it is quite a job out here — the restrictions are terrific, however I hope mine gets through. I hope he will be able to work his third pip — this is certainly no place for promotion for us subalterns anyway. Old Dad certainly deserves it. Now fancy you and my little Kay meeting. I am so glad and imagine you both had lots and lots to talk about. I know Kay will tell me all about it in her letters so that is something else to look forward to. That's life out here, as I am sure it is at home for you.

Today is a bad day for the 89th. The Colonel has been posted to command a Brigade. We are all so pleased he has at last got promotion — Brigadier — but will miss him. I will more than anyone, I think, he has been so good to me. The new Colonel is quite young and to date know little about him. It will never be the same though Peggy.

205 have moved on and John Talbot has gone with them, so all the batteries have left the Regiment. (The others you know about) so I think you will agree, "woe is us" the old boys.

Are you about to become a F.A.N.Y.? Were you able to get a direct commission? You spoke about it in your last letter.

Life is much the same out here but much cooler, quite a good thing. News is scarce in fact mostly routine, and my only pleasure now is riding my horse. He's quite a dear now and I spoil him with sugar (don't tell a soul) and biscuits. We have lots of officers together and now practice polo. I had three days leave in Cairo recently with Stuart but could only enjoy that place with Kay. We were both there on forced leave — doctor's orders and all that and had a quiet time mostly sleeping and seeing a few good flics. I think "we four" could have fun and games there; really it is a most wonderful place. I am afraid your savings would diminish rapidly — gosh, it's expensive! Phew! That's why we only had three days!!

Always save a corner to give old Dad my best when you write, won't you. I bet the food is foul. Poor old Hukins — "what, ain't you got no cake!" I have not heard from Pam, and I hope she is bearing up. Is she still at Bobbing? Looking forward to hearing from you again.

My best wishes to all.

Yours,

Charles.

Prisoner No. 3275. Oflag VI B.
9th November 1941.

The number of letters I have had make me the envy of the room. I get one from you nearly every other day and if they knew the contents, they would envy me still more for your letters are always so cheerful and paint just that picture of home we all love to visualise. Oh beloved, how I long to see your smile again, to hold you in my arms, to feel once more, your kisses on my lips. The man who said we shall be strangers when we meet can know nothing of a love such as ours. You will not see much change in "the old man", a little aged perhaps but the twinkle is still there and his love unchanged. So far, he has had no letters from Joans, Violets, Veronicas, Daphnes or Ingas, but lives in hope! He is very glad about the birthday present to his wife for not being able to send one was a great disappointment. But joking apart, finance has worried me, but you seem a marvellous manageress and have put me at ease. I know though how difficult things must be and I am powerless to help. Please do not go to any more expense for me as I am really well looked after. We have very good orchestras here and a fine library, so time passes quickly and pleasantly.

Hatton Cottage, Lubbock Rd, Chislehurst, Kent.
17.11.41.

Tomorrow Pop has invited Pat and I to lunch with him and his girl-friend's parents! The first time he's offered to take his children out for many months — he muttered something about two celebrations, one his, the other our wedding anniversary. I dread it if he gets sentimental. Just back from my lunch in town and found my marching orders for Thursday 20th. Dear me you know, very mixed feelings — glad to begin a job because I must work these days and will be able to save our pennies darling. Then my sweet it's a bit hard to begin work on our first wedding anniversary — it should bring me luck.

Gore Court, Otham, Nr. Maidstone, Kent.
20.11.41.

Well, here I am, all I can say at the moment my precious is that I am in a beautiful old country house nearly ¼ mile off the road. I share a room with about a dozen others, who really aren't on my job, but cooks, etc. and have broad accents ranging from Cockney to Scotch but I gather I won't be with them so very long — it's quite an experience. The actual F.A.N.Y.s like me, seem a decent sort of girl. Oh darling, a lot of bottles, including gin have appeared on the scene! It's a bit thick beginning a job on our wedding anniversary. If I get a chance after supper, I want to run outside for a walk round on my own. It's damp you know just like it was last year when we went out for our first walk as man and wife; how sweet a memory darling.

21.11.41.

My thoughts are so full of lovely and yet rather, I should say, very sad thoughts — a telegram came this evening from you and Mother saying, "Heartiest congratulations and God grant happiness next year". He will I know. Oh, what sweet heaven darling. Before letting my thoughts run away with my pen, I am going to tell you about what I have been doing today: woken up by a gong at 7.30, parade 8.25 at which I was only an onlooker, breakfast 8.30, then made beds and did our rooms, then I cleaned a truck's engine, then fitted out with clothes. It's really amazing just how much one is issued and quite good quality things. This afternoon I took my shirt, tunic and great coat into Maidstone to a tailors, to have them altered

— a few shillings well spent. I hope so, I'll be completely khaki clad by Wednesday, then I had tea in the Star and came back here about 5.30. One of the officers is an old friend of mine. I nearly collapsed when I saw her. Last night was parade dinner and tonight a buffet supper, with Walker this friend of mine and two corporals, so I am well in so to speak.

Prisoner No. 3275. Oflag VI B.
21st November 1941.

My beloved darling, I have saved this, my third letter, for today. In spite of time and space you are as near to me now as you were a year ago. How I have lived to bless that day, darling, and thank God we decided as we did. Next year, with luck, we shall celebrate the day as it should be celebrated. Now I can only write "I love you" knowing that only you can read into it all that I mean. I had ten letters the other day from you, Mother, Cyril, Diana, Mrs Winter-Lotimer and Charles. Will you thank Diana and others please? Darling, thank you for sending the jacket and bagatelle. I look forward to getting my first parcel and when they have all arrived, I shall have all I need. Please don't send anything else unless I ask for it. Food invalid comforts parcels are about all. I am glad you enjoyed your stay at Rivers Hall and hope the new job will not be too much of an anti-climax. I must send a letter next week to your aunt. Please do not worry about that last cablegram. It is quite unnecessary. Mother sent some snaps of you all with Mary Rose. She looks very sweet, I just long to see her again. How lucky they are! Geoffrey Towse and I often talk over a cup of cocoa in the mornings. He is a charming fellow and very pleased about your friendship with Carol. Well, my sweet one, I just long for that holiday you are planning and am all in favour of the arrangements, particularly changing khaki for tweeds.

All my love,
Alan.

Gore Court, Otham, Nr. Maidstone, Kent.
24.11.41.

Here's a copy of a letter Michael sent to me this morning. I am keeping it because I think it's awfully nice. *(Michael was Peggy's brother and twin of her sister, Pat).*

"It may seem somewhat unusual receiving a letter from me, boasting its own envelope and stamp complete, but I feel that this occasion merits something with just that little extra distinction. This coming Friday will be your first wedding anniversary. It should have marked the end of your first married year with Alan. A year in which you would have lived together in your own home, had not the war taken him away. Paradoxically enough, this war, though it has been cruel on you, in the latter respect, it has smiled upon you in two marked occasions. Firstly, it was the means of bringing you and Alan together in the first place, and secondly it has preserved him miraculously through a veritable hell and thus allowed him to still be with you in his thoughts, though he is far away, but it will not be long, it cannot be long, before he will be with you again, safe and ready for a peaceful and happy life. I myself am looking forward very much to that day so I can appreciate how much you will be wanting him back. You may consider it strange your younger brother writing to you in this vein, but nevertheless, I am your only brother and thus have your welfare very much at heart."

Darling, don't you think that is a very good letter? I do. Again, I've had a very busy day in the open air; cleaned under and over and in a truck and opened the wrong axle oil nut and ½ pint thick slimy oil flowed out missing my face by inches as I was lying on my back under the truck. This afternoon I drove some 30 miles on my own in a 3-cwt truck in the rain and now have a very healthy complexion and appetite. All this outdoor life suits me grandly.

28.11.41.

Well, well, here's me all dressed up in khaki from lunchtime today and I had my first drill — Oh! Saluting and drilling, however I am asking for an outpost job where there's none of that and one's, one's own master. I like my independence. I wear my greatcoat like an officer and really, I look quite decent. My tunic's a lousy fit. Another girl and I are looking for horses as we think it would be so heavenly to ride sometimes rather than go to the pictures. Her brother is with you, a Captain Howard.

3.12.41.

Saluting still muddles me — who I do and when I don't salute? Then it's too easy just to salute like an officer and not smartly like a troop. Last night I was 2 minutes late in bed and the orderly officer was furious — silly twerp! I'd been on an errand of mercy helping a very nice new girl settle down in her room, but that's the only thing I kick at really hard — indoors by 10 p.m. and lights out by 10.30 p.m.!

Prisoner No. 3275. Oflag VI B.
4th December 1941.

My very own darling, I hope this will reach you in time to wish you a really happy Christmas and a reunion in 1942. I want you to buy yourself a present from me and give yourself a big hug and a kiss when you unpack it on Christmas Day. Next year I will be there to deliver all three myself. I had five letters from you yesterday, one from Cyril and one from one of the Sandwich staff. I hope soon to get my parcel. Geoffrey had his so it should not be long. I am still very fit and play hockey frequently. Last night I saw "Behind the Scenes" a local production and very good. I have got hold of a good German Grammar and a standard work on Banking, so I am not wasting my time. Since my last letter I have heard from Sonia — please thank her and I have been requested to ask you to write very clearly and not more than three letters a week to save the censors. I am yours now as always,

Your Alan.

Gore Court, Otham, Nr. Maidstone, Kent.
6.12.41.

I was called out of bed at 7.30 am today to take an ambulance to fetch a maternity case (Urgent) to a hospital. My dear I reached the hospital with the patient at 9.45, the baby was born at 10.30 am. I just flew that ambulance there — what life one sees in the army.

Prisoner No. 3275. Oflag VI B.
6th December 1941.

My own beloved darling, although it is some time since I wrote last, I hope now to continue a weekly letter to you again. There is so much to say and so little space I don't know where to begin. Firstly, and most importantly, I have just had eighteen letters from you and others. To answer them is impossible. All I can say is I am very, very proud of you and the more I read your letters and those from our friends, the more I thank God for your love, your spirit and your example. I am sure Peggy that the Gunners never had a better officer than Mr 'orton's nurse. I had letters too, from Pop, Cyril, Jennie, Mother, Lady Minter. Please thank them all. Thank you too, for all you have done.

9th December 1941.

Excuse card but I have used one letter to answer Cyril and Jennie's. I get your letters frequently and read them over and over again. You write just the things I want to know about. Yesterday I had the one of October 10th mentioning my Invalid's Comfort Parcel. It sounds grand. You sound in fine form — good work Peggy. I too am very fit — chin up and back straight.

All my love,
Alan.

Gore Court, Otham, Nr. Maidstone, Kent.
15.12.41.

You know darling, when I drive the big 15 cwt truck, I get a proud feeling of elation when I have to perform some awkward manoeuvres in yards where many men drivers are congregated with their trucks. I feel as though I am every bit as capable as them at backing into corners, and when my head pops out, I do see occasionally a few amazed faces to see a female head protruding.

16, Craven Terrace, Halifax, Yorks.
Dec 16th/41.

Dear Madam,
I must ask you to excuse me in writing to you totally unknown as I am.

Recently on a visit to Elland your name was mentioned as having been in communication with Mrs Bradley and Mrs Garside who each had a son as Gunner in 234/89 A.A. Regiment, R.A. of which your husband was an officer and now unfortunately a prisoner in Germany. I had a son too, Battery Gunner John Hoyle (44158) who after Crete was reported missing and not until November, did I hear anything, when alas I received from the War Records Department the news that he was killed at Carnea, Crete on 20th May and that the Department had received information from an officer of the unit now a prisoner of war in Germany. My object in penning this note is that I would like to know a little more than the bare fact of my dear boy's death. Such as, was it by dive bombing or otherwise? Did he suffer long, were his discs recovered, was he interred alone or in a joint burial? To thinking Mr Horton being the officer who informed of the end, I would ask if when next writing to him you would kindly name my queries. Should he not be the officer may be such an one might be in his camp. If so please ask for any information available.

My boy was a tall, well built, dark complexion. I enclose a newspaper photo (not a very good one) and paragraph. Don't return it please, I have others and please refrain from acknowledging the receipt of this, but if any information as named is forthcoming in due course, I shall appreciate hearing from you.

Yours sincerely,

Alfred Hoyle.

Gore Court, Otham, Nr. Maidstone, Kent.
20.12.41.

Firstly, excuse my blodges, smears and grammar but it is 3.30 am and I am on night duty and here we do not sleep before night work, only 3 hrs afterwards. Actually, I do not mind night work. It gives me time to write my letters, wash, iron and mend my rags and tatters. We don't have to wear uniform, so I wear a pair of Pam's old navy-blue trousers, a white blouse and a grey sweater of Michael's. I am certainly learning "Life" as we have a very mixed bag here now. We've a great deal to thank God for. How you came out of that hell alive is still a great miracle to me for which I am forever thanking him and for your great love for me, for without it I'd just give up the ghost. Dear me, I'm slowly dropping asleep, and I still have the officers' brasses to clean (The night guard's job).

9, St. Michael's Rd, Maidstone, Kent.
26.12.41.

As you see its Boxing Day and though I scribbled a note to you from Hatton Cottage on 24th, yesterday you were so very near me and I had so much to do to help the Xmas spirit here, and as most girls were rushing to go out with their boy-friends, another girl (married) and I sat at night bemoaning our sadly over eaten stomachs and discussed our beloveds. She's very nice and knows a number of our friends north of London. Xmas Eve I went home at the crack of dawn to find letters from you and one from you to Poppa. He and the family were very amused to see you addressed it "Pop" as "My Dear Pop". It put him in a very good mood as usually we only talk about him as "Pop" between ourselves and use, "Daddy" when we speak to his face. Diana, in scarlet corduroy dungarees took me with her to decorate the church with Gwen Fehr. After lunch we decorated with holy, ivy, mistletoe, etc. and I took the pudding etc. out of the store cupboard and instructed Pat how to cook everything. Daddy took me at 6 o'clock to the bus stop and I was back here for supper. Yesterday though I was on duty there was no work beyond just warming up my ambulance, so we did all the necessary housework and helped to cook the dinner. We had a turkey, pudding and cake all given us, so we did very well. We all over-ate, and I had to go off for a walk by the river to get an appetite for even a small piece of cake.

29.12.41.

My very own beloved darling husband, Before I give you my news a Mrs Hoyle[23] wrote the other day wanting particulars of — 1) did John Hoyle die from dive bombing or otherwise? 2) Was he interred alone? 3) Did he suffer, if so, how long? I hate retrieving memories my sweet, but she has only just heard of her son's death as the War Office heard from one of you people and if it was you, I am to thank you. If it was a cruel death like Peter's and Coco's I'll not mention it. We've not told Pam anything beyond "instantaneous". Its extraordinary how quickly she's over it and beyond about 3 letters to Phyllis she's not written to any of her contemporaries. Now for some news my sweetheart, tonight, I am on my own doing night duty at the hospital. I have a wee bed-sitting-room to myself, and we can sleep half-dressed, so I am about to remove my tunic and shirt and roll up in the blankets. I'd like to remove more but we can't. I'll remove my face and if I go out, I'll go with a shiny nose, who cares, it's dark, though tonight it's barely necessary to use light there is such a wonderful moon. My pet aversion, an orderly, has brought me a cup of tea at 9 o'clock. But a friend who is a V.A.D. here and I are visiting the kitchen at 10 o'clock. One thing about this job darling is that the time just flies by and now I am away from Gore Court I'm not doing such heavy driving though an occasional outing in a big ambulance is called upon. In time another girl and I are aiming for a staff car job.

---

[23] The original letter was from Mr Hoyle although Peggy refers to his wife here for some reason.

1942 — Another Bloody Year

Datchet, St George's Lane, Sandwich, Kent.
1.1.42.

My very own beloved darling, what a lot has happened in the past year to us; what places you've travelled. Life's taught me a great deal just watching other people and the more I thank God for the tough principles we've had handed on to us from our parents. To see others, fall by the wayside, has a very stiffening effect on me — stiffening, not harrowing.

I'm sitting up in bed here, Mother's taken this place for two weeks and Jennie and Mary Rose are here too. I arrived by bus at lunch time. Cyril's been gazetted today, a full Major now. I'm meeting Mrs Lock in Canterbury soon — she's full of hope about Charles, like we all are. Here's a very great secret, Charles would have told you I know — he has a very serious girl-friend in the north who he hopes will wait for him.

89th Heavy A.A. Regiment, R.A. M.E.F.
2.1.42.

My Dear Peggy,
Ever so many thanks for your P.C.s They are so cheery and welcome. I have written to Daddy and given him little bits of news, but the restrictions are colossal. I spent a very pleasant evening with Gus and Alex before Xmas, and we talked of the good old days. He is quite liking his new job and lives in a flat with Barclays Bank

boys — complete luxury. Cecil and Corbett are still going strong in Haifa and now David Wilson has joined them. Malcolm has gone to Cairo. Stuart and Dice are the only 89th left here as 205 departed some weeks ago. They may yet return and that means the return of John, I hope.

Yours sincerely,
Charles.

9, St. Michael's Rd, Maidstone, Kent.
4.1.42.

My very own beloved darling Alan, Enclosed darling is something an old lady I don't even know has written and asked me to do for her. Her son, Derek Addenbroke, a Squadron Leader, was last heard of last April — he has a wife and a wee babe of 14 months, and she believes he has lost his memory — personally darling, I hate to disappoint her, but it doesn't look like the same face. The Telegraph says all his crew were lost too. So, I wonder in the course of your visits you'll meet him, but it will be very hard if he has lost his memory. He has a scar which causes his hair to part crookedly.

(Attached to the top of this letter is one tiny photo from the Telegraph *and another small picture sent to Peggy by the officer's mother).*

89th Heavy A.A. Regiment, R.A. M.E.F.5.1.42.

So nice to receive your long newsy letter today dated Nov 9th. I wrote to you a day or so ago so no doubt this will arrive at the same time. It is again good to hear of your visits to Kay and thank you for your watchful eye and do keep in touch — I am sure Kay is delighted to hear from you and the occasional meetings must help this awful life of separation. I have had news from time to time of the others. It is good to hear they are fit and well. Chernakoff is with me here and runs the canteen in great style. What news to hear that some of our men are still in Crete — Saddler of all people. I did manage to get my batman back with me, only to lose him. I now have a Sudanese servant Ibrahim, black as soot, but a good and attentive servant and speaks a pretty attractive line in Sudanese/English. Cator is a P.O.W. I understand and old Minter, still the cheerful rogue, has wrangled his name into a commission — I hope he gets it. Life here is much the same. The new Colonel is quite impossible!

Colonel Stebbings was such a dear and a joy to soldier with. I miss him, especially in my new job. He would have given me every assistance whereas now I am likely to be tripped up at every move I make — even Stuart and Bill have joined the opposition. Stuart, as I am sure you know Peggy, is a frightful snake in the grass, and a Bill without John a less snaky troublemaker. A little war would do them a lot of good. However, I am doing my best to cope and intend to do my job as well as I can until I return to real life with my sweet little wife. Forgive me for pouring out my woes won't you. Perhaps I have said too much.

Yours sincerely,
Charles.

9, St. Michael's Rd, Maidstone, Kent.
6.1.42.

The first part of this was written whilst enjoying a peaceful afternoon now I'm out 20 miles from home whilst repairs are being done to the engine and I am by the Swan fire, eating and drinking and just read a long letter from Carol Towse giving me Geoffrey's news of an aeroplane ride you had many months ago — were you sick darling? I'd love to fly but not under those circumstances.

12.1.42.

Here is some really wonderful news for you; Charles Lock is safe as a P.O.W. and I gather that won't be for long now, so all is well thank heavens. One day fairly soon I am meeting Mrs L for lunch. I've had a bath and am in bed by 9.30 still trying to rid myself of my lousy cold. It's been a touch of flu I believe and is now paying my sinuses a call blast it! I feel and look like a bloated herring and snort like an old sow! My darling I became a heaver up of coal today. 4 tons arrived and the lousy truck driver wouldn't shovel it so I set to and helped shovel some and ended up black, until a visit to the hairdressers on Wednesday my hair will be nearly black.

13.1.42.

Pam, my sister, has announced her engagement to a Ronald Edwiger, an extremely nice First Lieutenant Gunner (she's following her sister). I introduced them to each other Xmas '40 and Pam's been a beast to him for a year yet he, brave lad, has stuck to his guns and won. I hope Pam's serious for his sake. He is so nice, aged 27 years I believe.

Prisoner No. 3275, Oflag VI B.
15th January 1942.

My very own beloved darling. Many thanks for letters which still roll in. The last was 15th November and how it made me long to be back with you in our old areas again. No, darling, I do not worry about you — I trust your judgement perfectly and just wait as patiently as I can for the great day when I can take you in my arms again and we start life anew. Now for some news. It is for your ears only in case it should not come off. I have been recommended for, and it seems reasonably certain that I shall get, the M.C. I shall not know for a long time. I wish it were some extra pip, but it will do as a consolation prize. News of this and a pair of gym shoes were my Christmas presents. I hope you enjoyed Christmas my sweet. I attended Holy Communion and Evensong in our dining room, attractively decorated with two Christmas trees, evergreens and candles. We had a grand pantomime, "Citronella", carol parties around the camp and quite a good meal and party in our room. I made the Christmas Pudding and a Cottage Pie. The old man can now cook and darn — he scarcely needs a wife! No parcels have yet come to hand, but I hope to get one soon. Give my regards to Pop and Co, Mother and Co, Cyril and Co and Bobbing. Au revoir Pegasus my love and "chins up",

your own,

Alan.

9, St. Michael's Road, Maidstone, Kent.
25.1.42.

I have just returned to hear the loathsome news I've lived in fear of, my happy days at this place are over — tomorrow I go back to Gore Court and swarms of silly, giggly females, one never gets a moment of peace anywhere. However, I rang up Pop and told him of the plans and if it's to get me driving an open truck this weather, I am going sick and will have leave. I hope not to forfeit my day off on Thursday with Mother and Mrs Lock but to return to company where we have parades, etc. and lousy female N.C.O.s.

British Red Cross Society, Prisoner of War Department, 14, Carlton Terrace, London, SW1.
28th January 1942.

Dear Mrs. Horton,

WS/Lt. A. E. Horton. P.O.W. no 3275

Thank you for your letter and I hope it will not be long before your husband tells you that he is getting the parcels that we sent him in the autumn.

As you know, we are only allowed to send invalid comforts parcels for health reasons and the vitamin content of the standard Red Cross food parcels is carefully worked out to supplement adequately the German rations.

However, as your husband has been through so much since he was captured and you feel so worried, I think it would be quite in order for us to send him a special parcel of tonics every month for three months and we will therefore now arrange to do this.

Yours sincerely,

Muriel Bromley Davenport

Hon. Secretary Invalid Comforts Section.

Prisoner No. 3275. Oflag VI B.

28th January 1942.

Firstly, Mrs Fehr, Pam, Lesma Brown and Mr Benstead, the old newsagent at Sandwich, have written me. Can you please acknowledge to them and explain why I cannot? I have also had a parcel with a game of monopoly and two novels in it which I think came from Lloyds Bank Magazine. Several fellows in the room have had personal parcels so mine should come soon. It has been very cold here (45°F of frost) and my studies have come to an end temporarily until it gets warmer. Then too, I have been confined to the room for some days with a cold on the chest, but it is nearly OK now and I hope to start again soon.

5th February 1942.

Many thanks for the letters. There is also a games parcel in the camp for me, but I have not been able to draw on it yet. This is the first one to appear so I hope the others will arrive shortly. Can you please acknowledge for me letters from Michael, Angela and Harry Moxham and explain why I cannot reply to them? I have also had a letter from the General Manager of the Bank to which I have replied. The letter you had from Michael was certainly very charming, he is a grand fellow. I am glad the new job is not too bad, and certainly do not mind you going to dances. I want you to be as happy as possible so that time will be short to our great day. So, my past has caught up with me! Well, well! I hope you don't know it all! But the future, Sweetheart is for you, and you and I alone. Mac, Geoffrey and the Major wish to be remembered to you. The latter has left us now for another camp.

Hatton Cottage, Lubbock Rd, Chislehurst, Kent.
6.2.42.

The doctor came this a.m. and has armed me with a written statement forbidding the army to give me heavy work or drive heavy vehicles. The aches I've had have been muscular rheumatism. I am glad he has given me this statement for a little heavy work does me no harm, but they thought because I was big I'm tough, so I am in normal life but I'm damned if I'm ruining my health to please a lot of unreasonable females. So darling I am very fit and there is no need for you to ever worry over the missus. I then went to the dentist and how glad I went to my own. He wants me to get a few days leave to have two nasty stoppings done under a local and one out by gas. I'm furious at my teeth for behaving so badly all at once.

8.2.42.

I have 7 days leave from Tuesday. I applied for sick leave to have my teeth done but it has come out of privilege leave, blast it! Anyway, it will help rid me of this muscular rheumatism (not lumbago). We had a lovely time this afternoon with a truck. We went wooding in the sun and snow under a heavenly blue sky. The only snag was the truck got snowed in and we had to dig it out. I have terrific pink cheeks after the cold, fresh air.

Prisoner No. 3275. Oflag VI B.
19th February 1942.

First, brief answers to your letters. Gunner Hoyle's people have been fully informed by Hugh Clarke, Addenbroke is not here, photograph is of Captain Deighton. Thank God Charles is safe. We have been pals for such years that his loss would have been a very real one. I hope you manage to meet Mother and Mrs Lock and do not find Gore Court too bad.

Please congratulate Pam for me and wish her all the best.

Hatton Cottage, Lubbock Rd, Chislehurst, Kent.
20.2.42.

Just arrived home and found a letter from you January 15th. And oh, my loved one, all my loving thoughts and congratulations on the M.C. It's a very deep secret between you and I till I hear from you; but darling, I am prouder than ever of you. Tell me how it was won — was it for one action or the whole campaign. I am dying to hear all the details.

PS: Pop has heard from a friend at the War Office — your M.C. is official and has been for some time.

Oh, you brave darling.

Xxxx

22.2.42.

There is such a whirl of excitement in the family now — two things are the cause. First darling, your M.C. then Pam's wedding to Ron Edwicker on March 16th. At dinner on Friday Daddy said, "You know Alan has won the M.C?" Having that morning received your letter of January 15th with "Hush, Hush" written all over it I was amazed for him mention it. It appears he had lunch a little while ago with a friend from the War Office who told him, so it's official but I've not yet seen it in the paper or a War Office letter.

Sadly, despite the recommendation, and comments from Pop's friend at the War Office, Alan was never awarded the M.C. and he never once spoke about it to us. As a member of the Territorial Army, he did, however, receive the Territorial Decoration but did not explain why it was awarded.

Prisoner No. 3275. Oflag VI B.
4th March 1942.

Thanks for all the letters. I had one today written at Bobbing and needless to say all the references made me long for the old times again. Remember me to them and tell Treadgold I am sorry that her prayer book went west with all my kit in Crete. Remember me also to Foley. I always thought he regarded me as Bloody Fool! The news of Felton and Co makes me envious. How I wish I had a chance to collect some pips and medals. I cannot help feeling very bitter at times. The Doc sent for me the other day to answer an enquiry from the Red Cross about my health. You must NOT worry darling, I really am fit and keep the old brain in trim with my carving and studies. Time passes very quickly. I am making a Gunner badge from an old breadboard with a pen knife and a pin. I am very proud of it so far.

This carved, wooden badge returned home with Alan at the end of the war and was something he always kept in a prominent place in his study.

11th March 1942.

Firstly, letters received — Pop, Mrs White (Charles' sister), Holness, and a Christmas card from the Bank Magazine! And one from your friend Margaret Probert in which she praises you highly but refuses to mention any of your past! I had several from you and Mother yesterday, the most recent being February 14th. So, Wilson is a skipper — what a damn shame I didn't run faster!

19th March 1942.

My darling, great excitement yesterday for my first parcel arrived. It was actually the second you sent so the first has gone astray. Its contents are just what I wanted — the jerkin in particular. I am now very well equipped and was able to pass on some of my old stuff to others in the room less fortunate. We raffled them and had great fun. Razor blades are very scarce, so these prevented a beard in the nick of time.

All love,
Alan.

Hatton Cottage, Lubbock Rd, Chislehurst, Kent.
23.3.42.

Another letter February 19th, it's come through very quickly this time. Pam's wedding went off with a good swing, a sufficient reward for all the hard work Pat, Lesma and I had put in — 70 people on rations is no light job and we cooked till 10 at night. I was only cleaned and dressed before taking my seat in the front pew as matron of honour! God darling, I needed you at my side particularly at the reception. I gave them 3 guineas from us.[24] They are honeymooning at Grosvenor House and then Bournemouth, 2 weeks together.

26.3.42.

These last two days sweet, have been very full ones. Today I've had my first day of office work, my desk happily by a French window on the sunny, sheltered side. I've been doing pay — Whew, who'd have thought your Missus would make a pay clerk? It's been a terrific brain exercise, but that's what I want. Military Transport was a little tough on one and not enough brain work and consequently I had too much time to think. I had the awaited

---

[24] One guinea was one pound and one shilling, three guineas was three pounds and three shillings.

interview with Company Commander yesterday. She was very pleasant and has accepted my application.

28.3.42.

Just hearing the King make a good speech about tomorrow's day of prayer. I want to try and go to Evensong at 6.30; the local parish church has a very fine organist and choir.

29.3.42.

It's been such a heavenly spring day so after lunch another girl and I took bicycles and went miles through the country lanes past lovely old houses and through farms and orchards and ended up for tea in the local town and who do you think walked in? — Pam Stebbings, looking happier and prettier than ever plus Phyllis Hill and Wanda. After a good gas we went to church, at least the other F.A.N.Y. and I, to a lovely service that I came out feeling I learnt something great. It was Palm Sunday as well as a National Day of Prayer.

Prisoner No. 3275. Oflag X C.
3rd April 1942.

Good Friday. A comforts parcel is listed for me, so they are rolling up at last. Can I have some pipe cleaners please? In answer to the commission question, I can only say — do what makes you happiest. You will not avoid taking orders, for freedom is lost in service, though they may come from people more fitting to give them. With responsibility to kick, life becomes harder, but life has more refinements. The decoration was for services generally, not for any outstanding gallantry. I'm sorry it's so prosaic.

Hatton Cottage, Lubbock Rd, Chislehurst, Kent.
20.4.42.

A P.C. from you yesterday only a week after my last two letters, so imagine my excitement and surprise. I'm so very happy to know you've received one of my parcels; actually, it was the third; 2nd next of kin as the first went in September and also an officer's uniform, which had all khaki things. Now I know what you've got and what you haven't by my lists so in June I'll mail a shirt and undies and razor blades — I can still wrangle them from a canteen.

Prisoner No. 3275. Oflag VI B.
4th May 1942.

Your photograph has reached me at last. It was the highlight of a good week for two more tobacco and two more comforts parcels came for me as well as three book parcels and a large batch of mail. I have glazed the photo with cellophane and made a frame for it and it hangs at the head of my bunk. You look more lovely than ever. I take it down and gaze at it before I fall asleep, and immediately I wake. It has done much to shorten the distance between us but makes me long more and more (if that's possible) to have you at my side again. I am still very fit and play hockey fairly frequently. The garden is showing promise of some return for our labours but lately the wind has been cold from the east making life rather unpleasant.

I still struggle with German though with little success, do some French and read political economy. Strangely enough I have lost all interest in novels reading them only on Roll Call Parades whilst waiting dismissal. I cannot attempt to answer all your letters but read them again and again and love to know all that you are doing and thinking.

Hatton Cottage, Lubbock Rd, Chislehurst, Kent.
16.5.42.

I've got a stripe! For 3 weeks I've been acting unpaid, unwanted, etc. Lousy idea but then I hope to get 19/- odd hard money a week. Soon be paying income tax at this rate! I'm against a stripe for myself very much but you need one to protect yourself and the more I get, the better will be my job.

Prisoner No. 3275. Oflag VI B.
19th May 1942

Have played two games of hockey today. The weather is good, and I am very brown. Accounting textbook has arrived. I have lots to do so don't worry about sending any more handicrafts. I do hope you are better now and enjoyed the sick leave. Our garden is doing well, and we hope soon to have lettuces and radishes from it! Now for a report, first though I should congratulate you on an excellent choice! He looks marvellously fit, shows not the slightest sign of dysentery which apparently laid him low in the early days of capture. He is very cheerful, optimistic and receiving many parcels.

I don't exaggerate, I promise you. Sometime next year, perhaps sooner but I doubt it.

British Red Cross Society, Prisoner of War Department, 14, Carlton Terrace, London, SW1.
May 19th, 1942.

Dear Mrs. Horton,

You will remember in January last I told you that I would write to the Senior R.A.M.C. Officer of Offlag VI B and ask if he would be so kind as to let us have an up-to-date report about your husband's present state of health. I am now very glad to tell you that I have received his reply, an extract of which runs as follows:

Reference your MBD/HMS dated 4th February 1942. I have seen Lt. Alan E. Horton No 3275. Please tell his wife that he is very fit indeed and has completely recovered from the bad effects of his early days of captivity when he suffered from the same complaints as many other Officers from Crete. Since coming to this camp he has put on weight and has not required any special treatment or food for a long time. He will receive Invalid Comforts parcels when they arrive but there is no necessity for continuing these special parcels.

In view of what Colonel Levack says, I think you will agree that there is no need to send any further parcels for the present. With all good wishes and I am so very pleased to be able to send you such a very reassuring report.

Yours sincerely,

Muriel Bromley Davenport.

Hon Sec Invalids Comforts Section.

Hatton Cottage, Lubbock Rd, Chislehurst, Kent.
28.5. 42.

Just drilled 30 persons in front of the adjutant: my first efforts against a gale, aeroplanes, birds, etc. I was petrified but out of us 8, I was voted best! Me and my stammer, you could and can still, knock me down with a feather. Oh, but I got my own back on a Sergeant who was late on saluting to the left!

Prisoner 10852, Camp 329, Germany.
29.5.42.

Dear Mrs Horton,
Just a remembrance to you hoping that yourself and Mr Horton are both OK. Jack Bennie showed me a letter tonight from you giving details of Mr Horton's recommendation for the M.C. Please pass on our congratulations to him and also our very best wishes hoping to see him soon. He certainly deserves that medal. All the boys here join me in wishing the very best to you of the moment, hoping to see you soon.
    H. Field.

Hatton Cottage, Lubbock Rd, Chislehurst, Kent.
1.6.42.

Friday I took the parade at drill. It was amusing though I felt quaky at the knees. Your missus apparently has a good parade voice! A great relief that I didn't get stuck as everyone expected I'd do. Busied about and cooked as a cook was on leave, a very hectic day.

By the way, I'm now getting 14/- a week war proficiency pay! Sunday, after Commanding Officer's parade I gardened all day, dug and weeded and retired to bed at 8.30 tired and drugged with sun.

Prisoner No. 3275. Oflag VI B.
4th June 1942.

The whole room, including a barrister, are of the opinion you have given me grounds for divorce — mental cruelty! The picture of that large cream cake (was it chocolate?) has caused more mouth-watering than anything since we became gefangeners but, joking apart, my sweet I was delighted with the snaps. You look even more charming than in the last and it is easy to see how you get all the compliments.

Faversham Cottage Hospital, Faversham, Kent.
7.6.42.

Now please don't jump and grow agitated at the address and sit down quietly Alan and listen to what's happening. You know I came to consult Polly about something a week or so ago. He found I'd a bad appendix so by falling sick on my 7 days leave he is operating on me, Monday 8th at 3 o'clock. I only arrived at six this evening when Polly and his wife came with flowers galore. I have a wee two roomed ward to myself. There is absolutely nothing to worry over darling. Polly has arranged to have my operation and stay here paid for by the army otherwise he'd have to put me in a nursing home for 20-30 guineas.

Tuesday 9th 11 o'clock. Well, it's all over and done with and here I am upright in bed. He and Mrs P insist I go to them a week before travelling home and then Auntie Greeta wants me for a week at least. I've done nothing but doze today. Just had lunch — a cup of Bovril! Never mind, it's only for one day.

Prisoner No. 3275. Oflag VI B.
9th June 1942.

We had a busy day on Saturday spring cleaning our hut. We took everything out. Scrubbed the whole place and whitewashed the ceiling with a chalk solution and a shaving brush! When we had finished, we looked exactly like slap stick comedians who had been throwing custard pies. It is much brighter now though. No parcels have come in for me for some time. I hope the pair of shoes arrives soon as I now have only a pair of clogs. Apart from that my only other wants are shirts, a razor blade sharpener and two sets of "pips". Will the American Parcels materialise? They are very good and several fellows in the room get them. If you can fix them, they will be very welcome.

Faversham Cottage Hospital, Faversham, Kent.
16.6.42.

Apparently, there is some hitch, and no one has been officially notified that I'm sick therefore I'm 10 days overdue from leave! What's the answer please sir? Darling, some funny old thing was so ignorant about P.O.W. Camps that they supposed the cooking and cleaning were done by MAIDS! Later, Mother's been, she came at

1.30 and left at 17.30, very well and chirpy and calls me a "film star" surrounded by flowers and looking so well.

17.6.42.

Lots of things have happened today; Cyril, Jennie and Mother came and spent two hours with me this afternoon. All very well, but Cyril had a hangover! After they had gone, I was allowed out of bed, imagine the thrill, Darling, I stood up between two nurses and just couldn't stand. It's incredible how much it takes out of one and makes me wild to be so helpless. I am allowed to wash myself in bed still. Now for news of our furniture, we've acquired a genuine Jacobean, perfect condition, Welsh Dresser, also a pretty Sheraton oval shaped chair and occasional gate legged, low tea table, all for £20! And a beautiful new Ottoman single bed £10 — £25 in London!

Prisoner No. 3275. Oflag VI B.
19th June 1942.

Just heard of your visit to Canterbury and Faversham and dinner with Harry and Midget. I am glad the Faversham visit was successful! I heard from Midget today, please thank her, and your Granny a few days ago. I'll send her a card next month and congratulate the Doc for me! The weather has been cold and wet, rather miserable so activities have been restricted to reading and writing and I have produced a short story. It's not too bad, I think I'll try some more.

24.6.42.

Now this a.m. a grand letter from you, June 4th darling. I am so very sorry over the cake, actually it caused a great many comments here — a real treat — it was Diana's birthday cake; don't divorce me please, I won't do it again.

2.7.42.

Pat's just brought me up your letter of June 9th so now I know you can spring clean — what a useful husband! I'd love to have joined your gang of slap-stick comedians — would they have let me?

Prisoner No. 3275. Oflag VI B.
6th July 1942.

I had a letter from you a few days ago which took only a fortnight. In it you said you had only just got up, that the stitches were coming out and the scar small. This was the first indication I had that you were ill. Since then, the letters have come in in reverse order from the start, so you see Pegasus I knew you were better before I knew you were ill. When this reaches you, I hope you are on parade again and using that stripe (congratulations) in the best Horton tradition. Tell Polly Porter I am adding his name to my list of parties and if only I can keep on my feet, promise him a good "gin up" for looking after you. So, Midge is to have a baby. Well, well. I hope it will make them happier together. I am sorry about Pop's business but, as you say, post war reconstruction should give them a chance to start again[25]. C'est la guerre. Since last writing I have had another Comforts parcel and more tobacco but still no more clothes. As I normally wear only gym shoes, shorts and singlet except for check parades it does not matter though. By the way, can you send me some garden seeds please — particularly turnip, swedes, cabbage, sprouts, carrots, etc. We now have some bees which swarmed into the camp. They are the most interesting creatures.

19th July 1942.

I am very relieved to know that you are so well and will certainly write to Polly. Remember me to them and thank them for all their kindness. Since my last letter I have changed my room to 36/7. Something I have been trying to do for ages. It is much cleaner, brighter and better in every way. Being stone instead of wood I think it will be a warmer place in winter should we be doomed to spend another winter here.

150 Causeway Street, Boston, Mass, U.S.A.
July 19th, 1942.

My Dear Alan,
It was fine to hear from your wife, though we were sorry to learn of your being captured, and also of Mrs Sutcliffe's death several years ago.

---

[25] The architect's business closed in the war and my grandfather worked for the government. He did only a limited amount of work after the war.

Peggy's Uncle Bill and I were good friends over here 27-8 years ago and again in 1924 when my wife and I visited England. Then we met Peggy, 5 years old and cute as a button. Our family spent 4 grand days with their home as our home. What fun and what arguments we had!

What terrible times these are for the world, when fundamental differences in ideas clash in every field, economic, political, military, religious.

I trust you are getting the good treatment accorded always to a worthy foe and are in good health. A package of food, in fact 2, go to you at the address we got from Peggy, about 2 weeks apart. We hope you and your friends enjoy them, Cheerio and much luck.

Claudius G Pendill,
Lieutenant Commander, U.S. Navy

Hatton Cottage, Lubbock Rd, Chislehurst, Kent.

24.7.42.

A long letter from Carol today. Geoffrey apparently told her you were keeping more to your room because of clogs darling heart. Haven't your shoes got through yet? They went off last January. Another pair is going off in August. Oh why, oh why, should you have to suffer discomfort? God alone knows you have been through enough, both mental and physical, but your example of bravery darling inspires all and especially me, your missus.

Prisoner No. 3275. Oflag VI B.
24th July 1942.

Thanks for writing to America. You see, my Sweet, the position is this. Rations plus one parcel is fine but in winter, when weather makes transport bad, this sometimes fails for short periods. It is very useful to have a stock on hand for those occasions; some have terrific stocks. Unless we get parcels from secondary source it is impossible to build up this reserve. Switzerland, Portugal, Turkey and Egypt are the potential other sources. Talking of the last, I hope Morley and Co never do see the inside of an Oflag. It is no life for anyone who likes doing a job of work.

Underhills, Peter's Avenue, Oxted, Surrey.
28.7.42.

Here's me, dog tired and sitting up in bed in my old, flowered dressing gown and that thin pink nightie you like, all bathed and powdered and in a new home. I have a very pretty little house and garden all of my own to run — at least the house keeping for 7 persons, actually I am not so far from Magpie Cottage too. It's a new house built with lots of lovely old beams. My fingers itch to furnish it. However, I've already put in flowers and moved furniture. I've come here to take life easy until I'm tough again and during the day everyone is out so I will do my shopping in a pretty village, cook and sit in the garden this lovely weather — my first job in lone responsibility.

29.7.42.

The other girl in charge insists on doing the housekeeping and shopping and makes me a cook. I'm no cook and not receiving cook's pay and I have experience of housekeeping at home and at Gore for 40 persons and she has had none and is in fact supposed to run the Military Transport side. However, I know my own mind and job and no hanky panky. *(Peggy was an excellent cook!)*

Prisoner No. 3275. Oflag VI B.
8th August 1942.

It is ten days now since I had a letter, and it may be sometime before you hear from me. The reason is that the German P.O.W.s. are said not to be getting theirs and our in-goings and out-goings are regulated by theirs.

Hatton Cottage, Lubbock Rd. Chislehurst, Kent.
8.8.42.

Two long aerographs came in today from Martin. He has sent some food parcels off to you along with quite a number of letters. Yours to Boyd arrived OK after 3 ½ months, Clarke's reached Boyd by the way. Poor old Boyd's gone to H.Q. and Stuart's taken his place — are they mad? Leverton only got out by being three months in hospital and South African — but fancy being under Stuart! Before I forget, Midge's efforts to have a baby failed again. Did I tell you Cyril is Lieutenant Colonel, Temp but I can see him making it permanent!

Prisoner No. 3275. Oflag VI B.
12th August 1942.

By the way, I hope to take Inter BSc. (Economics) in December if I am still here.

19th August 1942.

The ban on mail has at last been lifted, at least temporarily and yesterday I had six letters, some from you, some from Mother and one from Diana. Please thank Diana and congratulate her on her exam results. I am still struggling with Economics, French, British Constitution and History and do PT in the mornings and play deck tennis in the evenings to keep fit — also because my tummy is getting rather large! My new companions in this new room are very pleasant and I am much happier here than in 37/6. We live together generally in surprising harmony considering how much we are forced to be together.

89th A.A. Regt. R.A. M.E.F.
September 6th, 1942.

My Dear Peggy,
It seems ages since I wrote to you, but I am afraid the last month or so has been a trifle hectic.

I am glad that Dad is well. I have written several letters to him, two to Leslie and Mac. — So far, no reply. So please tell him Peggy I am always thinking of them all, and now dear old Brigadier Stebbings — but we are so glad to know he is safe.

Stuart is now Major in 235 and Boyd is 2 i/c at Regiment. It is grand to have Boyd here, just the last link to those grand old days at home. David is Adjutant now, so we cling together. Cecil has gone east of his old place and that seems all the changes to date, except I may be going to a battery soon which will be a pleasant change. I am trying hard to get back to the battery where the few boys who came back with us are. I would like that no end. They are not far away from us so it may be possible.

Kay is at Hellingly and seems fit and well. Like you we look forward to those promised parties, hell! What fun.

Best wishes to all,

yours,

Charles.

Hatton Cottage, Lubbock Rd. Chislehurst, Kent.
7.9.42.

Herewith a list of parcel goods just going off: 1 Camelhair cellular (holey) rug, 1 pair black calf, sheepskin lined, crepe soled shoes, 1 pair long-legged pants, 1 vest, 1 face flannel, 1 box Yardley's shaving soap, 30 razor blades — if too many give Geoffrey Towse some, Carol can't find any — 2 sets of bronze pips, 3 Pears soap — no more of the transparent variety I'm afraid darling, 1 glass razor blade sharpener, 3 tins MacLean's tooth powder, 1 pair nail scissors, 1 tooth brush, 1 shaving brush, 1 pair khaki socks, 1 pair camelhair mitts, 5 packets veg seeds: carrots, cabbage, swede, sprout, turnip, each envelop has two 4'' packets in, ½ slab of Bourneville ration chocolate. Now hold your thumbs and pray they reach you, my sweetheart. Incidentally, I'm off to Sevenoaks not Oxted this evening.

9.9.42.

Here's Pegasus at our section office, desk of her own, Quartermaster Corporal. The officer here is a friend of Polly P's actually, has left me in charge of Quartermaster side, i.e., food, indents, seeing house is clean, stores, clothes. Whether it will bring in my second stripe or not, I've no idea, it ought to as it's usually a full corporal's job.

Eichstätt

From around this time, Peggy began to make use of her home address on nearly every letter she sent. She moved to different addresses throughout the rest of the war but found it easier if Alan's letters always went to her family home and were forwarded to her from there rather than being lost at various military bases in her absence.

Prisoner No. 3275. Oflag VII B.
11th September 1942.

My own darling, my new address is: OFLAG VII B, Germany.

19th September 1942.

Here I am in Bavaria! The camp is a barracks with the addition of some new stone huts, set in a lovely green valley through which meanders a narrow river. Quarters are cleaner and much better built than those at VI B and there are good exercise grounds. We travelled here in 2nd class carriages in good weather and enjoyed the change immensely. The towns and the country in this part of Germany are very fine indeed and I should just love to wander round here with you, my darling, as a free man. There are certain snags attached to our current "conducted tours"! I fear this move has put paid to my exam this year as at least a month will have elapsed before my books reach me, again censored. On the whole though, the change is good although this place like all others is not without its disadvantages. I must tell you since you ask that ███████████████████.

Navy Dept. H.E.C.P. Misaum Point, New Bedford, Mass, U.S.A. 12th September 1942.

Dear Old Peggy,

Your letter of July 1st which came 2 weeks later was so welcome. I was away in the Navy, but my family was right to work on the matter of the baskets of food for your husband, a P.O.W. in Germany.

We took it up with the Red Cross, the Quakers and the best grocery company in Boston, S.S. Pierce. I sent a check[26] for $2.50 for the first basket with the idea it would be best to send one at a time, at intervals, to ensure, if possible, the safe arrival of most of them.

Then the Quakers advised that they could not send it. And finally, S. S. Pierce returned my check, said they no longer send baskets, and that all food must go in bulk.

We are greatly disappointed that our efforts came to nought. I suppose that the food was not reaching the men for whom it was intended, and that the only way to get it there was in bulk lots, handled by an organization which can actually supervise its

---

[26] An example of two nations divided by one language! Check is American for cheque.

distribution. I wish it were otherwise. I hate to have to write this after getting such a wonderful letter from you.

I want to hear from you again as soon as you can take the time. Tell me what you are doing and news of Alan. Over here we are doing about as I imagine you did, slowly coming to realize what a terrific struggle we are in for and gearing up resources and especially our minds for the unpleasant and desperately tough methods we shall have to adopt to win. I personally have been on various details at sea and ashore — but the war is young, and I expect ample variety both in work and in the place I do it.

With love and more courage to you and good cheer to all.

Yours,

Claudius S. Pendill.

P.S. When this business is over, plan to come and see us. Best to your dad and Uncle Bill.

Hatton Cottage, Lubbock Rd, Chislehurst, Kent.
20.9.42.

Apparently, the vegetable seeds I bought you have been returned by the Red Cross! They are getting so strict about what one sends. The Royal Horticultural Society are supposed to supply all seeds you want in bulk.

Prisoner No. 3275. Oflag VII B.
23rd September 1942.

It seems an age now since I last heard from you — actually it must be nearly three weeks. This is one of the inevitable disadvantages of moving. We are now fairly well settled, and I have secured a comfortable bunk next to the stove, a great advantage, believe me, when winter sets in although I do not think we shall experience the same rigours as we did last winter. So far I have not done a scrap of work. The barrack room atmosphere is not very conducive to it and anyway my notes and textbooks have not yet reappeared.

27th September 1942.
My books have not yet appeared from the baggage store and entertainment has not got going. This sounds an awful tale of woe but will soon come right. Until then I have a very comfortable bunk and a terrific capacity for sleep. My new companions are very pleasant but very religious and serious. Oh, for freedom, the West End and money to burn. You'll need a tight rein my Pegasus.

Hatton Cottage, Lubbock Rd, Chislehurst, Kent.
28.9.42.

I now have a very responsible job, the feeding of 50 odd (mixed) persons — all ranks too and I hear unofficially that my two stripes are due shortly — 25/- a week! Wow, the most I've ever earned!

30.9.42.

Life does really get more and more busy. It's now nearly 5 o'clock in the evening and I am writing at my desk in Gore by a French window thrown open wide as the September evening and orange sun is lovely flowing in onto me. This morning I went to the

N.A.A.F.I. to spend ration cash money — a cold wet morning and I thanked heaven I wasn't the permanent truck driver like last winter, it was an open one and it was hell getting cold and wet every day.

Prisoner No. 3275. Oflag VII B.
3rd October 1942.

My June parcel came yesterday for which many thanks. Unfortunately, the drawing book was taken out. Can you possibly send the next in a kit bag? It would be very useful. The Pears soap and shaving cream is grand and as for the chocolate — Oh boy!

10th October 1942.

I am writing this because you may have heard that I am handcuffed. You need not worry. It is for twelve hours daily, quite loosely. The whole thing is a result of an obvious stupid mistake, and we find it rather amusing if somewhat irksome. We are freed to eat and exercise and can read and smoke without discomfort. The worst thing is we only get four inward letters monthly now. An agreement will probably be reached soon.

18th October 1942.

Today is my eighth day in handcuffs. We have had it explained to us that it is a reprisal for our treatment of prisoners at Dieppe and Sark, but the exigencies of battle are overlooked. Anyhow it sounds much worse than it is for we have plenty of walking exercise, tobacco and books and is only for twelve hours a day with an hour's break at noon. It has put paid to my exam for, of course, I cannot write and besides, I still have not got my textbooks and notes back. I suppose we shall soon know the motive. What with handcuffs and a number and triangle on my back I cannot see any self-respecting bank employing me after the war!

Despite saying that he could not write, Alan managed to send a regular hand-written letter to Peggy. As we shall learn, the handcuffs were on far less than one might believe from these letters, which would have been read by the German censors!

Hatton Cottage, Lubbock Rd, Chislehurst, Kent.
18.10.42.

It's an awfully great sorrow to me not to have written since last weekend. I've tried to several nights but have felt too worn out to write a cheery letter. You may know I've had to help cook here; 2 of us for 30 odd people all day and cookhouse fatigues to do as there were no official cooks or orderlies. It's been on for about 3 weeks now. I seized a half day Friday and flew to Polly's for tea as my side has been hurting. A raspberry from him as adhesions where forming! So, I reported sick to an army Medical Officer and wrangled at least 2 weeks sick leave. Beloved, I am really very fit and all I need is a holiday with you.

By the way, if you have the following ingredients, you can make an excellent "Daddies Sauce" — flour, vinegar, mustard spice, pepper, browning if possible. You make an ordinary gravy adding mustard, spice, vinegar, etc. It tastes like a very good sauce. I've tried it on the people here and no one's yet realised its homemade! Today I'm having a blitz on army issue, it's all in need of repair — you'd laugh to see us in our glamorous undies. The pants are so huge that if one put shoulder straps on, they would do for pants and vests all in one! They are extremely tough and wear well but mine are nearly a year old and due for renovations.

Navy Dept. H.E.C.P. Misaum Point, New Bedford, Mass.
19th October 1942.

My Dear Peggy,

Just a line to let you know that again there seems to be some possibility for getting a food package to your husband, as we have been trying to find some way. We are sending two, if we can, each a month apart. Let us know if you hear from either, won't you?

And there is one aspect that we want to square up now. We insist on paying for these, not only that we love the opportunity, but this — when we left England after enjoying the opportunity of 4 wonderful days with your family in your home, we sent a gift of silver back from the U.S.A. to our chagrin we learned long after, that your father had to pay a duty on it to get it in, so our "gift" was only another "cost". Now you give us, at long last, the perfect chance to make good, which we love doing.

Trust you and your family are fine and well and please give my very best to your dad and Uncle Bill. What is the news of them, and of your husband, and of yourself? Naturally, I can say nothing of my Navy work, save that it goes better and better,

Luck and love, Claudius S. Pendill. Lieut. Comdr.

Prisoner No. 3275. Oflag VII B.
23rd October 1942.

I am hoping this will reach you on or about the anniversary of that grand day two years ago. It seems an age and yet every detail is clear-cut in my mind. My heart is full of things I want to say but I can only send this card and leave you to imagine them which I think you will do without difficulty. New Year, with luck, no writing will be necessary.

14th November 1942.

I have just been released from handcuffs after five weeks. Cold weather and lack of hard exercise aggravated by my rather poor circulation, and I was released in consequence. It is pleasant to be back in my old room again. Have just had a large batch of mail — October 20th the latest. Wish I could keep the Cathedral date this year but hope to, next.

18th November 1942.

Quite a large batch of mail lately. I am the envy of everyone here. Good show about the paid stripe — I only wish I could have you on the carpet to congratulate you! Had a letter from Angela too, will you thank her please? But to try to answer letters is a waste of time. You know my answers only too well. First, I must wish to all the season's greetings and ask you to pass on mine with yours to all our friends and relations. New Year, my own darling, D.V. we shall celebrate our wedding anniversary together and keep that Christmas date at the Cathedral. Oh, what a hap, hap, happy day. As I write I am sitting around a table having a mug of cocoa and listening to a gramophone. The records are rather ancient but full of memories for all of us. Cold weather is making us think of home comforts and first one and then another, chips in with, "Reminds me of Sunday evenings in front of the fire" and so on. I've got a cold in the head and I'm thinking hard of hot whisky and lemon!

Hatton Cottage, Lubbock Rd, Chislehurst, Kent.
19.11.42.

My Dearest Alan, I am afraid I am rather late in writing again as at half-term I really had no time to write to you. Let me tell you I had work to do! I had to deal with all the calves and help with the cows. I rode quite a bit too on a pony called Tim. Several days later: I've just got into an awful row from the head-mistress; she is going to write to Pop about it! I am longing for the hols to come. We break up on Dec 16th, but I don't go home until the 17th because of the travelling. I am still longing for you to come home again and am looking forward to that very eagerly. I went to hockey again the other day, and I played goal! It was very funny as I have never played there before! Well, I suppose I must stop now so I'll say, cheerio, and I'll be writing in a week or two, so all my love old chap, Your loving Diana.

Hatton Cottage, Lubbock Rd, Chislehurst, Kent.
21.11.42.

This morning I went off into town to shop; old Offer, the draper, served me himself with pink shoulder strap ribbon and hair pins and when I got talking to him about the war, he happened to say he knew a grand fellow from Lloyd's now a P.O.W. I said, "He isn't by any chance called Alan Horton?" Offer replied, "That's the man, grand old fellow." Pegasus says proudly (you ought to have seen my pride darling), "He's my husband of two years today. My darling, Offer's eyes popped out of his head and said, "My, you are his wife, wonderful!" He was all overcome. This handcuffing darling — Oh God — you know for over a month I felt somehow it affected you and tried to keep cheerful, you see I've been feeling just as I did when you were in action, as though you were using all my energy to help you along, and proud I am to give it to you for it is right I should share your suffering.

British Red Cross Society, Prisoner of War Department, St James's Palace, London, SW1.
26th November 1942.

Dear Mrs. Horton,

Lieut. A.E. Horton

Thank you for your letter which we have just received. As the question of reprisals imposed by the German authorities is being dealt with by the War Cabinet it is outside the scope of this

Department, we regret we have no official information on this subject.

We can only assure you, however, that everything possible is being done to safeguard the welfare of all prisoners. All our information is derived mainly from prisoners of war themselves, we have not very much other news than that which you have received from your husband. We have seen many letters which have been written on this subject and all the officers who have written assure their relatives that the reprisals are enforced in a humane manner and under medical supervision.

We are very sorry that we have not any recent information to give you.

Yours sincerely,

E.M. Thornton.

Director.

Hatton Cottage, Lubbock Rd, Chislehurst, Kent.
27.11.42.

Your letter of yesterday was dated September 19th like all yours it is so lovely to read to my heart's content. I am very worried over your handcuffs — are they off yet? I long for a letter dated after October 10th from you.

Alan records little of this handcuffing incident but other sources[27] do shed light on what actually took place. Some Canadian officers

---

[27] Harwood, Lieutenant, H. C. F., typed account of service in 5th, Battalion, East Kent Regiment (36th, Infantry Brigade) including time in

were manacled and placed in segregated barracks following an incident in Dieppe. It was said that this was a reprisal for their treatment of German 'prisoners who, it was alleged, had been temporarily bound after capture'. The Germans announced that a group of one hundred and twenty British officers would have to suffer the same fate as a result of an incident that was supposed to have taken place on the Channel Island of Sark.

At parade one morning, British officers noticed that the camp sentry boxes had their flaps down and the guards had been doubled. They all carried automatic weapons that were trained on the prisoners. The commandant, a man that Alan would have called a 'right bastard', strutted onto the parade ground and informed the senior British officer (S.B.O.) that he had to produce the officers to suffer this humiliating treatment. Any trouble would mean the sentries opened fire. It was later learnt that there were also mortars placed around the outside of the camp. A consultation was held between the S.B.O. and the company commanders, each agreeing to provide men to meet the commandant's demand. They marched from the parade ground, collected their bedding and moved into the same block as the manacled Canadians. The process was carried out with discipline and dignity and the self-important commandant had no need to instruct his guards to open fire, something that might have been a disappointment to him!

Handcuffs were applied early each day and removed every night so the prisoners could sleep. However, the prisoners quickly learnt the handcuffs could be opened with a rusty nail and a boot used as a hammer. They could also be quickly slipped back on again should a guard approach. This meant that playing cards and

Eichstätt. Held by Department of Documents, Imperial War Museum, No. 84/33/1.

reading became quite possible. Each morning, officers would parade in their greatcoats, correctly manacled. Incredibly, later in the day, they appeared minus their greatcoats, something that could only be removed when handcuffs were off! This did not seem to register with the Germans. Indeed, after a time, a roster of volunteers was developed so that the same officers did not have to suffer throughout the duration of this indignity. So long as the Germans could inform their superiors that the correct number of P.O.W.s were manacled they did not seem bothered. The treatment did not cause great suffering but was a psychological blow to the men. After some time, a German officer announced that they wanted to use a more sophisticated type of manacle with an eighteen-inch chain. This would allow more movement of the hands. The British officer in charge took a moment or so to look over the German before replying, "When I want your opinion on comparative barbarity, I will send for you. Until then, get out!" It is understandable why Alan felt it expedient not to explain all of this to Peggy in his censored letters home! The indignity of wearing manacles would have inhibited discussion of it in later years. News of these problems was obviously upsetting for Peggy and so, like many other aspects of camp life, it was played down in letters Alan sent to her.

Captain John Mansell notes on Sunday 11th November 1942 that, 'Amusement caused to P.O.W. — amazement to guards — at sight of football played in handcuffs!' In a foot note an unnamed contributor adds: 'The reprisal ended very early, in fact, by the Kommandant requesting the British Officers to be kind enough, for appearance's sake, to slip the handcuffs on (the locks had been *ruined) should he send word of a visit of a General or other senior German Officer.* "[28]

Hatton Cottage, Lubbock Rd, Chislehurst, Kent.
21.12.42.

A list of goods in December parcel: pipe, Pears soap — after much scrounging but I love doing it for you, face flannel, Yardley's shaving sticks, 2 toothbrushes, 1 lb. chocolate, 1 nail brush, 16 Razor blades, shoe leather, gloves, gym shoes of tough and useful type, shoe cleaning materials, mending wool and thread, kit bag, 4 handkerchiefs, 2 packets pipe cleaners, 2 tins of tooth paste for a change, 2 pairs of socks from Mother, 2 pairs boot laces, 2 pairs shoelaces — all in calf. All went off except metal polish; it was a paste type too.

24.12.42.

Christmas Eve and two grand cards from you, October 28th and November 5th. My best Christmas present. Its grand how near a birthday or anniversary a letter or card turns up from you Alan. Bombardier Bennie wrote me a long letter yesterday. 14 out of your section are with him and altogether 29 of the Battery — all well and anxious for news of you, "Mr Horton". I've replied all with Lieutenant Horton's news. All remember me and I promised them on your behalf 1 pint of best as they hold you, darling, in very great respect! Callow, Field, Price, Marsh, Pettifer, Brown, Snelling,

---

[28] The Mansell Diaries published privately 1977, Page 85.

Johnstone, Tutt, Davies, Coles, Copson, Dunn, Derby and Gower are their names. A bunch of pink Chrysanthemums came from a local shop yesterday to me "with Alan's love". I suspect Mother — a very sweet thought. Next year we'll be together. Oh boy, how I'll wish you a happy Christmas!

Prisoner No. 3275. Oflag VII B.
25th December 1942,

My darling, full of thoughts of home I feel I must write to you. The camp has "gone to town" today — a real Christmas. We went to Communion at 07.15 and came back to a real English breakfast for the first time since captivity. Carol service next at 11.15 and then beer in the canteen. Tomorrow a panto and Sunday a concert. Everyone in grand spirits. A great batch of mail last week. You are my constant companion in thoughts and next year, darling, with luck, in reality.

All my love,
Your own,
Alan.

Hatton Cottage. Lubbock Rd. Chislehurst, Kent.
28.12.42.

I arrived here at supper time last night and found a new lot of promotions up. I miss them every ruddy time, excuse my language! But it is the limit. I suppose all my sick leave and now compassionate leave mucks it up so. However, amongst the new

Lance Corporals there's a girl who used to be a cook and caterer, so I want to bag her and train her.

Prisoner No. 3275. Oflag VII B.
30th December 1942.

Christmas has been an absolute "wow". The Red Cross Parcels had all the little Christmas luxuries and the final result, being unused to food in such quantity or of such quality, was that we were all ill! Boxing Day we had a grand pantomime and on Sunday a concert. Rooms and canteen were decorated with evergreens and streamers. Your photograph, too, is decorated as it smiles down on me now. A very different spirit from last year prevailed. Again, I had nineteen very cheery letters in Christmas week, eight from you and others from Mother, Cyril, Jennie, C.G.M. Lloyds, Diana and a very nice one from Commander Pendill saying he has sent me two parcels. I must write and thank him. I enclose a form from Lloyds Bank. Your letters are so grand and cheerful. Darling they make me think that great day cannot be far ahead — in fact, all letters sound very cheerful. I think and dream of that great reunion and never forget to thank God for our love. I know exactly what this long period of waiting must mean to you and the sacrifices you are making for me. I pray I shall never fail you.

1943 — How long, Oh Lord, how long?[29]

Hatton Cottage, Lubbock Rd, Chislehurst, Kent.
1.1.43.

Isn't it thrilling to write '43 in the date now? The year in which we'll have our sweet reunion. I've made a New Year resolution not to smoke a cigarette till after 18.00 hrs as recently I'd gone haywire and went to about 30 a day and felt it too, so that's to be stopped. I am doing a bit of nursing when people fall ill — I still love it.

4.1.43.

Oh, what a day — we have a Warrant Officer inspection 9 am tomorrow. What an hour! All my orderlies are away except one who has a disease of sorts, so I keep her on housework only and away from people. 2 out of 3 cooks are away! Company Commander refuses my application for more of each. "You'll manage Horton" is her reply! So, the "Q" Sergeant and I have spent the day cleaning and scrubbing. Evensong at 3.15 and then to the Gibbons to tea and met Virginia Gordon, a very gay little thing from America and we had terrific fun. She calls undies by such funny names and can't understand why they call BB Brassiere, and we call a grill room

---

[29] From Psalm 13 verse 1.

that! Pop Gibbons was a hoot and kept saying he was learning things!

8.1.43.

I have another cook at last — and class 1 so all's fine and dandy on my kitchen front and my Class 2 is ready to take her Class 1 any day, so for the first time I'm able to tackle my office work properly. I have huge battles with our R.A.S.C. Canteen's officer, a real twerp and perpetually drunk and sad to say darling, he's a Lloyd's Bank clerk. Turner by name — know him? He's a typical narrow-minded example of a Bank clerk! I like these battles – he's so twerpish. I'm on my high horse and he knows it. He rather likes to be called Sir — I ask you! He'll be madaming me and our platoon officer before we've finished with him

13.1.43.

Well, I have not gone to Polly's for 24 hours after all, a pity, but after seeing the specialist again today they've stopped my leave and they're sending me on 3 weeks sick leave. Now don't flap and worry my sweetheart. There is absolutely no need to worry; a mere case of over-tiredness and still a little run down after my appendix operation, the X ray shows nothing, and my blood test only shows I was out of sorts. However, I plan not to start my leave till after the weekend as I have to leave a complete bible of my job and get everything in order for someone to take over and I've asked Auntie if she'll have room for me.

Rivers Hall, Boxted, Nr. Colchester, Essex.
2.2.43.

My last letter from Rivers Hall for a while. I return tomorrow morning to Hatton Cottage and Polly's on Friday and Gore, Saturday. Oh dear, but time marches on and soon the great day we both long for. I feel after all this good air and sleep, 100% grand — could race you all the way to the lake and back.

Lady Minter, Rivers Hall, Boxted, Nr. Colchester.
7.2.43.

My Dear Alan, as you will have heard, Peggy has been staying with me. She was here nearly three weeks, on sick leave. When she came, she was very run down, tired and had a nasty cough, when she left, last Wednesday, she was very fit indeed, cough had completely disappeared and eating and sleeping well too, in fact was quite her old self. The first week she was here I made her go to bed every afternoon. It went against the grain very much, but it did her a lot of good. Don't worry about her, as I am certain she is quite all right, but I think the lack of exercise and being in doors tired her very much. She is very cheery and optimistic. John came home yesterday on leave, just having passed out of O.C.T.U. and feeling very thrilled with life. Fred is abroad now and writes cheerily. You don't know any of them yet, but I hope before many moons you will know us all as Peggy does. She has a very soft spot in my heart. I am missing her very much. She is just longing for the day when you can both have your home and can settle down to happiness. Before that you must come here and finish off your honeymoon! I hope you are receiving the cigarettes I am sending you periodically. With very best wishes for the future,

Yours sincerely,
Greeta C Minter.

Hatton Cottage, Lubbock Rd, Chislehurst, Kent.
10.2.43.

I'm having a good old fight with the sergeants — they will order all my cooks off to P.T. without telling me and so tonight they've only got half a supper! Have also 2 new cooks — mentally deficient. I'm also very busy nursing flu people — this I always prefer to feeding hogs.

Prisoner No. 3275. Oflag VII B.
10th February 1943.

I have my wedding ring on my finger again after 18 months. I was overjoyed when it was returned to me the other day after repeated requests for it. Can it be a happy omen? Secondly, I have seven letters from you, all about Christmas time. And thirdly we are now again back on one full Red Cross parcel a week. So, you see the last few days have been pretty grand. If Cyril's letters mean anything, perhaps I shall be home soon. I have had to use one or two letters lately to write to the Bank. They have been very good in sending me books, games and tobacco and I thought some letters in the right quarters would be useful. Oh, my darling, how impatient I am for that great day. I hate to think of what that bottle of bubbly will do to me after such a long abstinence — but that will be nothing compared with the sight of your sweet self, particularly in that red dressing gown. The winter so far has not been as bad as last, but heaven save us from another. I have been very lazy and do little work but with a friend now run the Company Cook House one night a week!

20th February 1943.

I am glad you have heard from Bennie. Ward and Blick came to this camp yesterday as orderlies. They have both been sick but are now quite well. Ward remembers you visiting him in hospital at Chatham. The last few days have been simply grand. The morning's clear and frosty and then really warm sunshine. We have got the medicine ball in action again and I am making fresh headway studying gold standards, exchanges, foreign trade as well as some French and German. It's grand news about the Everetts. Please congratulate them for me. I've had my annual injection this week. The Medical Officer did not say "KEEP OFF THE ALCOHOL"! You must not worry about me. I am very fit and just aching to hold you in my arms again.

44, Broad St. Newbury Port, Mass, U.S.A.
24th Feb '43.

My Dear Peggy,
Tough luck you had to again get leave to rest up — but the strain is terrific, we know. Its bad news, that we cannot send packages to Alan. They are out; all must go bulk to help all prisoners. So, we have sent some that way. I am writing him a line again.

Also got hold of an old shipmate of mine of the last war, Commander Thomas Keane, U.S.N.R. C/O: U.S. Naval Attaché, American Embassy, London. He's a jolly Irishman, visited us two years ago, can bring news of us. He knew your Uncle Bill, so get them together and you'll have a time.

Much love and courage my lass, let's have a line when there's news. We're piling into the war far harder than we were even at the end of the last war. Rationing, it increases weekly, with no complaints. We are beginning to taste what you all have had for years, but of course with no bombing, and we are prepared to stick there through the years.

Faithfully, G. S. Pendill.

████████████████████ Mass.

24 Feb 1943.

My Dear Alan, a word of cheer to you. Hope my last letter also reached you. The mails are a bit uncertain these days.

Find we cannot send you any food packages, but that bulk food can be sent, so have shared in doing that.

I hope your conditions of living are as good as those which your country and this are giving to prisoners of war. Unless such is the case, it will make it harder than ever to achieve a decent peace, if and when that day comes, for which we all hope, work and pray.

Here's to a reunion and a fine visit when this business is over.

Much luck and good health,

C. S. Pendill. ████████████ U.S.N.R.

Hatton Cottage, Lubbock Rd, Chislehurst, Kent.
1.3.43.

Great news darling, Judy Everett has given birth to a son! Aren't they lucky? Let's hope he lost his dreadfully worried look; for nearly these last two weeks Mother says he's looked awful with worry. I'm now writing to Poppy Everett, but soon our time will come.

Prisoner No. 3275. Oflag VII B.
10th March 1943.

So glad all is well. I forgot it is Pop who sends the Simmonds and hope he will not mind me asking for a change. The truth is they get damp in their boxes and out here Player's No. 3 in tins keep better. Player's medium baccy too, is my favourite. You may shortly hear from Lloyds H.Q. Darling, giving you a list of books to send me. Please let me have the list but do not send the books as I can probably find them in the camp — this is part of a policy of mine for the future! The weather is simply grand today, but the nights are still very cold, and I am very glad of the blanket you sent.

Lloyds Bank Limited, Head Office, LONDON, EC3.
13th March, 1943.

Dear Mr. Horton.
Thank you for your letter of January 31st which I have just received. I am glad to hear you are well and I think you are wise to try to make the best of your time in preparation for your return to this

country, which I hope will not be too long delayed. I hear from time to time from many of our men who are similarly circumstanced and quite a number of them are spending their time in studying for the Institute of Bankers' Examination and, indeed, some of them are going further in studying for the London University Degree. Such a wise employment of time whilst a prisoner of war will stand you and your colleagues in good stead when you come back to civilian life.

It is difficult for me to know what books are suitable for you, as I do not know to what stage your studies have reached, but I am passing your letter on to Mr Faull, in our Administration Department; he may, perhaps, be able to tell something from your record and will send you two or three books which might be suitable for you. I do not know what facilities you have, but my own suggestion would be to take every opportunity of getting a knowledge of German, which will be interesting to you and may be useful in days to come.

Yours sincerely,

Sydney Parkes .

Director and Chief General Manager.

Hatton Cottage, Lubbock Rd, Chislehurst, Kent.
13.3.43.

The Gore twerps kicked me out of my lovely sunny bedroom and bathroom — whilst I was away an officer we have, objected to a Lance Corporal sleeping in the same room as a sergeant! Blimey anyone would think I'm infectious, so I'm in a worse room halfway up the back stairs, too near the rowdy cooks and orderlies. By the way I have 2 jaws for you to punch on your return; one the Medical

Officer at Rosemount refused to bring his wife into tea as long as I was there. I laughed and said I wasn't intending to stay to tea (the Comers having invited me) and that it was a pity that we were so short of real men that others had to be dressed up in the uniform of an officer — he heard too!

Lloyds Bank Limited, Head Office, LONDON, EC 3.
13th March, 1943.

Dear Mr. Horton.

Our Chief General Manager, Mr. Sydney Parkes, has passed to me your letter of 31st January. I have discussed your case with the Institute of Bankers who are doing everything possible to assist young bank men, who are prisoners of war, to continue their studies whilst in captivity. The Secretary of the Institute informs me that he has already sent you a book on higher book-keeping and this should have reached you by this time. He recommends that you should direct your energies towards passing the Institute of Secretaries Examination or the Executor and Trustee Diploma rather than to the difficult task of obtaining a London University degree. He proposes to send you in the near future the following books, all of which would be helpful to you if you decide on the Executor and Trustee Diploma:

- Elements of English Law
- A Book on Banking
- A Book on Mercantile Law.

I believe that the Chartered Institute of Secretaries themselves provide facilities in the case of prisoners who elect to study for their examinations, and I shall be pleased to approach them on your behalf if I hear that your choice lies in that direction.

With all good wishes for your welfare,
Yours sincerely,
General Manager's Assistant.

Prisoner No. 11013 Stalag lll D.
21.3.43.

My Dear Mrs Horton, I was glad to receive yours of 23.12.42. and
to see by it that Daddy is all right. I can't make out who you say has
been recommended for the M.C. I saw Sergeant Carter last week,
he is permanent sick, and Sergeant Harvey is in hospital. Tell Daddy
we are still working away,
    all the best,
    Bennie.

Hatton Cottage, Lubbock Rd, Chislehurst, Kent.
25.3.43.

I am going to discuss something darling, with you that you must
promise not to worry over — soon I am going to have a medical.
Beloved — apparently, they'll downgrade me which may mean I'm
slung out! There is absolutely nothing wrong with me except being
continually tired which the Medical Officer and Officers here say is
not only because I have a very tiring job, both mentally and
physically and apparently after my appendix I worked too hard too
soon, and every sick leave I have I came back feeling 100% fit, then
get run down after 4-8 weeks and hence the Board to be — promise
me you won't worry? You can see they are very decent and say I
must be very fit for your return!

7.4.43.

At last, I can leave this lousy hospital. All my tests are negative you'll be pleased to hear so Polly will be satisfied. I personally have always put my tiredness down to just war and being away from you, a purely nervous functioning but unconscious enough not to upset my nerves, faith and hope in our reunion before long. Polly's just taking extra care of me as he says he feels responsible for me in your absence, and my job is pretty tough, i.e. being constantly tactful to stop constant bickering of orderlies and cooks ███████████████████ so you can see darling there is and never was or will be any need to worry about the old woman. Whilst I was out your photo was passed around and admired by all!

11.4.43.

I'm so very glad you have your ring back — so perhaps now our rings find their way to our lips at the same moments. I am sure it's a good omen darling. We had great excitement about 7 am today — the stables had a fire. Another girl and I were first out there. I wore slacks and a great coat only — no time for other clothes! The men were very slow, it was terrific. The fire engine had to come.

14.4.43.

On Saturday I'm off to Chartham, I hope for some while, for most of the summer. Grand among the orchards and will live in a rectory — a garden with a river, only 10 of us. Heaven after 40 bitches!

Excuse my language darling but can never abide a houseful of females.

18.4.43.

You'd love to be here with me — I'm sitting on a red checked rug by a river; daises, daffs, forget-me-nots grow in profusion around me. Behind me is an apple orchard in blossom; there's a scorching sun and wild wind and it's just heavenly — but oh how I miss you my own sweet Alan. My new home is a flat on the 2nd floor and we have a grand view. At the moment I have a large, sunny, airy room to myself, and I made them feel a new broom sweeps fresh and got them spring cleaning — the place was lousy with dirt and two badly trained mongrel puppies.

Prisoner No. 3275. Oflag VII B.
20th April 1943.

Last letter recently 10th March: it seems to take ages for letters to get home. First some wants. As the December parcel has not turned up will you please send me a medium sized light kit-bag and boot polish? They are the only things from it I need as the Red Cross have sent shoe leather. My pyjamas are falling to pieces so I should like some more please. Razor blades are always useful. Please congratulate the Everetts from me. I think the spoon is a grand idea. I am longing to see how the new brooch goes with your ring! The weather has been grand for the last few days, and I have been in shorts all day. The trees are all in bud and the valley looks simply wonderful. I heard the cuckoo yesterday — the first time for three years, I think. A friend of mine and I get up each morning early and do P.T. Each day too, I spend some time digging in the garden and am getting very fit and brown in consequence. The beer tastes much better after exercise! Incidentally, I live in the "Garden City" or Lower Camp — very exclusive. Work too, has its place and I keep up a steady three hours a day. "Let's go Gay" is running at our theatre; its two solid hours of laughter. We are going for the second time on Saturday. Sunday the choir is singing Elijah in the evening, and I shall go to that. You will be very near me this Eastertide. I am out of step with our five minutes as our clocks are on one hour and lights out is 10.30. Can you make this time too darling?

9th May 1943.

Do hope the new place will prove better. My December parcel has arrived intact and now I have everything I need. I have been given another blanket so please do not send one. A steel mirror, toothpaste and razor blades are my only wants. The weather has been rather poor, but I am very fit and getting very brown. Some American prisoners from Tunis came in recently so we had some first-hand accounts of things.

Hatton Cottage, Lubbock Rd. Chislehurst, Kent.
20.5.43.

Have won my battle with the horrid Sergeant Cook and he eats out of my hands — apparently, I'm the first to beat him in his 25 years army service! So, I'm going to the old village pub tonight for a pint.

23.5.43.

Now we have a Sergeant here on 2 weeks rest cure. I think personally she's here to snoop by the questions she will ask me. Well, she won't allow even the fiancé of a girl here, so they meet outside and go on supper picnics. I let their boyfriends in and will do so again when she's gone. Its better they entertain them here than in the fields in my opinion! You see darling I remember my youth with a young gunner! But these miserable middle-aged spinsters, even the Lesbian types like this one, seem so very narrow and out to cross people. Our sitting room here used to be fun and a lovely place where all ranks looked forward to spending a peaceful Sunday teatime and helped cook the supper. Now they are all out except two of us. However, I won't bore you with all this — I get red when these female b---s get so narrow and idiotic — sour grapes with a lot I feel.

Prisoner No. 3275. Oflag VII B.
31st May 1943.

I am trying club swinging, a very dangerous sport, believe me, my arms are covered with bruises, and I still haven't mastered it. There is one thing here which will amuse you. We perform our natural functions in the "Garden City 40-seater". I caused some amusement here by saying I shall find the normal ones at home too lonely and propose to have one made on a communal scale. There is some conjecture now of what the Horton ménage is like!

9th June 1943.

The weather has been foul and I've a devil of a cold but on the whole all is well. We had a grand sports day on the King's Birthday and a pipe band beat the Retreat. We also had a good parade on Sunday. Some men become intensely religious, though, thank heavens, only a few. We have got rid of this element from our mess at last so I can blind and curse when I feel like it without being reminded of everlasting damnation. The companions I am with now are all more or less normal. We do 15 minutes of P.T. immediately we get up (about 7.45 am). Then the routine is parade, breakfast and work in the garden until lunch. In the afternoon, indoors or out, according to the weather, I read English and European history, economics, law, accountancy and heaven only knows what. On the advice of the Directorate of Lloyds Bank in consultation with the Banker's Institute! I am sitting for the Chartered Institute of Secretaries examination and am reading still for my BSc (Economics).

Hatton Cottage., Lubbock Rd, Chislehurst, Kent.
11.6.43.

It's now about 8.15 am, the others are in breakfast, and I am at my desk looking out upon the garden, river, trees, a hill upon which the hay was cut yesterday — the cutter pulled by a horse, a big grey one. He looked lovely against the dark trees and green hay. The sky is heavy and misty; the sun is still low behind the house and promises to be a grand scorcher. I sunbathed yesterday after a plunge in the river and turned my navy-blue costume down as far as I dare. Today I'm beginning to prepare a big cold lunch for Sunday as we have about 4-5 girls staying here for tomorrow's officers' dance. It's really surprising what one can produce from army rations — pastry made with half mashed potatoes and half flour is really very good.

15.6.43.

It's a fresh sunny June morning, I'm writing as usual at my desk 8.30 am. I've just rampaged everywhere. The others stayed ¾ hour extra in bed and are still wandering around unwashed in pyjamas and great steel hair curlers in, looking the dirty slovenly lot they are. Most are quite unhouse-trained, no self-discipline at all. One's having a hectic affair with a married man and of all things; he gave her an electric clock which she sleeps with! A bit hard I should imagine.

Prisoner No. 3275. Oflag VII B.
20th June 1943.

Incidentally, at long last, I am having my teeth attended to — eight fillings but nothing serious so you need not worry that I shall return toothless and bald! Methinks I must watch my appearance, or I shall be totally eclipsed by my lovely wife.

Lloyds Bank Limited, Head Office, LONDON, EC. 3.
7th July, 1943.

Dear Mr. Horton.

I was very pleased to have your card, dated 24th May, and to learn that you have made up your mind to sit for the intermediate examination of the Institute of Secretaries. I have arranged through the Staff Association for the Institute of Bankers to send you Robertson's "Organisation of Industry" and "Monopoly" by Robinson. Both these books are recommended for the B.Sc. courses in economics. I understand that the Chartered Institute of Secretaries have also sent you, through the Red Cross, copies of the past Intermediate and Final Examination papers.

Please do not hesitate to let me know if there is anything else I can do for you.

With kindest regards and best wishes for your future.

Yours sincerely,

General Manager's Assistant.

Prisoner No. 3275. Oflag VII B.
9th July 1943.

There is little camp news I can give you. Parole walks and cinemas are off, we hope only temporarily. Weather is dull, but hot and sultry and I long for a sniff of real sea air. A Y.M.C.A. calendar on the wall bears the verse "Be ye also patient". Doubtless it was well meant but at times I could cheerfully strangle the designer.

Hatton Cottage, Lubbock Rd, Chislehurst, Kent.
14.7.43.

I have a ghastly day before me — I distemper and paint my kitchen and not a soul offers to help. Lazy b…..s, they really are and Jean Knox, queen bee of all is in the area today. I am composing a hefty notice for the board on laziness and slovenliness. I call them at 7 am, dress, wash, do my face and hair, cook breakfast for 7.45 and those so-and-so's then crawl out of bed in pyjamas, unwashed and a positive ironmongery of curlers on their heads — and that's how they come to eat!

17.7.43.

Mother and I went to meet Grandfather. Your Aunt Meg was there. Aunt Mary came to see me, and we had tea at Little's with Dorie afterwards. I had expected to see your grandfather rather wan after Mother's remarks on how he was failing. Actually, his eyes are very bad except outdoors when he was able to see me better and clapped his hands with approval! He knew too who I was without any explanation and stood up and said, "Welcome Peggy, I am very glad of this opportunity to meet you and I hope you'll come again often." We talked about you darling and the war, etc. I had my photo taken with him in the garden by the wall, then picked cherries to bring back here.

20.7.43.

It's queer, though I'm with people all day I'm very lonely, they seem miles apart from me. I loathe it when they make stabs at my more fortunate upbringing than them and my idea of cleanliness seems normal to us but not to them — cigarette ends lying on the floor, clothes drying over the sitting room fire, etc. is home to them — queer, definitely queer.

23.7.43.

Our geyser's broken-down owing to old age and the engineer says we are not entitled to hot water, only a primus stove for heating the water on! So tomorrow, as the hospital Officer Commanding is in a good mood I'm tackling him — whoever heard of M.T. girls with no hot water! However, I win most of my fights so hope to win this one. The Royal Engineer man asked rudely if I'd give my all for hot water! Dirty skunk, he had the right answer á la mode Horton. Later: Won my geyser and soon things will move for a new one!

Prisoner No. 3275. Oflag VII B.
1st August 1943.

I hope this will arrive in time to prove I've not forgotten your birthday. I only wish I could be with you but please get yourself something you will like as though from me and add a kiss to my credit balance (this should be pretty big by now!). The news from the paper looks very good. Mother sent me her photo from Liphook. She looks very well; the war seems to have given her a new lease of life. The gardens here are simply grand and add that very welcome touch of colour to things that is usually absent. I read and sunbathe on a patch of lawn we have laid down overlooking the river, surrounded by flowers in which the bees hum and which smell delightfully. To smell something sweet too is a pleasant change. Oh, for the whiff of Numero Cinq! It's amusing to hear of all the promotions. It must be grand to be in circulation and to win such laurels. My banker's exams start on 9th and it's rather amusing to wonder if I will be able to "cope".

14th August 1943.

I have taken four exam papers this week but will refrain from commenting on them until I hear the results. We are expecting the next lot of papers in any day now. It was a pleasant change to have something concrete to do although the old brain made heavy weather of it after so much inactivity.

Hatton Cottage, Lubbock Rd, Chislehurst, Kent.
19.8.43.

Poor Pam's been in the labour ward since 3.30 am this day and still no arrival — it must be a fat, lazy boy. 20th — Pam had a boy, 8lbs last night and all's well, but neither of them wanted a boy. So, we are an uncle and aunt and I think a beer tankard for a Christening present ought to start him off OK.

29.8.43.

Be prepared for a shock — I bought my birthday present yesterday costing 32/-! More than I meant to pay. It's a lovely piece of hand-made lace, 1 ¼ yards. It caught my eye and for a long time I've been wanting something to make a top for the white nightie you gave me, so now it will be a truly bridal one, all white and lace and hand sown to the silk part. It can always come off and be put on to a new one when the silk wears out — I know you'll love it darling. Your parcel goes off 2nd September — have you had your March one yet? Another went off early June. I'm sending a good deal of chocolate my sweet to encourage your corporation!

Prisoner No. 3275. Oflag VII B.
31st August 1943.

Commander Pendill has written again. He seems very concerned as to my welfare. Could you please assure him we are well looked after by the Red Cross? Lloyd's staff Association and the General Manager's Assistant have written too. I shall be grateful if you will thank the former for all they have sent me and say the gramophone records will be very acceptable (so long as they spare me from crooners and wailing women, sending only music!). I shall be glad, too, and if you can thank the Institute of Bankers for their parcel of books. My April parcel arrived safely on Tuesday. It really is marvellous how you manage to find the stuff these days. Pears soap again, a real luxury — and chocolate, oh boy! I can't think of anything else I'll need for months except perhaps a towel and a steel mirror. Like the Glamour Girl: "Baby, I've got everything".

By the Seaside

When Peggy returned from her leave, she was moved to Shorncliffe near Folkestone in Kent.

Hatton Cottage, Lubbock Rd, Chislehurst, Kent.
4.9.43.

My job is running six small houses, catering, etc. two cooks and 4 orderlies. One cook was at Crown Quay, a fat companionable woman of 45, the other an extremely nice young girl who takes things calmly — the others here seem a decent crowd and our "pipper" leaves me in supreme command and even obeys me herself! She just bought an adorable baby bulldog which, when she's out, is one of my many responsibilities. The orderlies take their time but work well, in fact I consider I am really very lucky, unhappily it is only temporary, but I feel if I do well, and the full corporal ever gives up the job I may get back and be all ready to welcome you to your dear old cliffs and quaint pubs.

Prisoner No. 3275. Oflag VII B.5th September 1943.

Parole walks have been started here and I am hoping to have my name down whilst this fine September weather lasts. The country looks marvellous, but I am going to miss somebody very much as I walk over the hill.

Hatton Cottage, Lubbock Rd, Chislehurst, Kent.
8.9.43.

I'm getting very tanned with this lovely air and yesterday I had to go to the doctor with several girls and sat and watched the lovely sea and came back burning terrifically. It's rather sweet, my orderlies and cooks want to ask for me to stay here permanently and not the other girl. They seem to like me! Strange, they usually hate people who supervise them. It's a lovely September this year — early mists on the cliffs and gorgeous sunsets and moon — isn't it a gypsy moon? As I write I can just see the sea and long for a bathe but have stacks of deskwork all afternoon and then orderly and stooge again — twice in one week. A bit hard.

Prisoner No. 3275. Oflag VII B.
10th September 1943.

I expect Cyril will be doing his stuff soon and if I know him it is a job he will do damn well. Oh, to be in circulation again. Shorty, by the way, is 39 has a wife and two sons and I believe cares for nothing in the world but them. He enlisted out of patriotism and was caught in Greece before he hardly knew "shun" from "easy".

Hatton Cottage, Lubbock Rd, Chislehurst, Kent.
12.9.43.

I've a desk full of work I've left for a week. It's dreadful but deskwork gets me. Tell Mac this job is a million times worse than in his day — more paper daily to make returns on. I've a man who camouflages the absence of my returns but he's beginning to pester me to go out with him — ugh, an old man of 60, so I'd better do my own chores for a change.

19.9.43.

I am rather browned off as I had a ½ day pass to go to the Locks but had to cancel it at lunch time as I took over 18 more girls and four houses and a whole rearrangement of cooking and messing to be made. However, I am damn well going to take one during the week, have my hair done, meet Mother for tea and do a flick with her; that is if she is better as she's had shingles, not very badly but it's a slow recuperation.

Prisoner No. 3275. Oflag VII B.
20th September 1943.

Please darling, do not regard me as being badly off here. We are at ease while the whole world is locked in a death struggle, and we have no claim to bravery whatever. Your moral courage Peggy far surpasses my own. The full difficulties you have in getting these things has only recently dawned on me. Please, I beg of you, don't send more chocolate. We live very well indeed, and in our idleness, tend to be greedy. Then too, I can make a razor blade last ten days by a method a German soldier taught me. And I can honestly say I have enough clothes for two years. Come to supper tonight darling. We are having a "bash" and I'm cook; egg, cheese and potato pie, raisin tart (You should taste my pastry made from ground biscuits), sardines on toast, coffee and real butter (Canadian). I think you had better earn the living; I'll cook and look after the children.

Hatton Cottage, Lubbock Rd, Chislehurst, Kent.
23.9.43.

Darling, be brave my prayers are very near you. Grandfather died quietly last night. Mother rang me a little while ago. I can't find any words to say darling except perhaps this, he died very, very proud of his grandsons as well he might be and happy to have met me so recently. I'll remember him as a very intelligent, handsome man full of praise for you — in many ways you are like him. I'm so very proud to have met him and can now talk to you of him. He had been ailing lately and death was the kindest for a man so active, and what an age he lived to! So darling my thoughts and prayers are very near you in your sadness — he did so long to see us together, and I like to think he found happiness in approving of me as your wife. Mother seemed very shaken by his death, but then her shingles won't help matters.

Prisoner No. 3275. Oflag VII B.
24th September 1943.

I'm glad you didn't come to supper on Sunday. My pie was awful.

Hatton Cottage, Lubbock Rd, Chislehurst, Kent.
27.9.43.

Before I forget here's the contents of your September parcel: 1 rug (small), 3 pairs socks, 1 towel, 1 face flannel, 3 "Coty" shaving sticks (nice smell), 2 toothbrushes, 1 tin tooth powder, 1 hairbrush, 2 dusters, 2 bundles pipe cleaners, 3 reels of cotton, black, white and khaki, 1 pair braces, 2 tins Soldiers Friend,[30] 4 boot polish: 2 brown, 2 black, 36 razor blades, 1 hair comb, 2 ½ lbs chocolate, chewing gum! Are your measurements the same as before in case I could get a uniform darling?

Prisoner No. 3275. Oflag VII B.
30.09.1943.

Incidentally IF I have passed in the four papers I took recently and IF I pass the two I am working for at present, the Bank should credit me with £30. We'll earmark that for your post war wardrobe. I hope to take the Inter C.I.S. early next month and the Inter BSc. in December but examination dates are always somewhat problematic.

---

[30] This is a brand of metal polish also used in World War 1 by soldiers to polish their buttons, belts, etc.

Hatton Cottage, Lubbock Rd, Chislehurst, Kent.
3.10.43.

Darling the worst has happened! Cyril has turned up half a mile away from me! We'll both have to mind our "Ps" and "Qs" now — what a job! He's very important and on the bus coming back from the Fehr's farm where I spent the afternoon two of his privates were passing very flattering remarks about him. I had to give them some apples to shut them up.

Prisoner No. 3275. Oflag VII B.
4th October 1943.

I have spent the whole day in the room overlooking the river. The C.I.S. papers are in at long last, and we are to take the exam next week, meanwhile I am making frantic efforts to relearn what I have forgotten in the last 3 months.

14th October 1943.

The exam went off fairly well, but I am not too happy about yesterday's paper — my mind is far too far from my body these days. Guess where and with whom?

Hatton Cottage, Lubbock Rd, Chislehurst, Kent.
27.10.43.

Here's something very unofficial from the Secretary of the Institute, she says you have passed: Death Duties, Trust Accounting, Practical Trust Admin, Wills haven't come through yet. Darling, many, many big hugs, I knew you'd do it. They didn't tell me the markings but say it's very good the way you have done so well in the circumstances. Oh boy you sure are clever — I never even heard of Trust Accounting, etc.!

The British Red Cross Society, Prisoners of War Department, The New Bodleian, Oxford.
29th October, 1943.

Dear Madam,

BR/LK-Lieut. A.E. Horton3275, Oflag VIIB.

As you probably know your husband is a candidate for various professional examinations. At his request we have sent him the necessary textbooks, of which please find the list overleaf. Despite the fact that all the Banking books are a gift of the Institute of Bankers, we have spent nearly £6 on his books, which is practically double the amount we usually feel justified in spending on any individual man. We are therefore writing to hear from you whether you could help us with the expense. Any contribution you feel able to send us will be very much appreciated.

    Yours faithfully,
    Director.

Prisoner No. 3275. Oflag VII B.
31st October 1943.

Your very sweet letter telling me of Grandfather's death came in on Monday. The news was not altogether unexpected, but it is sad to think I shall never be able to take you to see him. How lucky that you saw him when you did. Mother's letter came in the next day, and I have put in a request for some extra letters so I can write to all concerned. There seems to be some chance that I may be able to get out gathering some wood soon and may even get a visit to the local cinema! It will be a very welcome break — the first time out of the gate for a year. I have had some news of Morley. A newcomer saw him entrained for Germany where presumably he is now. A pity he could not get away. MacCormack has left this week for another district in the interests of his health which has been rather poor for some time. I do hope Charles is all right. From accounts it seems he may have a rough passage.

Hatton Cottage, Lubbock Rd. Chislehurst, Kent.
31.10.43.

Oh, oh, here come the drunks — you'd be amused to hear their songs! "Roll me over" is the one again tonight; it really is a vulgar song. I shoved a lump of carbolic soap in the mouth of an orderly the other day for singing that.

3.11.43.

I had an interview yesterday about returning to the V.A.D.s. I shook the woman by being so keen and most unorthodox — I paced the floor in front of her desk instead of standing at attention! Also had a chat with a very nice Medical Officer and his Colonel who called today to see some sick people and they advise me to return. This Medical Officer is extremely nice, his wife is a doctor too — Scottish they are, and he loves to stand in the sun and talk to me about her and everything in general. I'm off to bed in a few moments as I'm going to Cyril's Officers' Dance tomorrow all in my glory.

7.11.43.

Many, many hugs and kisses and congratulations, your last exam result reached me on Friday — you've passed "Wills" so now you've passed all subjects well. Oh, you are so clever and I'm so proud of you. I arrived at Jennie and Cyril's hotel Thursday teatime, slipped out and had my hair done rather specially, had a bath and ambled through my dressing. I was determined to be "it". Cyril disgraced himself by racing up and down the corridors, whisky in one hand, and wearing only a skimpy towel. However eventually he dressed and came down last to his party — typically Cyril. Pat, his secretary and several other friends from town were there and he remarked to me later, when he was a little tiddly, that Pat's behind was very nice! Really, he is dreadful! Are you the same when you're away from your wife?

Prisoner No. 3275. Oflag VII B.
14th November 1943.

My July parcel arrived yesterday. It was absolutely magnificent, just the things I wanted. How do you manage to find them in these days? My mess-mates all want to know where you get Pears soap, razor blades, pipe cleaners, chocolate, etc. etc. It is only when I hear such questions that I appreciate the enormous amount of trouble you go to, to get the parcel together.

21st November 1943.

Now what can I say to you today? I have searched the camp this morning for a rose to put on your picture, but all are gone. I hope to find something else when I have written this. Your letters of 14th and 20th October came on Friday. I just know how you feel when you see Cyril and Jennie together and Cyril with his command. I too, have to fight bitterness when I hear of promotion of my juniors and remember my past work and hope which came to nothing. But it is life and must be taken on the chin. Soon the wheel will turn full circle and our time will come, meanwhile I am repaid in full by your love and understanding. On Tuesday I went out into the woods on parole to gather fuel. I had half an hour to wander alone, freed for a moment from the eternal sentry and his rifle and bayonet. It was a day such as we love — sunshine in the open and frost in the woodland rides. The leaves thick underfoot and that long missed but never forgotten smell of damp trees. You were very near me that day. I longed to lead you by the hand to share my joy. "Shorty" has asked if you would like to spend a few days with his wife and boys and has asked his wife to write to you. I have no idea of course, what they are like. They run a building business but among us it is reckoned that the world would be better for a few more "Shorties". I have another Banker's exam on 29th and I'm working hard. It is so very cold in the quiet room, and I sit wrapped in scarves and blankets.

Hatton Cottage, Lubbock Rd. Chislehurst, Kent.
21.11.43.

Our thoughts are very close today darling, 3 years your wife, in these three years I've grown to love you many, many times more than I ever thought possible. My heart literally beats within you. I feel so close always my darling, how glad I am we became man and wife. I'll always remember that night at Cobham, there was something very wonderful about it — but a different sort of wonderfulness to our sweet reunion.

23.11.43.

Would you believe it, I'm in bed. I think it's just over tired for with all the sick last week I really was pretty busy. My 24 hours at Mrs Lock's rested me greatly but this morning I just couldn't stand for long. I felt woozy but after a day of sleeping I feel fine. An orderly has been looking after me beautifully — built me a fire, bought me cups of tea and said, "What a pity your husband isn't here to look after you"! My manners are awful, do forgive me. A great bouquet arrived Saturday for me of lovely pinkie, mauve chrysanthemums — "Dearest love Alan". Thank you darling, if only you were here to deliver them, but they look really lovely in my room. Next year that great anniversary will see us together.

28.11.43.

Michael's being married Tuesday next to Jill — poor darlings they'll have 48 hrs together only. I am giving them a cheque to help them for now from us both. I think we can afford five — I gave Pam three, but we have £170 — £180 this month I believe for I've only drawn about £3 and £6 for your books. I'm orderly stooge and have washed my hair as I want it to look nice for Tuesday — have managed leave from about 6 o'clock Monday night to 23.00 hrs Tuesday. Jill's house is near Oxted. Pat's home on leave, Diana's home as you know.

Prisoner No. 3275. Oflag VII B.
30th November1943.

I have been to the cinema! Last Tuesday we marched into the town and saw quite a good film with English captions, a newsreel and a good film about horses. You cannot understand the thrill unless you have been shut up. Then too, the cinema decorations were very attractive. They reminded me that it is three years since I walked on a carpet or sat on a padded chair. What will it mean to me when I see you again, is more than I can begin to express. I managed to find a posy for your photograph on 21st but since then the weather has been foul, snow and sleet and the garden is finished for the year. I did a paper yesterday on "Investment" and think I did rather well. A solicitor in the mess is instructing me for the "Real Property" paper on Friday. It is a very difficult subject, and I cannot approach it with the same confidence.

Hatton Cottage, Lubbock Rd. Chislehurst, Kent.
2.12.43.

Now news of Michael's wedding. It was a very nice one, Jill looked lovely in white, and her sister was bridesmaid in white. I'm sending you the photos when I get them. Michael has a ribbon up for some service ███████████████. They were married in the pretty old church in Limpsfield. Uncle Billy, Pop's older brother, came — I'd not seen him for years. He saw Pendill recently when he was over here, and P asked very kindly after you.

Prisoner No. 3275. Oflag VII B.
5th December 1943.

The real property paper on Friday was a horror and I fear I've failed in spite of much work. Anyway, I'm taking a rest until Monday and then getting ready for the third jump. My September parcel arrived safely on Friday. The rug is absolutely ideal and arrived just as the hard frosts set in. As usual you have anticipated my wants marvellously.

10th December 1943.

Yesterday we went to the cinema again and saw a film about the Strauss family, a "Tour of Dresden" and the weekly newsreel. The last is like our own and very interesting. They differ in that ours prove the undoubted superiority of the English and these, the undoubted superiority of the Germans! In the interval we went to the Roman Catholic Cathedral — a very beautiful building indeed. Which reminded me of another, even more beautiful, and a date I have with a certain young woman, she is married too! These trips out are a great boon. Standing in that building yesterday I could drink in the beauty to the full. One has to sink to the very bottom before one can really start to live.

14th December 1943.

Two grand letters, Oct 26th and 31st. I give you full marks for getting my exam results so quickly. They were a pleasant surprise and I hope the luck holds for the others. We too, have but few hot baths, at present we get one hot shower a week, sometimes only one a month, but I have become something of a Spartan and go under the cold tap (sometimes!) in the morning. My gramophone records arrived yesterday but it will be some days before I get them — just in time for Christmas. What memories they will conjure up.

Hatton Cottage, Lubbock Road, Chislehurst, Kent.
16.12.43.

This is a series of ridiculous interviews so I'm pumping them hard to see if I can get back to the V.A.D.s. 17th This epistle ended abruptly last evening, the room was full of yapping women talking guns, M.T. and a hundred other silly things each trying to outdo the other. After tea we had one interview and all day we've had one test after another, all mad psychological ideas, tests that schoolchildren are better at than older people. One elderly C.S.M. can't do a single test yet she is a clever woman. However, all this may lead to my transfer. Later: just seen the Medical Officer and she insists I take a commission and put me down for that so I'm more muddled than ever. What a life. Her argument is that I have every qualification for a pip, more than most people and why not use it. I agreed but what about my release on your return? My intelligence tests have come — maths bad, everything else including spelling, good and I'm earmarked for a pip for intelligence — all sounds too important to me.

19.12.43.

Here I am at home finishing off my leave that was cut short by the course. I've got an extra night by haring away at 6 o'clock last night and came home to my comfy warm bed. It's dreadful to say that when you sleep on a hard bed and probably none too warm darling — forgive me? My final interview was with a very nice, high officer. She was married and more human — I was one of the honoured two girls out of 20 to see her! She's very keen for me to get a pip and says I could get out on your return but meanwhile I have to leave my company and study admin from all angles. Actually, I'm hoping to pull a few strings and work in town on something really vital and interesting in the office line under a man like Cyril. I told her I'd rather be under a man, they are more logical. Today I went over to see Sonia at Egham and came back after tea. She's very fit and sends you her love. She has a grand job in luxury as I pulled her leg but a lot of responsibility. Martin apparently expects his majority soon, Charles S has his, but Martin wishes it was you as he says Charles isn't half as good as you would have been. I heartily agree. Oh darling, you'll be amused, at one of my interviews they told me I obviously had the social background, education and experience to be an officer — ugh! Smarmy lot. 20th — I'll certainly contact Mrs Stokes and try and get up on my next leave. Burford's a lovely part of Oxfordshire too.

25.12.43.

Christmas Day and all day you've been very near to me my sweet. My hopes are all out for our next Xmas together. Yesterday was very busy getting in food and last-minute baking for which I enlisted the help of a driver as the cooks hadn't time. By 6 o'clock the other N.C.O.s ordered me to stop and go out to an E.N.S.A. Concert with them. It was very amusing, one of those four-star companies like you used to have — not as smutty as I had expected. They then made me go on to a hotel in which the officer's club is — we literally fought our way in and stood whilst 2 and 3 pippers gave us the once over. Our main aim was to get a lift home afterwards out of one of our partners, but the place was an absolute paradise for drunks — you walked on broken bottles, men lurched into you. Being with friends we felt it was the first "do" of that sort and it was an education, but once was sufficient — we walked home! This was very pleasant under the stars and a distant Salvation Army band playing carols to which a huge number of people were singing as they walked past, a white frost, it really was lovely. This morning was up early for we took the girls tea in bed and cooked their breakfast, built fires etc. Then I had two visitors, a couple of Medical Officers with whom we are going out tonight. Lunch we had with the men — very amusing. Pop rang up today, the first thing I've heard from my family at home, not even a card!

Prisoner No. 3275. Oflag VII B.
26th December 1943.

In spite of the date, I am actually writing this on Christmas evening. As days go here it has been a good one. We went to Communion at 7 am and a carol service, with choir and orchestra at 10.30. "Tucker" has been very good and there are several recumbent figures on the bunks around me as I write. But the great thing has been five letters from you and the records. I have read and re-read the former and played over the latter time and again.

1944 — Nearly There!

Prisoner No. 3275. Oflag VII B.
2nd January 1944.

I've so much to say I don't know where to start. I've had a big bag of 14 assorted letters since my last, so you see how impossible it is to attempt an answer. I do hope your flu is now better but expect by now you have forgotten it. The dance sounds terrific. I'd give anything for a night on the jazz like that. As for my dear brother I've something in my locker to deal with him when we next meet! I hope he doesn't forget his running shoes as I did! I hope you get some news of Charles soon; I'm getting rather concerned about him. On Wednesday we went to the cinema and saw "Baron Munchausen",[31] a new German colour film. It was a magnificent spectacle with some magnificent cuties. In the camp we've had our own Panto. It was an absolute riot. "Lights out" was not until 12.30 and we all went quite mad. I could not get a certain woman out of my mind until nearly 4 o'clock this morning. Guess who darling? I have learnt to combat ice and snow with a cold bath every morning. I am almost indecently fit again.

---

[31] *Baron Munchausen* — a fantasy comedy film made in Germany in 1943 and directed by Josef von Baky.

PROGRAMME

Bobby Loder

presents

"DOSSING DULCIE"

A
Pantomime
in
Three Acts

Book & Lyrics by Bobby Loder
Tim Munby & Frank Stewart.

MUSIC
by
ERIC ARDEN

Eichstätt – Christmas 1943

Hatton Cottage, Lubbock Rd, Chislehurst, Kent.
2.1.44.

I meant to write to you late New Year's Eve sitting by my bedroom fire, but I cut my thumb badly opening a tin of corned beef; however, it's healed enough to hold a pen today. I'm orderly stooge so how long I'll be left in peace I don't know. But darling a very Happy New Year, it will be a special year for us, I know. I don't believe in signs or as you would say, "women's intuition" but as Big Ben on the radio struck twelve, New Year's Eve, something snapped within me, and a great joy made me cry for I felt so certain our waiting is nearly over and '44 is the year we've been waiting and hoping for all these years. Yesterday I trailed by bus all the way to Gore Court for an interview with a big-wig. I let her have her say first which was that my selection board had recommended me for O.C.T.U. and it's rare a girl is recommended. In her opinion I ought to go up and try it! There's no getting out of it now but why they should recommend me of all people I can't imagine.

14.1.44.

Another interview over, this time our Commanding Officer. Rather hale and hearty but married and definitely reeks of whisky that may humanise her. She said, "My Dear Horton, old thing, you'll sail through your O.C.T.U." Blimey! Wish you were here darling to help me.

25.1.44.

I'm up in the office now and have a grand view of the sea over the fields — a little bay between two lovely sloping hills. I like the work better and my brain, even after 8 hours, feels it's having more use. After 7th Feb I'm alone to run it as the other girl goes on leave and I have to do it, minus the stripes and no doubt in a week or two will have to go on my O.C.T.U. Board. Hold your thumbs darling, I feel now, strange to say, I just must get through.

Prisoner No. 3275. Oflag VII B.
25th January 1944.

I had a grand walk on Tuesday. We were allowed to wander at will for nearly two hours in a beautiful valley of pines and beeches. You cannot imagine what a treat it is to be alone for a while with no noise other than the soughing of wind in the trees. Noise is inseparable from camp life, solitude, an impossibility. But I felt again, very acutely, the longing for a certain companion of mine. How much longer, my beloved, before I can stretch out my hand and feel yours steal into it? One other excitement, a fellow who sleeps in the bunk below me went "nuts" the other day and had to be carried away. I think some of these fellows regard this life as a major and insurmountable disaster instead of a trial of faith from which they can and should emerge all the stronger. But perhaps I judge too harshly. Perhaps they have no Pegasus on whom to lean. I thank Him and you for all you are to me. I still keep up my cold baths — the bathroom is a brick room in the centre of the hut, with a concrete floor, a drain in the middle and a tap about 3 feet from the floor against one wall. The postures of nude Spartans crawling under it in the cold light of a winter's morning are too funny for words.

Hatton Cottage, Lubbock Rd, Chislehurst, Kent.
2.2.44.

Incidentally my O.C.T.U. Board is next week for 48 hours, either the 8th or 10th. Tomorrow night I'm going to watch a play done by some of the girls in aid of the Red Cross P.O.W. Fund. It should be very good.

6.2.44.

I am glad to have got away here this afternoon to collect myself as I have my O.C.T.U. Board Tuesday. It's scaring me a little. I go home late tomorrow night as I'm not allowed a long journey before it. One has to arrive by 11.30 all fresh and oozing self-confidence. The moment you enter the doorway you are watched, stripped of your character and personality and if you react favourably to hours of gruelling psychological tests just as certain individuals lay down a female officer should be, you pass, and as a leaving present are given your character back till pre O.C.T.U. which is the worst of all, up at 4 am cleaning latrines — all very good for one no doubt but no bloody man or woman will remove what character I have, and I mean to do my upmost to get through.

Prisoner No. 3275. Oflag VII B.
9th February 1944.

I am delighted about the O.C.T.U. You will be a great success, I know. I will write more on this tomorrow. Glad to hear letters are getting home better. We've been rather worried about this. June and September parcels arrived safely. We're getting some real winter weather now, today the snow is thick and the sun shining — rather pleasant but cold.

Hatton Cottage, Lubbock Rd, Chislehurst, Kent.
11.2.44.

I'm on tender-hooks now for the result of my Board — they pass some extraordinary people and why the hell they fuss over my stammer! It will send me crazy if they fail me on that. One testing officer is the wife of a man with you called Bailey. Her rank is Junior Commander, and she is very nice, but oh how I loathe it all at heart, but if I have passed, I mean to do all I can to bring you home soon. Incidentally, I hope to go to staff-college!

Prisoner No. 3275. Oflag VII B.
14th February 1944.

Winter has descended on us in earnest. Through the window I can see long icicles hanging from the eaves opposite, one is quite 4 feet long. Everything looks really lovely under the snow but it's damnably cold. I am longing to hear some more about the O.C.T.U. Perhaps more mail will come in next week — Good luck anyway.

Hatton Cottage, Lubbock Rd, Chislehurst, Kent.
18.2.44.

Just heard I've passed for O.C.T.U. I need some help and shall have to have some Dutch courage. Just been doing pay for nearly 50 people and my brain's weary — only paid 5 people wrong! Gosh, you are grand — cold baths in this cold. I am so proud of the way you combat the boredom and weariness of just waiting, it's magnificent.

After Peggy's interview board, she returned to her duties at Shorncliffe to wait for the O.C.T.U. itself. She was given the rank of private but expected to do the work she had done as a lance corporal. She remained in Shorncliffe until granted her discharge late in 1944. She was never called to attend the O.C.T.U. partly, one suspects, because, despite working very hard, she also had various lengthy periods of sick leave.

Prisoner No. 3275. Oflag VII B.
20th February 1944.

Have no fear about that commission, darling. It is as good as yours. I have remitted £145 home and hope to send some more from time to time. It will help towards our home. Tell Everett that this is regarded as income arising abroad and not to subject it to income tax. The "old lags" from France and Norway are getting very excited as rumours have arrived in letters, saying that negotiations for their repatriation are in progress. Have you heard anything about it? We are having a Musical Festival in the camp which promises to be good. Noel and I still keep up our Spartan activities in spite of the cold and are very fit. This fortnight has been very cold, and our huts have the most magnificent icicles. The record one is nearly 7 feet.

I was overjoyed to hear about your O.C.T.U. for long past I have been very concerned about your being so open to insult from troops and having to live with people having so little in common with them. I know you will be much happier and make a great success of it. But if you are a Colonel when I see you next, I promise my salute will hardly accord with Rules and Regulations! However, whatever it is will not be for long. We have great maps of Russia and Italy on the walls and amend the battle fronts daily from the papers — the perfect arm-chair soldiers without the arm-chairs. My records are in great demand, and we have all fallen in love with Marian Anderson's[32] singing. Good records are few here but occasionally we borrow some and have a concert in the mess.

---

[32] Marian Anderson 1897-1993, a black American contralto, the first to be invited to sing at the White House.

THE MUSIC FESTIVAL

EICHSTÄTT
FEBRUARY 1944

Hatton Cottage, Lubbock Rd, Chislehurst, Kent.
23.2.44.

Got up about 11 o'clock — the Medical Officer came this afternoon and saw me outside and said, "Thought I ordered you to bloody well stay in bed till I came." I said, "yes, but I didn't agree. The man went off muttering, "Your poor husband having such a disobedient wife!" Whilst in bed I finished off completely that white nightie I've had on the go for years. It looks lovely and fits well where it touches beautifully. One of the orderlies saw it and said, "You better not wear that on your first night, or it will be too much for your husband!"

5.3.44.

This afternoon I went with a friend to the Fehr's farm by car as she had a job nearby. We had a lovely lazy time and wandered around in the sun — daffs are in bud and many other spring flowers. In spite of the terrific cold lately spring seems early. Mrs Carslaw gave us a lovely tea and gave me some logs for my fire and 6 eggs to bring back! My first almost since Xmas issue of one each.

Prisoner No. 3275. Oflag VII B.
20th March 1944.

One fellow has heard he has passed his Inter. I.C.S. so we are all hanging on for ours. I shall be very disappointed if I fail for I have worked very hard for that and the finals. The second Banker's results should be available soon too. Incidentally, if you get any bills for books do not pay without referring to me. Please congratulate Everett on his promotion. Please tell him I will be in active competition with him soon for jobs.

31st March 1944.

My January parcel arrived safely this week. The chocolate was marvellous and Pears soap again. How do you manage it, darling? You really must not stint yourself of chocolate we honestly do ourselves pretty well. If you have to send one in July, can I please have a Gunner's Beret and 2 shirts? I shall probably want some by then. I hope the 48 hrs with Mrs Stokes materialises and you have a good time. He (Stumpy/or Shorty) feels very keenly his boys growing up while he is away. It is damn bad luck. His bed is surrounded by photos of his family, and he marks his boys' heights on his bedpost every time he gets a new measurement. It's strange how he and I have become friends for we have nothing in common except a loving for family life.

I have packed up study except in the evenings and get as much exercise as I can. But I have a new hobby — embroidery. I made myself some cloth "pips" and did the job so well I have been inundated with orders. I earned 9 Marks with my needle in 3 days and have orders for about 15 Marks more. Will you please see if you can get my exam results from the Bankers' and the Secretaries' Institute? The results will decide my course of study. I enclose a programme of Hamlet as this was absolutely magnificent in acting and staging. I only wish you could see one of these shows.

Hatton Cottage, Lubbock Rd, Chislehurst, Kent.
14.4.44.

A letter arrived this evening. The Master of Balliol and Miss Herdman of the New Bodleian wish to congratulate you on passing your Intermediate C.I.S. so very well. God, I'm pleased darling. Imagine my terrific hug of congratulations and add them to the balance a/c to be settled up on your return.

20.4.44.

Darling, great news — The Bodleian, Alan have written again to say you have passed successfully; Law of Real Property, and Practical Trust Administration with distinction — I am very thrilled and almost feel like saying "I told you so, darling!" With all these grand results you must not feel you have wasted these weary years — I am just longing to hear all your plans for our future. You'll make a good job of whatever you do I am convinced.

23.4.44.

Incidentally darling your April parcel contained: 1 bush shirt and tie, 3 pairs socks, 2 toothbrushes and powder, 3 bars of soap — one Pears, 1 shaving bowl refill, 1 nail brush, 3 black boot polish, 3 brown, 1 Soldiers Friend, 2 pairs oxidized pips, 1 large packet Eversharp heads, 37 Razor Blades, 1 large duster, 2 face flannels, 4 handkerchiefs, 6 pairs boot and shoe laces, 1 skein khaki mending, 1 double photo frame, 1 khaki beret and badge, 1 hair comb, 1 bundle (large) pipe cleaners, about 4 ½ lbs chocks. Daddy made it up to the maximum amount with Red Cross chocolates. I can just hear the cuckoo and we heard a lark today so beautifully and it is grand to think dreary winter is over and also the winter of our lives. There's so much to look forward too so keep the old chin up my brave darling.

29.4.44

Talking of my O.C.T.U, I've still not gone and in many ways I'd far rather stay on here although I'm unpaid, acting rank etc. and I shall never get any further. This annoys Pop — he's always on about my education and brains but when commissioned £. s. d. will no doubt need more thinking about. Apart from the financial side, life here will be much more interesting and friendlier, then too it will take at least three months to go through it all and I'd barely put my pips up, that is, IF I get through.

Prisoner No. 3275. Oflag VII B.
4th May 1944.

We have had no letters in since I last wrote. We hope it's only a temporary hold up. This, with cold, wet weather, has made life rather dull and today I am feeling rather sorry for myself as I have had a tooth extracted and disgraced myself by passing out. It was my old friend from Crete — or rather "so and so". During the bright intervals Noel and I do great work in the garden. We now have a patch of our own. It's a great life for saving money if nothing else.

Anything, even unpleasant, bringing relief from "each day the twin of that which went before"[33] would have done. And then, Hey Presto, a circus came to town, and we went on Friday morning, 1,200 of us. It was a perfect spring morning, meadows gay with flowers, birds singing. The circus ran true to form — good turns, clowns, and animals under a "big top". I am sure we each got as much delight from it as small boys seeing one for the first time (and I could actually understand the clown's jokes in German!).

But that's not all, nor yet the best. We heard on our return that 5,000 letters had arrived and since then I've had 5, yours of March 26th, 28th and 30th and Mothers of March 26th and April 2nd. What delight to see your writing again after so long.

The visit to 'Circus Hellas' was celebrated in the camp magazine, Touchstone, *in July/August 1944. Page eleven contains a selection of drawings showing clowns, acrobats, horses and scantily clad females under the title 'An Impression of the Circus'. The work is initialled 'PH' and drawings are listed under 'contents' as coming from a number of contributors, including P. L. Hansen-Bay (The King's Royal Rifle Corps). Lieutenant Harwood explained the circus included a mangy lion close to death, two bears that were 'not on speaking terms' and a llama. The ringmaster was German, but the others were Poles, Austrians, Czechs and Slovaks. There was a trapeze act, a strong man and woman performing balancing acts, two clowns and a tuneless band dressed in tattered uniforms and unable to keep time. To the men, however, the chance to be out and see a show was a great treat, made all the more memorable by*

---

[33] Christmas 1943, Poem by Captain Randall Sly, Royal Warwickshire Regiment, 23rd December 1943.

a girl whose attire was briefer than her limited equestrian abilities and whose juggling with bowler hats deteriorated the more the men cheered!

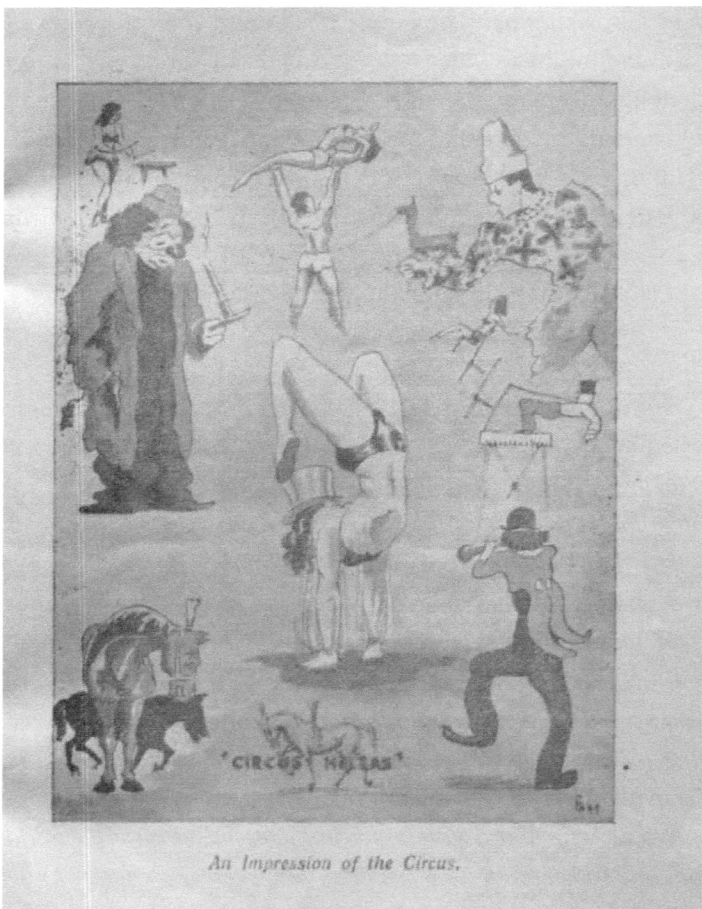

An Impression of the Circus.

Touchstone recalls the visit to the circus.

Hatton Cottage, Lubbock Rd, Chislehurst, Kent.
19.5.44.

Can you imagine what Pop's done? He's selling the house in August. He's threatened it so often and told me to clear out all our things and we've laughed and said it will never materialise. Pam knows no more than I do. Dear me, I have forgotten all about the P.O.W. Exhibition. A picture of one of the villages near here I recognised having walked there for tea one Sunday. I saw your name up for passing your exams. VII B figured mainly in the religious hut, several pamphlets on "life and prayers" which I like awfully darling. Several photos of boxing matches — tried hard to make one spectator look like you. He was laughing and tall but somehow wasn't quite you. Kettles made out of tins, blankets that made one still! — is that so? The most wonderful tapestry and wood carving efforts.

Prisoner No. 3275. Oflag VII B.
25th May 1944.

I can never see your handwriting too often. My Banker's exam results came in last night so there will be another certificate for our collection. As for "Distinction", I think there must be some mistake! There remains now only the Inter I.C.S. if I've cleared that jump, I shall take the finals and call it a day *(See Appendix 2)*.

Hatton Cottage, Lubbock Rd, Chislehurst, Kent.
3.6.44.

In an earlier letter I mentioned I wasn't going on my course for a while and didn't mean to say why until after my visit of yesterday to the specialist. You see the Medical Officer stated I was too tired to stand all the heavy physical work on it and wanted a better opinion. After 2 visits to the specialist — a very clever man incidentally. He has come to the conclusion it's a lack of vitamins, that's causing my terrific desire to sleep and dizziness, and gives me bad attacks of pain at times. I believe he's right and hence the reason for all the talk of physical disability since my appendix operation, so he sent me to buy some tablets including pretty well every vitamin — 16/6 per 100! — and for six weeks. I have to take it pretty quietly which is pretty hard.

Prisoner No. 3275. Oflag VII B.
6th June 1944.

Needless to say, overshadowing all else these days is the invasion, and the camp is seething with excitement. After waiting so long we became almost delirious on seeing the headline in the paper, "Und so began die Schlat im Western". Tomorrow (Sunday) we are having a good bash of food we have saved for the occasion and, incidentally, are celebrating the King's birthday. I hate to think I cannot fight at a time like this. It is all wrong that the family should not be represented. However, we think and hope it is the beginning of the end and soon I shall be holding you in my arms again Peggy.

Hatton Cottage, Lubbock Rd, Chislehurst, Kent.
11.6.44.

Incidentally, here's your exam results to date from Lloyds H.Q. they wish to be remembered to you. Institute of Bankers' — the whole of the Executor and Trusteeship Examination has been successfully completed. Chartered Institute of Secretaries, the Intermediate Examination was passed last year. Papers for the final examination have been sent out and the examination is expected to take place this month. Good luck my darling, you'll pass. You really are wonderful to have passed so well, you must be a very brainy man!

Prisoner No. 3275. Oflag VII B.
11th July 1944.

I am very brown and spend nearly all day outdoors when the weather is good. We had a very hot period recently, but it ended with one of the biggest thunderstorms I have ever seen on Saturday night. Since then, it has been lousy. Our flower garden was knocked flat, but Noel has done some good work on it, and it is recovering slowly. The Brigade Garden is flourishing too, and we get lettuce and onions regularly. It is a real treat to have green vegetables regularly after so much tinned food.

Alan used to tell us that to prevent them getting scurvy the prisoners were encouraged to eat the leaves of an acacia tree in the camp grounds when fresh fruit and vegetables were scarce.

Hatton Cottage, Lubbock Rd, Chislehurst, Kent.
13ᵗʰ July '44.

A perfectly grand letter yesterday, May 31ˢᵗ and that enclosure by the Warwickshire Captain is most amusing — Duke! Funny you were nicknamed the "Duke", I remember how I was nicknamed the "Duchess". We must look a rather snooty pair.

Prisoner No. 3275. Oflag VII B.
31ˢᵗ July 1944.

Our garden is a mass of flowers; from my new seat under the limes, I look up from my books, across the garden and the sports field below, over the river and the meadows to the wooded hills beyond. On parole walks the country is gay with flowers and wild fruits. On cinema visits the old town sleeps in its quaint streets and sun-bathed squares. But nothing has for me any depth or fullness. All beauty whether of sight or hearing, reminds me of you and that empty place at my side. Noel sometimes thinks me heartless, and I've heard myself sometimes described as "grim" and "terrifying". The truth is that I dare not display any emotions at all. The camp is full of kittens and our George lives in our room and visits me when I read on my bunk. I had seven playing around my chair in the garden yesterday.

Hatton Cottage, Lubbock Rd, Chislehurst, Kent.
31.7.44.

I was told the other day I'd never manage people till I become b---
-- minded! I ask you. As I had to be slightly respectful to this
dignitary I coldly replied, "I have no desire to be looked upon as an
old bitch!" It shook her but I turned on a very charmingly artificial
smile and no more was said. Kindness and tact is the way to treat
"difficult girls".

Prisoner No. 3275. Oflag VII B.
24th August 1944.

I told you about two weeks ago 14,000 letters awaited censoring
and I was hoping for some late dates? Well, I'm still hoping. The
last 200 yards take nearly as long as 500 miles. But tails are up, and
hopes are high and if we don't celebrate our wedding anniversary
together, I shall be very surprised.

Hatton Cottage, Lubbock Rd, Chislehurst, Kent.
27.8.44.

Bloomire and I spent yesterday afternoon sunbathing and bathing
in the sea and coaxed the bulldog into the sea. It was heavenly and
today the owners of the "Kent" have invited us to use their private
beach and have tea there too. This is something we appreciate
greatly — no undressing in corners of offices behind towels with
the fear of prying male eyes! I'm off any date soon for a month's
rest at Rivers Hall so you never know we may continue our left off

honeymoon there. A senior Doctor friend of mine (no special friend, more business actually) has been a real wrangler and said I needed a rest as I'm taking thyroid for three months to tone up again and need a holiday. He really said to me that it would be a good thing before you return! But the thyroid is the excuse. I feel guilty at this great time having a holiday, but he insisted that it was no reason for a guilty feeling and that you come first which is so true darling one.

Prisoner No. 3275. Oflag VII B.
28th August 1944.

Four grand letters today, May 9th, 14th 29th and June 11th. Each day means more letters from early May to late July, and it will be days before it is all censored so you can imagine the bewildering order in which we get them. The idea of a house for our leave is grand and you are quite right to insist it is far from relatives. That is the main reason I do not intend to return to Sandwich branch and I know you will approve. As the time draws near, I can scarcely contain my impatience. Reading and study are well-nigh impossible; sport helps and sunbathing, but my eyes keep wandering to the hills and sky and my mind and spirit leap the distance to be with you. How true was it written, "Where your heart is, there will your treasure be also".[34] You are my treasure, you have all my heart. Spirits and optimism are still high but only a miracle can get me home for your birthday, perhaps mine or for our wedding anniversary and then that terrific day! I shall be the fellow swimming ahead of the ship!

---

[34] "Where your treasure is, there will your heart be also" — Matthew's Gospel chapter 6 verse 21.

4th September 1944.

One more letter from you, 7th May, which had taken 4 months! I feel sure that soon I shall write a letter to you and be home before the card. I wonder if this is the one? We dive for the papers daily and adjust our battle lines. Lately they have gone so fast and have caused such tension it is impossible to concentrate on anything but the question "when?" I am so madly excited, my darling that I can do nothing but roam about the camp like a caged beast.

Hatton Cottage, Lubbock Rd, Chislehurst, Kent.
6.9.44.

My sick leave came through yesterday. I had a terrific row, and it came through in under four hours after that, so home I came. I'm going to Rivers Hall Saturday afternoon by train. How I wish you were on it, darling.

Rivers Hall, Boxted, Nr. Colchester, Essex.
17.9.44.

I have applied and, for some miraculous reason, have been given another 14 days leave — 28 in all! Actually, I'm very glad and I'm fully occupied which makes the time fly by. I churn butter, do housework as Auntie only has a daily help from 9–12 o'clock, arrange flowers, read and sew. I'm making a very pretty powder blue blouse at the moment — some material I bought with my trousseau silks early in '41.

Prisoner No. 3275. Oflag VII B.
18.9.44.

Optimism here has been somewhat damped by recent events but not so my own. I still think and hope we shall be together for Nov. 21st for leap years have usually been significant in my life and I see no reason why this should not run to form! I am still working in the wood-yard with axe and cross-cut saw and keep very fit. Weather is changing but good for the moment.

When I thought mail was at an end, letters of June 23rd, September 3rd and 10th arrived. I have got a stiff neck from somewhere and in consequence have had a touch of the blues. It is always the same when the weather is cold and one is a bit below par, it seems that the damned war will never end.

In spite of what the papers say I still hope to be with you for our anniversary or, at the latest, by Christmas. As I said before I have great faith in leap years! The valley is turning gold and brown again with autumn and looks very lovely. Although there are no parole walks or cinema walks now, I hope to go with a party soon getting tree stumps for firewood. This is the object of my present job in the wood yard. Last year's party say it is very hard work indeed, but it is a change and should toughen me up after all my studying. I have given up hope of taking my finals here and physical labour is a pleasant change. Yesterday we had a visitation from the protecting power and also medical board which passed 29 for repatriation. It is very nice for them, but I am thankful for my health and strength.

Hatton Cottage, Lubbock Rd, Chislehurst, Kent.
8.10.44.

It's just as well to be away from duty whilst my unorthodox application for resignation is going through, though I will no doubt have a stormy interview, but who cares? I can take this particular so and so on. We dislike each other, anyway she says I've too much of a mind of my own. I think she's too sodden with whisky to be any good, so there you are.

20.10.44.

Mother's arriving at Bromley at 5.30 and I have got a taxi to call for me and to go on and fetch her. Its dreadful weather so it looks as though the fireside will be our main activity. Daddy went off today on his trip. I've found out why he's gone earlier, one job is near where his girl-friend is, hence a weekend there I suppose! 21st Well Mother arrived safely looking very fit and very much fatter, quite round in fact. She certainly has a very large appetite and seems to be summoning up my cookery to see whether I'll feed you well. She keeps saying, "Yes, Alan will eat this," or "He will like this."

22.10.44.

Dr Moore came yesterday to see me and had tea with us — he's stopped my thyroid that the Folkestone man gave me. It's likely to do more harm than good and I've felt better without it. He won't let me return yet — there's no wrangling with him, but he says after all my time done, I need to rest and get ready for your return.

25.10.44

Mother's washing some clothes through before she goes on to some relatives at Wallington tomorrow. We had a good day in town yesterday — went up on the 10.30, shopped. I found a suspender belt from the place where I've always bought 5 guineas ones at 15/-. A utility but all you can get; well-made but no lace trimmings and not so well cut! We only had time for a sandwich lunch in Harrods which was a pity as I wanted to take Mother to Vanity Fair, but the picture began at 1.20. An excellent film with Katherine Hepburn in Pearl Buck's novel "Dragon Seed".[35] We were home by 6 o'clock. Later: Just really blown Mother up sky high. She was saying how Cyril's given her hundreds of pounds as well as ours. But she's not spending it! Blimey, I said we weren't giving her money to save and be returned to us in her will. We GAVE it for her to use and spend now! Or, I said, if it is more than she needed we'd keep it! That woke her up, and I said it was only right for Cyril to give more — he'd had more spent on his career and was earning 5 times what you had, so that's that darling. I've a will and rod of iron if anything pricks me about you darling heart. Let me get at any enemy of yours, they'd be a bloody corpse, not mine either!

Prisoner No. 3275. Oflag VII B.
5th November 1944.

Four letters from you: 9th, 17th & 26th July & September 22nd. My July clothes parcel arrived safely too, and I drew it yesterday. Many

---

[35] *Dragon Seed* — from the book written by Pearl Buck in 1942 and made as a film in 1944 starring Katherine Hepburn and directed by Jack Conway and Harold S. Bucquet.

thanks, darling for all the good things in it. I know only too well all the time and trouble taken getting them together. Please thank "Pop" for the shaving brush — it's really grand. The April ones have not come yet but are expected soon. Noel and I are bashing chocolate, a real treat these days. We saw a grand show last night put on by the orderlies and centred on a coffee station on the embankment. What memories!

Hatton Cottage, Lubbock Rd, Chislehurst, Kent.
12.11.44.

It was announced yesterday that all our Xmas letters to you had to be mailed by Nov 14th. I can't believe you'll be there for Xmas, and I pray so hard you'll be home darling, but all the same, if the great misfortune happens and you are there, it is most certainly the last, in fact you'd better pack your belongings that day. I hear too, the sad news you may not get your usual Christmas parcels.

Prisoner No. 3275. Oflag VII B.
14th November 1944.

Have spent two wonderful days working in the forest and I'm at it for a week. We leave at 08.00 and return about 17.00 having lunch out in a hut built of spruce logs. Snow is on the ground and the woods are lovely, but it is very hard work. Tonight, I have had my (fortnightly) hot shower and will turn in immediately after supper. A grand letter from you was waiting for me when I got back last night, 29th September. Glad some letters are home. The 21st draws near — oh for that grand day again!

Much as I hate to do it, I feel I must bow to the inevitable and send you my Christmas greetings in this letter. After our recent optimism it seems a "bit 'ard" but so long as the old country comes out on top and the principles of freedom for which we fight are maintained it is well worthwhile. You must rest and keep well and cheery — it will be fine if you can get your discharge — and preserve your faith and courage a little longer. I still take a cold shower every morning and work with an axe and saw in the wood yard. Next week I hope to spend in the forest digging up tree roots. The party leaves about 8 am and returns about 5 p.m. It is very hard work but well worthwhile for a change. Indoors now it is too dark to read until the lights go on at 4.30 p.m. and the coal ration has been cut so much it is uncomfortably cold. Exercise outside is the best way to keep warm. Going out too, we can bring back a pack of wood every night.

21st November 1944.

Would that I were back where I was four years ago tonight! But as you have pointed out, then we had separation to face; now it is a reunion. What a lifetime these years have been. God grant the end is now near. I have had one grand but very old letter from you since the 14th July 22nd One wonders where it has been and what adventures it had before it reached me. My week's work in the forest ended on Saturday and a very pleasant change it was although very hard work. We had a march of about 3 miles mostly uphill, through the woods in the morning. Our job was to grub up the roots of felled trees, carry them over about 200 yards of rough, muddy ground to the road and load them onto the truck which is towed to the camp by tractor. At 11.00 hrs we paused for cocoa, at 13.00 hrs for soup and tea and packed up about 16.00 hrs. Each night I brought back a pack full of wood for the room. The forester who appeared occasionally looked just like a musical comedy Bavarian Huntsman, green hat with feather, green coat, ruck sack, shot gun and shooting stick. We saw deer at times and the country looked wonderful with snow and morning frost.

A letter from the Institute of Bankers contained a request for applicants for the "Eastern Staff of the British Exchange Bank." Neither the name of the Bank nor its countries of operation are given. These may be anywhere from Egypt or Palestine to Persia, India, or the Far East. On the principle of having as many chestnuts in the fire as possible to choose from when I come home, I have applied. It is very unlikely that my application will even be considered in the circumstances, but I have also asked for all communications arising from it to be sent to you so that you can see what country it is in and decide whether or not it is a suitable country for white people and so on. It commits us to absolutely nothing at all but might offer something attractive. The only advantage a job abroad can offer us is more pay and a higher standard of living. Against this must be set the disadvantages of leaving our old friends and the problem of education for our children abroad. I should not dream of going to any godforsaken or ungodly spot neither should I dream of taking you away if you did not like the idea. I applied to give us something else to consider should the chance arise. If you hear anything, darling, let me know what you think of it. I have been granted these letters specially to apply and to write to you about it.

Hatton Cottage, Lubbock Rd, Chislehurst, Kent.
7.12.44.

Pop announced he'd asked one of his girlfriends and her mother and Red Setter dog here for Xmas. She's an absolute gold digger after Pop and loathes us. Not out of the same drawer and says it's so lovely to have people working for her — she's a shop assistant! I'll be bug…! If I'm cooking for them unaided, I'm on sick leave, and Pat and Bill will clear off, Pam will too with young Mike. Diana will sulk as we all loathe her artificiality and insincerity. Otherwise just being ourselves, Pat and Diana would have helped me cook, housework and bed making. God — men of Pop's age are the end — fancy expecting us his children to run after and spoil his— Well, I've got that off my chest to you, I'm sorry but I know you will understand.

Prisoner No. 3275. Oflag VII B.
14th December 1944.

Already the Xmas programme is up — boxing, fun fair, auction sale, theatre show, etc. The posters would do credit to any poster designer at home. They are real works of art and all in colour. My final papers have arrived and so we sit in early February so I must get to work. If I pass, I shall have an impressive array of letters after my name — eight in all.

I shall be jolly glad to know that you have got your discharge. Christmas here promises to be a festival according to best traditions for we have been ordered to consume all stocks of food by January 14th. Noel and I are going to make a cake and a pudding and live royally for 3 weeks. After that — well it's up to the Red Cross. If nothing turns up, I shall feel inclined to ask you to stop our subscription. Winter has set in early this year. Snow covers the valley, and it has frozen steadily for several days. I have had to turn down a week with the wood party in the forest so that I can get on with my studies. I hope to go out after the exam and meanwhile work 2 hours daily inside sawing or chopping. Like you, I miss you more with every passing day and love you more and more. There is no such thing as getting used to this life. Each year it seems to get worse and if I let myself think too much of you and home it becomes almost unendurable, and Christmas makes it worse. God grant we shall not be much longer apart. I had a walk with Freddie the other day. He has not had your letter yet. He is in good form but fed up like the rest of us.

THE CHARTERED INSTITUTE OF SECRETARIES

PHONE: KELVIN 4471
GRAMS: SECRETARYSHIP-CENT-LONDON

TEMPORARY ADDRESS

PRINCES HOUSE
95 GRESHAM STREET
LONDON, E.C.2

22nd March 1944

Dear Sir,

I have pleasure in en-
closing a copy of the pass list
in which your name appears as a
successful candidate in the
Intermediate Examination of this
Institute held in June 1943.

The Chartered Institute
of Secretaries sends you its best
wishes for the future.

Yours faithfully,

C. H. Odell Carpenter
Secretary

A.E.Morton Esq.
Oflag VII B
GERMANY.

Exam results confirmed by the CIS

Hatton Cottage, Lubbock Rd, Chislehurst, Kent.
19.12.44.

Just heard I have my release — grand, isn't it? I feel you'll be pleased, but I feel a bit awkward when I think of Thelma and Bloomire and their lousy jobs. But Dr Moore advised me I have heaps to do here, even when the family aren't at home and only Miss Foster. Daddy has a great deal of secretarial work for me to do, his own private work which he can't do in his present office and job. Anyway, I'll soon be looking after you which is definitely full time! Darling, have you ever met a man in No.1 Company called Harry Langdon? A Royal West Kent man — his wife and I often see each other on my Thursday trip to Bromley. We've known her and her sister for years, not well but they used to come to Mop's (*Peggy's mother*) bridge parties and the keep fit classes Mop and I went to keep the extra inches under control!

21.12.44.

Would you believe it — Cyril is on his way home for a 28 day leave and a job! Mrs Lock told me in a letter yesterday that poor Peter isn't as lucky. These d…n marines as you'd say. Mother had a lovely bunch of big yellow chrysanthemums sent to me today with your dearest love. It was very sweet of her and thank you, darling Alan.

25.12.44.

Christmas Day and now much of my thoughts are with you and how much I love you and miss you — only you can know that Alan by the longing ache in your heart. I was up early to go to 8 o'clock Communion today, it was bitterly cold and one of the whitest frosts I've ever seen — like a white Christmas from snow, it was really rather lovely. We hung our stockings up and I had apple, orange, nuts, soap, and a nice small torch. The King spoke this afternoon after a radio tour of the Empire. It's so wonderful to realise that it's soon 1945 and it will be when you get this, and it's the year we will have our sweet and wonderful reunion in. This time I'm so absolutely sure. Last year it was a very big hope.

Prisoner No. 3275. Oflag VII B.
25th December 1944.

We have just finished tea and I feel I must write to you although cards are not due until later. Its real Christmas weather, sunny and freezing hard and skating started this morning. As things go we have had quite a good time — various entertainments have been organised and there have been the usual visits to friends. Yesterday I went to evensong and this morning to Holy Communion. Tonight, we play "Monopoly" after supper. Food is plentiful as we have got to "bash" out all we have here. But Peggy, all my thoughts have been with you, what might have been and what will be soon, God grant next year.

Belvedere, Dola Avenue, Deal, Kent.
Christmas Day.

Here comes a line to you on Christmas Day. It's nearly bedtime but I want to write to you before going up — such a lovely day as regards weather especially as we couldn't have had a better one. John and I went down to St Peter's for early service and walking down in the darkness with streaks of light as the sun was beginning to rise and the sparkling frost on the ground, really it looked lovely. I was picturing you perhaps coming out early to exercise but in very different setting. Please God it will be the last one out there. Good night and dearest love to you,

God bless,
Mother.

Prisoner No. 3275. Oflag VII B.
31st December 1944.

It is terrible to sit here writing to you with yet another year drawing to its close and my promise still unfulfilled. To write again "1945 for sure", "soon", "chins up" and "soon" seems to have become meaningless. What can I say to you Peggy? There seems but one thing sure, one thing I can say which nothing and no one can better and that is I love you and long for you more with every passing day and hour and treasure your love for me above everything. Yes, maybe we missed much before we were married but I am sure in the end we gained more. I loved you too much to take you before you were wholly mine and have never regretted following the dictates of my conscience.

The Final Stretch

Hatton Cottage, Lubbock Rd, Chislehurst, Kent.
1.1.45.

Well Alan, here we are, New Year's Day and this year we will for CERTAIN be together — what a wonderful thought. A Very Happy New Year! I am getting so very excited to see you again and be with you forever and to hear your dear voice and feel your arms around me and hold you in mine, to share even the minutest triviality of the daily round with you. Yes, my sweet I will even look forward to seeing your face at the breakfast table every day!

3.1.45.

Now a little about your application to an Eastern Bank — there's not enough space for much so will write more prolifically next time. I have no objections to going anywhere overseas with you no matter how godforsaken, but with children to consider it will have to be a good country for white people — a big Exchange Bank should hold good possibilities for you my sweet, if anything crops up I'll get old Harry Hoare and see what he thinks and he can get more gen from the Lloyds General Manager. But it would never be a hardship to go abroad if I am with you. I love your wonderful companionship so very much. I love our good friends too, but you are my life forever.

Prisoner No. 3275. Oflag VII B.
4th January 1945.

It is still very cold indeed, weather that does not suit me at all. Skating is in full swing, but I do very little. I am still trying to study but the silence rooms are like refrigerators and our own room is like bedlam. If only the papers had come in the summer, it would have been easy. I feel too that more of me is at home with you than remains here, so I don't feel very optimistic about the exam.

Max Gate, Lennox Road South, Southsea, Hants.
5th January 1945.

Here I am again at last. Mother and Jennie have kept me well informed regarding your activities, and most of your letters to them were later forwarded to me. Heartiest congratulations on passing all your exams and we trust it won't be long before you can reap the advantages of all your work. I have not heard from Peggy recently, but my recent high-speed movements have left my mail weeks behind me. I hope to be able to see her before long. Mother was looking very well when I saw her for a few hours yesterday — I don't think you will think she has changed at all when you see her yourself. She is hopeful about getting her flat in Victoria Road before very long. I know you were hoping, and indeed expecting, to be home again by now; when I was away, I was almost convinced that you would be home before me. Nevertheless, you may, even now, return with the same short notice that I had, and we all believe that you remain very optimistic. Since leaving home I've "had my hair parted" once or twice and am not a little fortunate in being here at all! However, I am fitter than ever and am very much enjoying the English winter. You will be interested to hear that I am now going to be a teacher — at the establishment for which I worked so hard and long before the war.

All the very best to you and an early return.

Cyril.

Hatton Cottage, Lubbock Rd, Chislehurst, Kent.
7.1.45.

The Institute of Bankers replied to your letter of November 26th, Friday last, 5th January stating they believe the vacancy in the Foreign Exchange Bank in the East has been filled but have written to the bank concerned for further information. I quite agree that if ever a job sounding attractive and in a white man's country turns up it's a good plan — for you to do such a job well, as I know you will, it will carry better promotion back here when we return — am I right in that?

Prisoner No. 3275. Oflag VII B.
9th January 1945.

I have just finished a book of poems, "Such Liberty" by John Buxton, an officer in this camp. It was published by MacMillan & Co in 1944 and I would like you to get a copy for he expresses beautifully thoughts which pass through my mind but which I can only clumsily express. Many might refer to you and I, and of his sonnets Numbers 9 & 13 I like.

14th January 1945.

I've had the usual winter visit from my old acquaintance and have spent a week feeling sorry for myself. We've had no more letters and hear that 28,000 for Oflags and Stalags were destroyed in an air raid. Today sees the end of our food "bash" but another week's buck has arrived which has to last us a fortnight. Oh, to be able to shop again! The winter so far has been very severe but when the sun comes out it is quite warm. One thinks of spring, of blossom, of Kent, of all sorts of good things!

31st January 1945.

Inward mail has virtually ceased but out of the blue the other day came a letter from Mother, December 3rd. It was fine to know all was well at least up to then. The Arnhem fellows brought us good news of home — two are in our room as I write being closely cross questioned about everything. They are in great demand and in return for a cup of tea they are expected to undergo a bombardment of questions like a counsel's examination. The news is very good but after so many disappointments we are all afraid of being over optimistic. The thought of being on leave with you Peggy, during an English springtime is almost too delightful to permit my mind to dwell on. But the day must come and meanwhile anticipation and hope carry me beyond the wire, forward and into the future and over the sea to your side. The winter is very severe, but we are all weathering it fairly well. I would hardly describe conditions here as home from home but compared with many we must be in clover.

11th February 1945.

A letter at last, December 10th, all about your trip to Thelma. It was wonderful to see your writing again after so long. A whole month's mail is missing which may turn up even now. We have been in luck, for Christmas parcels turned up too and we've had half a week for two weeks. The stuff in them is very good indeed but at half rations, tickles the pallet too much and reminds one how much a square meal would be appreciated. What we have, however, is sufficient for our needs. The weather changed suddenly with the beginning of the month. The temperatures jumped and the sudden thaw brought floods. There is still some snow but at present it is dull and damp. The reprisals continue so my exam is off. It is very annoying after 15 months work, but I may take it when I come home (That's if you will let me!) I am doing a bit more German meanwhile to pass the time which drags deplorably now. I still do an hour a day in the wood yard and I'm getting a day out next week with a loading party. Getting on a working party is the only means of getting a day out these days so I am looking forward to it. Alastair Pilkington has moved into a room above us, so I am having him down one afternoon for a brew and a talk. He's a very charming lad indeed. I can now read the German papers after a fashion. The news is great but even now none of us can think of seeing England in under six months. I hope to God we are wrong.

20th February 1945.

Letters these days are as rare as Red Cross parcels. A propos the latter, the British Red Cross sent us a message recently; we can go on to full parcel issues. This has caused hoots of ironical laughter as we now have none at all and the chances of getting any seem very remote. I hope you got my letter suggesting we halve our subscription for we have been on half rations since September and now we shall be lucky if we get that. It seems stupid to pay for what neither I nor any others in Germany are getting. I had a really splendid day yesterday. We left the camp at 08.00 hrs and spent the entire day until 18.00 hrs in the woods. Our job was to load the trailers which bring the tree stumps into the camp which we split up for fuel. It was a fine sunny day with just a slight sharpness in the air. The woods and the surrounding country looked lovely and the hard work a real joy. The midday break was taken, and we had it round a great fire on which we roasted potatoes. Now that the parole walks are stopped and the theatre closed there is very little variety in life and hence, I enjoyed it to the full.

28th February 1945.

I've just finished supper after a very strenuous day with the wood party. So far, the weather has been almost too good to be true and today was so warm we worked bare-backed. We leave daily at 08.00 hrs, cross the valley, and climb a very steep hill on the top of which is our site. The rock is only just below the surface and digging out big stumps is terrific work. Once up, they have to be lugged down the rides to a tack where the loading takes place. After all day at that we carry home army packs of wood. The first two days leave one as limp as a rag but after that it's easier. But work is offset by being in the freedom of the forest, which is lovely and alfresco meals round a great fire between shelters of spruce boughs. We get extra soup for our labours and believe me we need it. Again, we are not shut in during air-raids, which is a great thing these days. I shall be very sorry when my week is over.

Alan recounted to us that on one of these working parties in the forest he heard a sound behind him. Looking round he realised, only just in time, that some Germans were felling a tree and it was about to fall on him. They offered no warning and only a quick sprint saved him from a very nasty accident. Whilst Alan wrote to Peggy about how much he enjoyed these days out he never mentioned the more dangerous situations for fear of causing her unnecessary worry.

11th March 1945.

Two grand letters to answer — December 7th and January 2nd. In view of the missing ones, however, I cannot understand your references to Mike. It's nice to know we are on the Roll of Honour though what I've done to deserve that I can't imagine! I was glad to know some letters have got home too, for up to November 26th I've 20 letters sent to you and not yet acknowledged. There must be dozens of yours I've not yet had. We had a stroke of luck last week. Apparently, the Red Cross are now sending parcels by lorry convoy and one bound for a camp further east broke down near here and we got it. As a result, we've got ½ a parcel per head so our turnips and spuds will be varied for a few days. We have just heard that our rations are all to be cut by 1/5 and spuds by a 1/3 from this week so we are hoping that the Red Cross will get cracking again soon. The weather is dreadful again and as I am just recovering from a bout of 'flu things don't look very cheery at the moment. I spent two days in bed with Noel as nurse but still feel rather shaky. On the whole though we are in good spirits and spend most of our time forecasting when the war will end and how many more days we shall be in the "cooler". It seems to vary from four weeks on a sunny day to six months on a wet one! We are like children and very tiny things send our spirits up or down. You're going to have something of a problem child to look after when I get home Peggy, but I think if you take as a motto "Feed the brute" perhaps he won't be too difficult.

Sunday 18th March 1945.

First, a large batch of mail is in, and I had 4 grand letters from you: Nov 12th, 22nd, 29th & Dec 21st also 2 from Mum, 1 from an aunt & 1 from Sheppard. Will answer these in my letter. Glad more letters are home. Secondly some more Red Cross parcels have come in and 8,500 more are on their way. These mean a hell of a lot these days even at ½ a week. Thirdly after 5 false starts and with a hangover from flu I have taken my finals! If the papers ever get home, I think (and hope) I've a fair chance of success. The weather too has been good. With sunshine one feels the war may end sometime.

All letters sent by Peggy to Alan between 4th March and 13th April 1945 were returned with a stamp saying, 'This letter has been returned by the Swiss Post Office who were unable to forward it to Germany because of the interruption of communications'.

It was thought that the plane carrying Alan's examination papers home to the UK was shot down for he never received the results of his final examinations.

Hatton Cottage, Lubbock Rd, Chislehurst, Kent.
25.3.45.

Remember I always said "I've got my eyes on you" — I still have it seems! — Though you may have explained in another letter which as, yet I have not received. Your postcard of January 24th didn't mention it, i.e., the reason for the chaotic state of the camp. Nora Stokes wrote to me the extract from Noel's letter of January 21st telling her all the reasons and why — God you know my thoughts upon the subject. My thoughts if expressed would no doubt jeopardise the transit of this letter. Keep your chin up and your thoughts and dreams of that great day so near now my own dear heart. Cut my glamour bed jacket out last night. Its pale duck egg blue voile, i.e., transparent! High necked and long, full sleeves, Bishop style and yet glamour! What's the saying, "the art of revealing in the art of concealing"! I feel I must hurry up and finish all my making and renovating or you'll be home before I've done everything. I'm saving some of my clothing coupons so you can buy anything you want to save waiting for yours.

Alan makes no mention of any incident in his letters at this time, presumably not wishing to worry Peggy. However, The Mansell Diaries contain a lengthy entry for 15th January 1945 explaining that the S.B.O. and another senior officer were notified on the evening of January 14th that the camp commandant wanted to meet them at 08.30 hrs the following morning. At the morning roll call, it was clear that the number of sentries had been doubled whilst a party of Germans entered via the far end of the camp. Fairly rapidly, vast numbers of S.S. troops appeared and took up their positions, blocking the approaches to the Garden City. Off duty guards and plain clothes individuals also arrived. The flaps on the sentry boxes were lowered and machine guns were trained on the P.O.W.s. All troops carried weapons. The S.B.O. took up a prominent position and motioned for all the prisoners to gather round him. He then said that he would read the German order issued to him, adding a few additional comments as he proceeded. Mansell notes that the S.B.O. spoke magnificently.

It seemed the British had apparently mistreated German prisoners in Egypt for two years, forcing them to live in tents, without sufficient food or water, bedding, tables, stools, etc. The Germans were not going to reduce the food rations or supply of water, but all furniture was to be removed immediately and all Quiet Rooms were to be closed, thus creating similar conditions for the British. It was clear to the S.B.O. that this order came from on high and was in line with other reprisals such as the handcuffing described earlier. In other camps, the heads of P.O.W.s had been shaved and belongings confiscated. The intent behind these actions was to reduce the morale of the prisoners. Mansell describes the relief clearly visible on the faces of the S.S. when, early in the S.B.O.'s speech, the British P.O.W.s laughed, and the mood changed. For some two and a half hours afterwards, tables, stools, mattresses, etc. were piled up outside the housing blocks whilst the prisoners played ice hockey, skated, or walked the campgrounds! The Protecting Power and the Red Cross were informed of the reprisal by telegram. Captain Mansell noted in his diary the following day, 'Spent v. cold night without mattress, but not too uncomfortable'.[36]

---

[36] The Mansell Diaries, 1977, Printed Privately — pages 137-138.

Hatton Cottage, Lubbock Rd, Chislehurst, Kent.
1.4.45.

Oh, I must tell you, Gwen and I have just recalled a funny incident that happened this afternoon. Keith and I had just jumped off a five-foot stone wall onto the beach and run inland away from an incoming large wave and turned to see Gwen hanging to the wall for dear life and the wind had lifted up her mac, skirt and white frilly petticoat showing her large white bloomers. God, we did laugh. We ache all over and are so sleepy from buffeting against the wind that we plan to go to bed early and snore away the night hours.

2.4.45.

Here I am home again after a perfectly grand weekend at the Fehr's farm. It was so lovely to be amongst friends and family who really seemed to want me and enjoy my company. We came home after an early lunch via the Kent County Football match won by the Gunners, and we were back at Hatton House by 6.15, had a cup of tea and Egglesfield, their groom, helped me down here with my baggage to find no meal prepared, windows shut and such a stuffy house and groans to welcome me, for whilst I am away, they eat all the rations and laze in bed and have meals at odd hours. This I don't mind for two people but for 6 as they are now it's hopeless. However, I will get down to brass tacks tomorrow. I informed Pam I was taking a few days on strike soon to get ready for you, and was promptly told, "in that case you must leave here, I'm not cooking for you when you don't earn your keep" — nice sister!

13.4.45.

We were all shattered by the death of Roosevelt, but that can't stop the daily routine. Carol Towse wrote today in answer to a letter I wrote last week enquiring from her why there had been such a long silence from her — she's been in bed since October last with T.B. in the right lung but is better now. She doesn't say whether Geoffrey knows or not, poor girl, what a worry.

At this point, the letters between Alan and Peggy come to an abrupt halt. The Americans liberated Eichstätt and most of the prisoners were marched from there to Moosburg (Stalag V11-A) amidst considerable chaos as they finally departed Eichstätt. Some found easier modes of transport, as a note to Alan from Noel Stokes indicates:

My Dear Alan,

I have been fortunate in being selected to go tonight by motor to Moosburg. I sincerely hope you are progressing favourably. Please get in touch with me.

Yours,

Noel.

Noel's note was accompanied by another (undated) letter written by Robert Powell of the Argyll and Sutherland Highlanders and signed by a number of other officers.

Dear Alan,

Enclosed is a note from Noel, who is leaving for Moosburg tonight by bus, as some extra transport is being provided for lightly wounded or older people. Noel was pretty badly shaken, I think, when we first got back, but Jim got him some dope from the hospital, and now, after a rest, he is a good deal more like his normal self. Robin is also going with him as he has a broken rib, due to so many people having lain on top of him at one stage in the proceedings!

And now for yourself, Robbie Roberts and Dudley — we haven't heard much of your condition, but C. I. B.[37] hope to publish bulletins later on this evening, so we pray for more cheering news of everyone. This note is just to express to the three of you, and anyone else we know, the sympathy of everyone else in this room. We hope it will give you all a little extra encouragement to know that everyone sends their good wishes for a speedy recovery, and most important, an even speedier return to England.

Kind regards and good luck,

Yours ever,

Robert Powell.

G Charlton, Ollie Taylor, Harry J Willis, "Fish," Len Guest, Gregory O'Neil, H.S. Rowland.

Keep your pecker up Alan — you'll be fine, I know, Jim.

---

[37] C.I.B. — Central Information Bureau. I am guessing that this is what the officers meant by this abbreviation and that they are referring to the senior allied officers of the camp but there is no full explanation of this in Alan's papers.

Right at the end of Alan's logbook, there is a name and address. In his much later, typed version of this log, he notes: 'The signature is that of Lieutenant John O. Baptiste, Madison 5, Wisconsin, who when leading a patrol of Patten's army into Eichstätt, after the town had been shelled all night, burst into our ward in the German Hospital where we were being cared for after being wounded in an American air raid. He was brandishing a tommy gun and his first words to us were, "Say, are you guys all right?" That was towards the end of April 1945, and I had been a P.O.W. for almost exactly four years.'

Those who marched to Moosburg experienced the kindness of the local population and met other prisoners of war en route. All of this, however, must have been marred by the 'friendly fire' incident which was alluded to at the very start of this book, and which was the trigger for the letters of Noel Stokes and Robert Powell.

Alan was among a number of men killed or injured by the Americans. He very occasionally talked of being in the hospital in Eichstätt. In the bed next to him was a man who asked, "Alan, could you spare me a cigarette please, this hurts a bit?" "This' was the amputation of one of the man's limbs and it seems that the anaesthetic was either minimal or non-existent! What a cruel twist of fate for these men who had waited so long for freedom only to be killed or injured, at the eleventh hour, by their American, overzealous liberators. To see the lives taken from those whose captivity they had shared for so long and with whom they had built up such camaraderie must have been a shattering experience.

The papers of another officer provide more detailed information about this shameful incident.[38] *The camp had been*

---

[38] Wright, G. B. Lieutenant, Durham Light Infantry, handwritten diary entitled "The Last Days of the War or How the Hell to Pass the Time",

informed that they would march out of Eichstätt for Moosburg at 05.00hrs on Saturday 14th, April 1945. The parade ground was crowded with men, many of whom had their possessions in perambulators, go-carts, wheelbarrows or on other types of wheels that had been begged, borrowed, or stolen from neighbouring rubbish tips by orderlies or working parties. The P.O.W.s were ordered to leave by battalions or companies and to line up on the road outside where they made a column of about a mile in length. As they did so, men were aware that one or two American planes were circling overhead. An American pilot in the camp thought they were Mustangs, others disagreed, thinking they were Thunderbolts. One flew especially low, dipping his wings from side to side. The men waved to the pilot, pleased to have them overhead. Moments later, about half a dozen planes appeared, circling and wheeling around the camp before the leading plane dived. A puff of smoke was seen from beneath its wings and a burst of machine gun fire was unleashed.

The men below assumed at first that a German fighter plane had infiltrated the group and that they were about to witness a spectacular dogfight. Lieutenant Wright vividly describes the awful sound of machine guns as numerous planes flew low along the road blasting these men with all the power they could muster. He was absolutely disgusted that after five years of war, his comrades in arms had been either killed or injured by the Yanks – supposedly on the same side![39] He goes on to explain how he eventually gained a position of relative security and was able to watch as a pair of mad horses, broke lose, bolting free

---

written in Eichstätt. Held by Department of Documents, Imperial War Museum, No. 98/4/1.

[39] Wright, G. B. Lieutenant; Held by Department of Documents, Imperial War Museum, No.98/4/1.

along the road, how a small German car was blasted to shreds by bullets and a lorry was getting the works further along the road. 'This', says Wright, 'is the most terrible bit of warfare I've ever seen'. The planes turned and came in for another swoop leaving a column of around 1,300 officers completely broken up and unable to proceed that day to Moosburg. Wright estimated that around nine men were killed and approximately fifty were wounded. An unknown number of Germans also suffered the same fate, and it was incredible that more were not injured or killed, considering the lack of cover.[40] Wright's diary explains that, that night, some people were transferred to Moosburg whilst the main body left the following day. This is borne out by the notes sent to Alan, and others in the hospital, informing them that Noel Stokes was to depart that night with others who were sick. He is not, however, able to provide an explanation as to why this terrible incident ever occurred in the first place. Perhaps the cruellest, most unjust, answer to this question came from the camp commandant, who had the audacity to explain to the S.B.O. in Eichstätt that it was his fault! With commendable restraint, the S.B.O. is reported to have responded that such decisions could only be made once the war was over! April 14th, 1945, was a sad and bitter day for the prisoners of Eichstätt.

It is interesting to realise that this most dreadful of incidents proved of value to the British officers, and those of other nationalities, who, by now, were passionately longing to end their years of incarceration in the infamous Colditz Castle. In his wonderful account of Colditz,[41] Henry Chancellor explained that

---

[40] In 2003 a plaque was erected by the side of the road where the terrible "Friendly Fire" incident occurred, and it states that 14 men were killed and another 46 were injured.

[41] Chancellor, Henry; Colditz, The Definitive History, ISIS Audio Books, ISIS Publishing Ltd; Oxford, England.

news of this incident reached the supposedly impregnable mediaeval fortress where so many legends had developed. Jock Hamilton-Ballie, who had himself been in Eichstätt, where a number of his friends had been killed or injured, was by now in Colditz. He narrated what measures they took to prevent such an incident. Here the prisoners started to make for themselves their national flags (Polish, French and British) as protection against so-called 'friendly fire'. The P.O.W.s found making the Union Jack a very emotional experience after years of life under the Swastika. These flags were eventually employed and, mercifully, no incident of the sort recounted above took place at Colditz.

For Alan, this darkest, and most bitter of clouds, possessed a silver lining. The next item in the file is a telegram, dated 2nd May 1945, less than a week before V. E. Day, and despatched by Peggy to Newbury, Berkshire. It reads:

"LIEUT A E HORTON 98 AMERICAN HOSPITAL
HERMITAGE NEWBURY BERKS = BE WITH YOU FOREVER SOON ALL LOVE HUGS AND KISSES PEGGY."

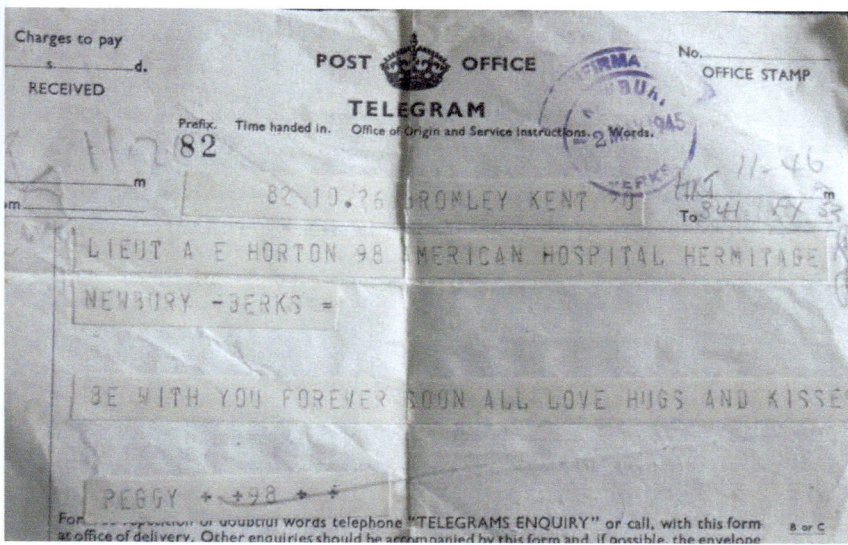

```
Charges to pay                    POST        OFFICE              No.
  s.        d.                                                    OFFICE STAMP
RECEIVED                             TELEGRAM
                    Prefix.  Time handed in.  Office of Origin and Service Instructions.  Words.
                    82
                                                                              11-46
                        82 10.26  BROMLEY KENT              To 841

   LIEUT A E HORTON 98  AMERICAN HOSPITAL HERMITAGE

   NEWBURY -BERKS =

   BE WITH YOU FOREVER SOON ALL LOVE HUGS AND KISSES

     PEGGY + +98 + +

For ... ... of doubtful words telephone "TELEGRAMS ENQUIRY" or call, with this form   8 or C
at office of delivery. Other enquiries should be accompanied by this form and, if possible, the envelope
```

On discharge from hospital, Alan returned home to find that, compared with many, he was very fortunate to have safely returned to his home country.

47, Fielding Street, Liverpool 6.
May 2nd '45.

Dear Mrs Horton,

No doubt you will be wondering who this letter is from as it is quite a while since I last wrote to you, in fact it was the August of 1941 when both you and I received the bad news regarding our husbands. My husband was at the time serving under Lieutenant Horton.

Forgive me writing but I was wondering if your husband had arrived home and also if he knew the whereabouts of Gunner

Wright. At the time of writing, I feel very worried as I have not heard anything from him at all since last Xmas Day and at that time, he was a P.O.W. in Stalag 344 in Germany, which as you no doubt know, was liberated in the latter end of January.

If your husband is home Mrs Horton, I do hope he is well, please if you can possibly find the time to reply to this letter, and let me know any news.

Sincerely,

E Wright.

P.S. We may not have to wait very long now, but you can well understand how anxious I feel.

On the back of Mrs Wright's letter, Alan drafted his moving reply:

Dear Mrs Wright,

My wife and I found your letter when we arrived home together the day before yesterday having just met again after these fateful years.

I was in camp at Eichstätt Bavaria and was left behind in a German hospital with a bad leg when the other British officers were marched south over the Danube. Because of this I was liberated early and being sick was flown home within a few days.

Unfortunately, I can give you no news of your husband neither do I know anything of the whereabouts of any of the other boys of my troop. The Germans separated officers and men immediately after capture. I understand however, that British P.O.W.s liberated by the Russians are sent home via Odessa. This means a very long journey and there must be thousands of them to find transport for.

Because of this you must not worry if it is some time before you hear news of him.

I hope most sincerely you will have him with you safe and well before long and know the happiness which is now mine. I shall be very pleased if you will let me know as soon as you have news, and I will also be glad to know anything your husband can tell me of my comrades. To know they are well will mean much to me for it hurt me very much that I was unable to bring them safely out of Crete and thus cause you these long years of anxiety and separation.

Please accept the best wishes from my wife and I for good, speedy news and all it means to you.

Yours very sincerely,

A. E. Horton.

There is no further record in the correspondence of what became of Gunner Wright.

Because he was injured, Alan was flown home and arrived earlier than many of his fellow prisoners. Peggy had gleaned this news and contact was finally established. As he had been told by a German soldier, years earlier, on the beach in Crete, as the last British battleships sailed over the horizon for home, "Vor you, Englander, zee war is over." This time it was almost true! After a period of recuperation and leave, Alan was despatched to Beaver Camp, Hounslow, as depressing a place to end the war that might be found.

Tuesday 21st August 1945.

What hell it is to be here without you. A whole day and not even the sound of your voice. This place is the devil of a hole. The Depot is nothing but a great packing factory for M.T. stores and employs thousands. I have been posted here on the "technical side" which is just too stupid for words. It will take at least two months to learn my job and then I get my ticket. How typically army! But this camp is where all the male military workers live; they go to the Depot daily by lorry. It is grossly understaffed by officers, so I am trying to get a job as company commander. It will be partly administrative and much more my line of country. The commandant has been away, but I shall see him tomorrow and meanwhile hope for the best. What I have seen of Hounslow and Feltham leaves much to be desired. It all looks just "bloody" but so far I have not seen very much.

I forgot to tell you in my letter yesterday, darling, that your husband has been mistaken for Field Marshall Montgomery! Just as I was leaving the station at Feltham yesterday afternoon an old man leapt on to the running board and thrust his head through the window. He stared at me for a moment and then said, "Gawd blimey Guvner, I could have sworn you were our Monty." Do you think it is any use me buying a black berry with two badges on it?

Wednesday 22nd August 1945.

I saw the Brigadier this morning and went in all set for a fight. He received me very cordially. Shook hands, granted my request and we parted good friends. I have been sent to "B" Company which consists of about 500 odds and sods of a very rag-time battalion. It would seem that shortly I am to take it over and I am supposed to smarten it up. What a job for one who has never been in a company office before — but how much better than being a factory foreman as I should be at the depot.

The officers in this place are quite a passable crowd and the Major is very pleasant. I am in quite a jam about uniform, unless Cyril's will do, for Moss Bros. and Alkits have none and it will take at least a month to have some made. I told the Major the position today. He was very sympathetic but says I must get some. I have arranged to go to town tomorrow evening to see what can be done.

Thank God we have only one A.T.S. Officer here and she appears only at lunch and tea. Further we are cared for by two batmen, so my morals are in no immediate danger!

Oh Peggy, my precious, how I miss you. Instead of being one of the "keen types" I am very bolshie indeed and hate the whole show for keeping me away from you even for a short time.

Thursday 23rd August 1945.

Last night after I wrote to you, I was persuaded in the mess to go to a dance (Troops) in the gymnasium. My company commander, an old ranker captain called Moon, had to go as O.O.D. and most of the others went because the Officer Commanding went. It was really quite fun and very useful to get an idea of what the troops are like. Some typical ordinance "twerps" were there; one Major whom I flatly refuse to call "Sir" except in front of his own clerks in his office and several other odds and sods and some appalling A.T.S. Officers.

The men are mainly ordinance, but many are returned P.O.W.s from various regiments who have been drafted in. These (and I don't blame them) take a very poor view of having to be here at all. They want to be in their own unit, and many have the fighting man's contempt for the base Wallahs. Some are very smart, some are very slack. They are a motley crew and scarcely "happy".

It is not clear how much leave Alan was given on his return to England in May, but in his Release Certificate, dated 23rd November 1945, he was granted one hundred- and eight-days leave, commencing on 20th October 1945. In December, Alan received the following note from the War Office, dated 5th December 1945.

Sir,

Now that the time has come for your release from active military duty, I am commanded by the Army Council to express to you their thanks for the valuable services which you have rendered in the service of your country at a time of grave national emergency.

I am, Sir,

Your Obedient Servant.

WAR OFFICE

P/71325

5th December, 1945.

Sir,

Now that the time has come for your release from active military duty, I am commanded by the Army Council to express to you their thanks for the valuable services which you have rendered in the service of your country at a time of grave national emergency.

I am, Sir,

Your obedient Servant,

[signature]

Lieutenant A.E. Horton,
Royal Artillery.

For Alan, the war was finally over! Alan and Peggy rented a small bungalow in Ashford, Middlesex for the duration of Alan's posting to Beaver Camp, Hounslow. Later, Alan re-joined Lloyds Bank, working in their Guildford branch, until he was moved to his first managerial position at Cheltenham in the late 1940s. At the time, he was the youngest manager in Lloyds Bank. They became parents to twins, Anne and John, in 1949. In 1956, Alan suffered from tuberculosis and was seriously ill for about a year. It was felt that his years as a prisoner of war undoubtedly contributed to this illness. Alan died from cancer in 1993 and Peggy, ten years later.

The Horton family.

Appendix 1 — Another Bloody Week

Several pages of Alan's logbook are devoted to describing the detail of a typical week in a prisoner of war camp. In a note added many years later, when he typed his logbook up, he records: 'A fairly representative week chosen at random. Rations are half Red Cross parcels and from German rations. The latter are cut 30% when we are on full Red Cross parcels. Noel prepared the food and fetched the parcel and I washed up. Next week we change over. The plane incident on Sunday was unique. Air raids are now frequent, but this is the first time our planes have been seen so low over the camp. It is typical of between seasons, when wet and gloom make periods of idleness frequent. It is also from an unsettled period when studying seems impossible. The private parcels were the first seen since about May. A show too, is scarcely a weekly occurrence.

Sunday 29th October 1944.
07.30. British coffee with Klim[42] — no sugar.
A cold foggy morning. Had a restless night. Felt lazy and got up at 08.50 — flunked a cold bath. Washed, shaved and put on best battle dress.
09.30. Appel.[43] Everyone late as usual on Sunday.

---

[42] Klim — Milk Powder.
[43] Appel — Roll Call.

09.45. Breakfast; 2 slices of black bread and margarine. Treacle on one and "Goon" jam on the other (½ parcels!).

10.00. Cup of Cocoa. Usual period of gloomy disorder till orderly cleared up. Too dark to read in room. Went to silence room and wrote "When ignorance is Bliss" in this book. Very cold and miserable there but empty as its Sunday.

12.00. Air raid alarm. Confined to block.

12.01. Cottage pie arrived. Fairly good issue and a pleasant change after the eternal soups. Last day of week as "J.C."[44] for Noel and I. Laid lunch.

Lunch; Cottage Pie (every 3rd or 4th week). Extra Goon rations to ½ parcels. 1 ½ slices of bread and goon jam. Cup of tea (with sugar). Spent afternoon mending Dudley's sweater (4 Reich Marks) and making mittens for work on wood pile.

13.30. All clear. No excitement.

15.50. Made toast. 1½ slices each with margarine. ½ litre of cookhouse tea with Klim. No sugar.

16.00. Heard three planes go over very low. Great excitement, said to be one M.E.110[45] pursued by two British planes. Machine-gunning salvo.

Reports as usual very varied.

    1. 2 mosquitoes. Saw circles and tracer. German shot down.

    2. Definitely fighting but saw no results.

    3. Saw stars on under-wings of pursuers! And so on.

17.00. Evening parade. Old German officer was on, arrived late and was very slow. Weather very dull indeed but warmer.

---

[44] J.C. — The meaning of this is unclear

[45] M.E. 110 — A German Messerschmitt plane from the Second World War.

17.15. Evensong in theatre with Padre Cave (The Rev. Eric V. Cave, Royal Army Chaplains Department). Familiar hymns and good reading of lessons by "The Brigand" (Captain Fraser).

Continued sewing until —

18.45. Laid supper; cooked spuds (fried) and made omelette (1 tin egg powder). Very slow and our rocket fuel is damp.

Supper, Spuds fried, (double whack ½ parcels!), omelette, meat sauce (extra from the cookhouse). Dried Apricots and Klim. 1 bread and margarine. Cup of tea (Sugar).

Things looked a bit brighter with lights on and room warming up. Also had an optimistic letter from Peggy (August). Started "Drums along the Mohawk".[46]

20.00. Silence room again to write in this book, "Sidelights on Banking" and this note but mainly to get some peace and quiet.

Air Raid Yellow 20.45. All clear 21.00.

21.20. Heated argument in progress. German Reich Marks are being recalled (issued in place of Lager Marks!)[47] and a 10 Mark levy is to be made to cover all charges as there will be so many available. Equitable or not?

Prepared cups for early drink washed and turned in. Continued, "Drums along the Mohawk" and read two chapters from Genesis before "lights out".

Monday 30th October 1944.

07.30. Goon Coffee (½ litre). Klim but no sugar.

A better night and brighter but cold morning. Read another chapter from Edmonds' book.

---

[46] Drums along the Mohawk (1936) by Walter D Edmonds.

[47] Lager Marks or Lagergelt — money used in the camps whereas Reich Marks were the German currency.

08.45. Under cold tap in ablutions, dressed, shaved, laid out bed linen for changing.

09.05. Parade. Late as usual.

09.30. Breakfast; 2 slices, margarine; treacle on one & Goon jam on the other. ½ litre Cocoa.

Usual morning chores in room so went to silence room at 10.30.

Rumour that "the Brigand" had cut off his side-whiskers has proved false.

12.00. Lunch; ¼ litre Brattling soup and ¼ litre "seconds". 1½ slices bread, margarine, treacle. 1 baked potato and ½ litre tea with sugar. Sun shining!

12.45. Noel starts queue for orderlies' shower — I wriggle out as I provide wood for fuel!

Filled in tobacco indent for week.

Story of German plane shot down yesterday said to be true.

Gave "Fish" my laundry list. 1.25 Marks. Paid in Reich Marks.

Afternoon finished off mittens — quite a good job and got an order from Dudley for a pair!

Prepared porridge for supper, Noel having forgotten as usual.

15.50. Tea; ½ litre unsweetened from cookhouse, 1½ slices of toast and margarine.

Took a walk round the camp. Weather grey, damp, cold.

17.00. Parade on Lagerstrasse.[48]

17.15. Returned to bunk to read. Lights switched on at 7 o'clock.

Read a novel for an hour and one hour's law.

18.00. Two letters for me; 24th September, Mother and a July one from Peggy. All well thank God.

19.15. Supper; Boiled spuds, porridge, 1 slice of bread with margarine and treacle.

---

[48] Lagerstrasse —Camp Road.

20.00. Went to see a bridge match between England and Canada in the theatre with Fish, Robby and Tom. Noel deep in the 'blues' refused to come. Very well staged but quite beyond me. Calling and play quite incomprehensible. Very smoky. Glad to leave at 21.35. England won easily.

Moonlit night and promise of frost in the air.

Washed, etc. turned in on return. Heard our orderly leaves tomorrow with 29 others. Sending us 'Kranks'[49] to replace them.

More novel and finished off Genesis, can't think why I have never before fully appreciated the Old Testament.

Tuesday 31st October 1944.

07.30. Goon tea, ½ litre. Heated argument in the room about an officer who wrote home that men here collected snails on parole walks and ate them. Does this worry people at home? Kept well under the blankets!

08.30. Under tap in ablutions.

09.05. Parade on Lagerstrasse. Dull, wet but warmer. Everyone late as usual. Russ and 2nd in command furious.

09.10. Shaved as Noel is always so late getting breakfast and there is nothing else to do.

09.30. Noel fetched our Canadian Red Cross parcel.

No orderly and place chaotic. Got hot water for ½ litre of cocoa on his return.

Chocolate good!

George and Bob reorganising our fuel supply — disorder, dirt, and noise.

10.30. Silence room to write this and my letter to Peggy.

---

[49] Kranks — people who were unwell.

12.00. Lunch. ¼ litre cabbage soup, I Canadian biscuit & 2 cubes cheese. ½-litre coffee (sweetened).

Read my novel. An interminable argument going on between George and Len. "Is Germany's economy inflated?" One day I shall slay these two!

Robby collected our Reich Marks, which should not have been issued. German officer responsible is said to be having any shortages deducted from his pay. By the "souvenirs" it looks as if the poor bugger will go without his pay for some years!

14.00. Took textbooks I am sending home to parole hatch. No queue for a change.

14.20. Called at Brigade Exchange for matches. Usual queue. Too low on list and must wait till next week.

14.30-15.10. Took two turns round the camp. A typical autumn afternoon with sun just struggling through the clouds. Valley looks lovely in autumn coat. Yellows, greens, browns, mauves and blues struggle for supremacy. Flowers in camp still very pretty. Scheiss-panzer[50] in to empty 40-seater. Oxen look very picturesque but the smell.......!

Returned to dull room at 15.10 feeling warmer and more at peace.

Read Mercantile law until —

15.50. Tea; ½ litre (unsweetened) 1½ slices of toast and butter.

Vote taken at tea as to whether the camp levy (to be raised if no camp money is provided) shall be at flat rate or according to rank. Being a subaltern, I voted in favour of the latter!

The damp and dullness make me bloody minded (as it does to everyone) so took a walk until —

17.00. Evening parade.

---

[50] Scheiss-panzer — sanitary men emptying the latrines. This is a less than complimentary name for such folk!

The sunset tonight is worth recording. The hills turn black as the sun disappears behind them and sky colours appear in all the glory of contrast. Tonight, the fiery red was truly magnificent. Eastwards the sky was green, mauve and purple. One notices such magnificence when living quarters are so drab.

17.20. Silence room with Steven's Mercantile Law.

The inadequate food makes the damp cold seem to sink into the marrow of one's being.

18.30. Walked on Lagerstrasse till 19.00 feeling very "browned".

19.00. Found four letters waiting for me; Mother July 9th and Sept 2nd, Peggy 17th July and 22nd Sept with two photographs.

Supper; ½ salmon, beetroot and spuds; 1 Canadian biscuit fried; ½ litre tea, sweetened but lukewarm.

German cheese ration cut by 50% today!

Washed up supper things and played bridge till 21.45 when all lights went out for air raid. Got a homemade Carbide lamp going in the aftermath, turned in.

Repatriation rumour again cropped up.

Wednesday 1st November 1944.

07.30. German coffee (½ litre). Morning cold, foggy.

Second frost of the winter. Stayed in bed till parade bugle went. Washed, dressed and went on parade.

Fog so thick could scarcely see companies opposite. "Herman" read out German order about "approaching German women incompetently".

09.15. Put laundry on piles opposite the block.

09.20. Shaved.

09.30. J.C.

09.45. Breakfast and cocoa (2 slices with butter and marmalade).

Washed up as still have no orderly. George and Bob still dealing with fuel, and we had to sweep the room. Complete chaos so took a walk in the sunshine till 11.00 when returned to write this.

Read Mercantile Law until—

12.15. Lunch, ¼ litre Irish stew, 1 baked potato, 1½ slices of bread & butter. 2 ccs cheese, ½ spread with marmalade, ½ litre coffee.

After lunch, Noel played some gramophone records — washed up.

14.00. Took a chair into the sun and read more law until —

15.45. Tea; ½ litre unsweetened, 1½ slices toast and butter. Washed up. Walk around the camp and saw a load of clothes being unloaded — rushed back with the news.

17.00. Evening Parade. Late as usual.

17.15 — 19.15. Read my novel. Letter from Peggy July 9th one in room Oct 9th.

17.15: Supper; ¼ 12oz tin of bully beef mixed with spuds and baked, prunes and raisins, 1 slice of bread and goon jam, 1 Canadian biscuit, butter and goon cheese (very smelly!).

Washed up — filthy business in almost complete darkness and in cold water.

Evening very cold. Read novel till 21.00 when I washed and turned in, as lights out is now 22.00hrs. Read several chapters of Exodus till 22.00hrs.

Thursday 2nd November 1944.

Very good night's sleep without the usual interruptions!

07.30. ½ litre goon tea.

08.25. Cold shower in bathroom. Raining hard.

09.00. Parade on Lagerstrasse.

09.15. Shaved.

09.25. Breakfast; 2 slices bread, butter and goon jam, ½ litre cocoa.

Room very dark and gloomy. No orderly so complete chores. Washed up and walked in the rain on the Lagerstrasse. One Canadian Red Cross crate of wood being issued to each room. Low clouds drifting up valley look very attractive.

11.10. Returned to room and read law.

12.15. Lunch; ¼ litre curried (?) vegetable soup, Potato, 2 Canadian biscuits with butter and goon jam. ½ litre of coffee (Sweetened).

Heated discussion on music with dogmatic Robert and Dudley being very rude to each other. Noel played some records, but these almost drowned by the din. Randall (D. W. M. Randall; Royal Signals) called in to define 'symphony' — a typical kind of discussion.

Low concentration ruined by Len's humming and whistling.

Washed up. Parcel slips round but sweet F. A. for Noel and I. Tom and Robert only winners.

Load of roots in for splitting up so will have a job daily in future. Robert warned for outside party next week.

Red Cross Cigarettes delivered 25 per head (½ rations).

Read until 14.30 then rain eased up and I went to wood yard. Split logs until 15.50.

Washed and got ready for tea.

16.00. Tea; two slices toast and butter, tea very late (16.30).

Room too dark to do anything until —

17.00. Evening parade on Lagerstrasse. On these days it is pleasant when parade is over, lights switched on and the blackouts are put up. The room warms up; one thinks of supper to come and can see to read fairly well without straining one's eyes, although continuous humming and whistling by Len is somewhat disturbing.

17.30. Put in tea store indent for Saturday:

International Committee of the Red Cross — Sardines

International Committee of the Red Cross — Meat Roll

17.35. Clothes parcel slip for me (whoopee) and one for George. Piece of chocolate from Tom who collected his before parade (Goody-goody!).

Lie on my bunk and read law for an hour and then some more of "Drums along the Mohawk."

18.45. Supper, ¼ bully and spuds baked, 1 fried Canadian biscuit, 1 slice of bread and butter with goon jam, ½ litre of tea (sweetened), 4 squares chocolate ration from Robert.

Read my novel till 21.00hrs. Then washed and turned in.

Have got a very definite "DOWN".

Read several chapters from Exodus. Would that I could bring plagues down upon these people to affect our release!

22.00. Lights out. Much banter and backchat before the room became quiet.

Friday 3rd November 1944.

Very good night's sleep without the usual disturbances from various causes, which seem to come from this diet of potatoes.

07.30. German Coffee, ½ litre unsweetened.

08.45. Up and washed.

09.05. Parade. Company very late and awarded the usual punishment much to Noel's annoyance (on field).

09.15. Shaved.

09.30. Breakfast; 2 slices with butter and goon jam, ½ litre of cocoa.

New orderly, Brock, reported — been 7 months free in Italy. Looks promising.

Usual morning chaos cleaning up.

10.30. Reported to wood yard; sawed wood till 11.30. Came back and read law until—

12.15. Lunch; ¼ litre pea soup, 1 baked potato, 1 slice of bread, 1 Canadian biscuit, butter and goon jam. 2 squares of chocolate from Robert. ½ litre of coffee (unsweetened — out of sugar!).

Pay balances came in; mine OK. Read some more from Edmund's book.

Rumours from Dudley:

"Working Commandos" to go out for cones this winter as parole walks not allowed this winter. Source — 2nd hand, from Von Fetter (?)

All being repatriated next year (what again!). Source — very indefinite.

I am trying to make up my mind whether or not to intensify my studying. Will the papers arrive? Is it worthwhile anyway? If I don't, can I continue work in the wood-yard in spite of short rations? If not, how the hell can I spend my time? Fish has entered for a German exam today. What the hell is a man to do for the best? Prepared and put in the tin a chit to send home, 315 Marks.

Walked once around the camp and stopped at the wood-yard. Got an axe and worked until 15.30.

Returned, washed and read until tea.

16.00. Tea: ½ litre unsweetened, 2 slices toast and butter.

Lights switched on earlier so read until parade.

17.00. Evening Parade on field.

17.20. Bridge.

Letter card handed out, 3 P.C.s and 1 letter. No post for me tonight.

18.45. Supper; spuds and carrots; barley gruel (¼ litre from the cookhouse), 1½ slices bread, butter and goon jam. ½ litre tea (sweetened somewhat!).

Washed up. Evening very cold and raw.

Washed and turned in early and read my novel.

Jack Priestly (The Queen's Royal Regiment) and Buck in to play bridge with Noel and Robby.

Reich Marks handed in were 4,000 short! Germans threaten continuous searches until discovered. After heated discussion, Noel was persuaded to part with his "souvenirs".

Read several chapters from Exodus.

22.00. Lights out.

Rough, cold and disturbed night. Up twice from natural causes. Noisy count by the Huns at 23.30, which woke us all up: disturbed several times by Noel banging on bed-boards because I was snoring!

Saturday 4th November 1944.

07.00. — ½ litre Goon Coffee — unsweetened.

08.30. Cold shower in canteen bathroom. Morning wet and cold.

09.00. Morning Parade. Noel very early this morning! Parade on Lagerstrasse.

09.15. Shaved.

09.30. Breakfast; 2 slices bread and butter, one with goon jam and one with marmalade, ½ litre of cocoa (slightly sweet!).

New orderly got room cleared up quicker than usual.

10.10. Left to collect parcel with George. Both like schoolboys but ardour damped by having to wait in the queue for nearly an hour. Quite a thrill watching parcel opened — something very intimate about the things Peggy has so obviously collected with such loving care. Makes me very glad I am married and more thankful than ever that war has brought her to me. 4½ lbs chocolate!

11.00. Returned, sorted my stuff and got out some spare underwear for the orderly who is short.

11.45. Air raid — red alert. Planes heard overhead several times but cloud too low to see them. Soup up early because of warning.

12.00. Lunch; ¼ litre potato soup, 1 baked spud, 2 slices of bread and butter; one with Goon sausage, one with marmalade. (Had a long thin loaf on Thursday hence extra slices). 4 squares of chocolate from George. ½ litre of coffee, sweetened.

Room full of smoke as chimney is blocked — everything filthy. Rumour that spud ration is to be cut. This is serious as we are on ½ parcels.

Major Hogg collected tin store this morning. Owing to rain and long wait he returned in a pique and refused to do it again because Majors Nelson, Pelham-Burn, Janson and Dewar never get it. After heated discussion, we decided to carry on. It saves us many journeys collecting it this way. "Twicer" Hawkesworth, however, was caught out at racketeering and will have to fetch his own in future.

12.50. All clear.

Read for a while and then went to the woodpile. No work owing to the shortage of tools. Walked around the camp and returned to clean my boots for the weekend. Fish had a parcel slip and collected it during the afternoon. Read until tea — feel much too restless to study.

Tea: 2 slices toast and butter with 5 squares of chocolate. Cookhouse tea very late (½ litre unsweetened).

Gave four squares of chocolate to every man in the room. We have got more chocolate now than any of us have seen for months owing to the influx of "clothes".

Lights switched on at 16.30 so read till parade.

17.00 hrs. Evening parade on Lagerstrasse — field too muddy. Great queue at the theatre entrance immediately afterwards for first of a series of "Prom" concerts by the orchestra. Was hoping to go tomorrow but queuing dampens one's enthusiasm!

Richard Beamish came in with a foul cold and, in spite of my hints settled down to talk until 18.00. He was returning 30 Players cigarettes we had lent him.

"The Mart" bad debt collector came around, for our one point overdraft. Robby has promised to put one in for us on Monday.

18.00. Letters up. One for me from Peggy — July 12th.

Managed to get rid of Richard on pretext of wanting to read it alone. Hope I haven't caught his ruddy cold. The air is thick as it is.

My book parcel came in from the censors — some good reading from Harrods. Obviously from Peggy. Acknowledged on an acknowledgement form and posted this with acknowledgement of my clothes parcel.

Roger Mortimer (Coldstream Guards) came in and asked if I would like to go out with a wood party the week after next. Would I like? You bet I would! Will know definitely on Monday. Hope C.I.S. examination papers for the finals don't come in when I am out.

Several German "Kultur" magazines are in. These are very good.

Issue of raw cabbage today.

18.45. Supper; ½ small tin of sardines with boiled spuds, prunes and a little Klim, 2 slices of bread, butter and marmalade, 5 squares of chocolate, ½ litre of tea slightly sweetened.

Washed up afterwards and we all went to the orderlies' show "Coffeestyria". Very good show indeed but reminded us too much of good old London and the embankment.

21.20. Back again, washed and turned in.

Read novel and several chapters from Exodus.

22.00. Lights out.

Appendix 2 — On Passing an Examination!

On 31ˢᵗ May 1944, Alan posted home a poem written by Captain Randall Sly of the Warwickshire Regiment, whom he describes as 'a writer, sailor, soldier, farmer and student of mysticism! He really can write well but knocks off these efforts whenever anything happens for our amusement'. *Alan spent quite a bit of his younger life in the village of Mongeham, near Deal in East Kent.*

> They've put out the flags in great Mongeham today
> For news has come through that the duke's on his way,
> With garlands of flowers and a herald who cries:
> Make way for the mighty, the strong and the wise!
> The hockey-field hero has done it at last —
> He took an exam, and, by heaven, he passed!
> So, bow all ye maidens with worshipping glance,
> And come all ye yokels and join in the dance:
> And all little shop girls raise eyes to the sky,
> And pour out your hearts as the hero goes by!

Appendix 3 — Some Background Notes

The Battle for Crete

Crete is an island, one hundred and sixty miles long by thirty-six miles wide, tapering to just seven miles in places. It is mountainous, rising to about nine thousand feet. The Cretan people have a reputation for their warmth and hospitality.

The Cretan harbours were undeveloped at the time of the German invasion in 1941, although there were functioning airfields. Communications and other facilities were limited but the island had strategic potential, especially for the Eastern Mediterranean, where it could help access the Balkans and North Africa. Suda Bay, a large natural harbour, offered great possibilities to whoever held it.

Hitler had conquered much of Western Europe by spring 1941 but wanted to occupy Crete to protect the southern end of his domain. His desire to master Crete became more pressing following defeats inflicted on Mussolini's forces in Greece and North Africa. Against the wishes of his generals, Hitler desired to occupy Crete before opening the Russian front.

For the Allies, General Wavell was responsible for the defence of both Crete and Greece, but he was handicapped by shortages of military supplies and equipment. His men were dispirited and worn out following earlier fighting in Greece in 1940.

Allied forces were drawn from Britain, Australia, New Zealand and Greece. Shortly before hostilities were due to start, a New Zealand general, Bernard Freyberg, had taken command of Crete.

He arrived on 30th April 1941 and discovered little had been done to strengthen the island's defences. This was less than a month before the German invasion commenced on 20th May. Freyberg had been appointed as a distinguished general, used to action. He accepted the role, despite reservations about the Allies' lack of preparedness for any battle.

Intelligence from code breakers at Bletchley Park indicated the Germans would launch a full airborne attack on Crete, aiming to take possession of the airfields as soon as possible. Local commanders were unconvinced and prepared for a seaborne invasion. In fact, the Germans intended that only later would reinforcements arrive by sea.

The Royal Navy did much to thwart the sea invasion and was crucial in delivering forces and equipment to the island before the Germans arrived. They evacuated many allied troops after defeat by the Nazis. Sadly, much less was done to prevent the main air invasion. Events in Crete helped establish the principle that naval operations are more difficult when enemy forces control the skies. Some wanted to increase the number of Allied aircraft on the island, but in reality, the few remaining on Crete were removed only days before the German invasion commenced.

Operation Mercury was seen as a landmark in the history of airborne warfare as the Germans used paratroopers in unprecedented numbers. Seven hundred and fifty men arrived by glider whilst ten thousand were parachuted onto Crete, with a further five thousand delivered by air transport. The remaining seven thousand arrived by ship. The arrivals were to be in two waves, one in the morning, the other in the afternoon of the day of invasion.

The Allies, expecting invasion from the sea, did not sufficiently protect the airfields, but the Germans were unaware of the resistance that they would encounter on Crete. This resulted in an extremely bloody battle. The final part of the battle for Crete began five days after the initial invasion. It proved a costly victory for the Germans, who lost five thousand, five hundred men from an invasion force in excess of twenty-two thousand. The losses were so great that Germany never used such large numbers of airborne troops again.

The Allies sustained three thousand, five hundred casualties with one thousand, seven hundred killed. It was estimated that twelve thousand Allied troops were taken as prisoners of war. Their failure to win a battle that took place across hillsides and in olive groves has been described as 'a story of a lost opportunity'. Military historians agree Crete was not a place where the Allied forces acquitted themselves in glory. The lack of men and resources seriously hampered the defence.

The Cretans developed a courageous resistance to the Nazi forces although General Freyberg never armed them, possibly because there were not enough arms for the regular forces — something Alan mentioned on several occasions. The Cretan resistance's help in hiding and evacuating Allies left behind on the island was outstanding. The first such group left the Island in July 1941.

Prisoners of War — P.O.W.s

The life of a prisoner of war is unbelievably boring compared with that of a fighting soldier. As with many generalisations, this neglects the fact that those held in prison camps need great physical and mental stamina to survive the ill treatment and death that surround them. Hope, courage and humour are also vital weapons for any P. O. W.

The Treaty of Westphalia (1648) first established the idea of releasing prisoners taken in war. Before, prisoners seized in the crusades and other wars were exterminated brutally. The Napoleonic and the Anglo-American wars heralded an improvement in the treatment of P.O.W.s. The 1874 Brussels Conference led to an understanding that the treatment of prisoners should be more humane.

A system for exchanging prisoners of similar rank developed, reducing the number of captives whilst ensuring skilled personnel could return home. Many felt that the detention of large numbers of the enemy reduced their numbers. It is illegal to interrogate prisoners under the Geneva Convention; prisoners need only provide their name, rank and number. More detailed information for the treatment of P.O.W.s emerged at the Hague Convention (1907) whilst the Geneva Convention (1929) went further and there was a review in 1949, following the Second World War.

From 1939-1945 the Soviet Union, Germany and Japan were noted for their mistreatment of P.O.W.s. The Koreans and Vietnamese were known for their brutality whilst more recently, the Americans have been criticised for their treatment of prisoners at Guantánamo Bay and Abu Ghraib prison in Iraq. There is widespread condemnation of the recent practice of displaying prisoners taken in war on the media.

During the Second World War, the treatment of American, British, French and Commonwealth soldiers by the Germans and Italians accorded with the Geneva Convention. Germany's treatment of prisoners from the Soviet Union was much harsher. The Japanese and Soviets did not espouse the Geneva Convention. The main complaint of British troops held by the Germans concerned the poor quality and scarcity of food, especially in the final years of the war. There were also grumbles about harsh treatment by those on forced marches towards the end of the war as the Germans moved prisoners away from the advancing Allied forces.

The most brutally treated soldiers of the Second World War were the ninety-one thousand Germans captured by the Russians at the Battle of Stalingrad and taken to Siberia, where poor health and bitter cold killed many. Only five thousand survived the ordeal, returning in 1955 to Germany following the death of Stalin.

The Germans and British used other ranks for manual labour and recompensed them for their work. The Allies took a pride in trying to ensure that all prisoners were well treated. Indeed, for some it was an encouragement to surrender towards the end of the war when supplies in Germany were short. Officers did not usually perform manual labour.

Housing for most prisoners in the Second World War was usually in single storey huts with two or three tier bunk beds. In the middle of each room would be a wood or charcoal stove.

During both World Wars, all sides held significant numbers of civilians. Less is recorded about these people although some believe they were treated better than military personnel. Despite this, it is clear their lot was not good and on occasions, they were less able to withstand the hardships they experienced, especially in the case of women, children, or the elderly. The wives and families of all prisoners who remain at home endure their own pain and suffering.

Allied officers incarcerated in Germany stayed in Oflags, hence Eichstätt's name. Stalags were camps for other ranks. Some camps were set aside especially for air force or naval personnel. Prisoners were moved by train and Alan once mentioned a 'loo stop' when a poor, elderly, peasant woman offered fresh bread to the bedraggled soldiers who had disembarked from their train to relieve themselves. The bread tasted wonderful, and the men were immeasurably grateful for this lady's simple act of generosity.

In every camp, a parade for roll call took place at least once a day.